When **Virginia Heath** was a little girl it took her ages to fall asleep, so she made up stories in her head to help pass the time while she was staring at the ceiling. As she got older the stories became more complicated—sometimes taking weeks to get to their happy ending. One day she decided to embrace her insomnia and start writing them down. Virginia lives in Essex, with her wonderful husband and two teenagers. It still takes her for ever to fall asleep.

Discover more at millsandboon.co.uk.

THE DETERMINED LORD HADLEIGH

Virginia Heath

MILLS & BOON

First Published in Great Britain 2019
by Mills & Boon, an imprint of HarperCollins*Publishers*
1 London Bridge Street, London, SE1 9GF

© 2019 Susan Merritt

ISBN: 978-0-263-26916-1

MIX
Paper from
responsible sources
FSC® C007454

This book is produced from independently certified FSC™ paper
to ensure responsible forest management.
For more information visit www.harpercollins.co.uk/green.

Printed and bound in Spain
by CPI, Barcelona

For Frankie and Shell.

Thanks for all your support
since I started my writing journey.

You are awesome!

Prologue

The Old Bailey—May 1820

She had attended every single day of the trial. Alone in the gallery, her face pale, sitting erect, her slim shoulders pulled back as she stared straight ahead. Her hands were hidden among the folds of her skirt. It had taken Hadleigh almost a week to realise that she hid her hands because they provided the only clue to the way she was truly feeling as they twisted a ruined handkerchief into tight, agitated spirals which she kept proudly from view.

She had a child, he knew. A son who was a little over a year old. Yet she never brought the babe to the court as some did in a bid to elicit sympathy. Nor did she give any indication she noticed the hordes who had come to gloat at her tragedy. The blatant pointing and unsubtle whispering; the shameless newspaper artist who frequently perched himself directly in front of her and sketched her expression incorrectly for the breakfast entertainment of the masses—such was the gravitas of this case that everyone wanted to know about it. And about her.

The traitor's wife.

That quiet dignity had both impressed him and humbled him because it was eerily familiar. Her honesty, yesterday, had shaken him to his core. In a last-ditch attempt to save her husband and prove his good character, the defence had called her as a witness at the last minute. Unexpectedly. They asked leading questions, to which she could answer only yes or no, then stepped aside so that he could cross-examine her.

'Was he a good husband?'

She had looked him dead in the eye. 'No.' He had expected her to lie, but gave no indication of his surprise. Her gaze moved tentatively to the furious man in the dock. 'No. He wasn't.'

'Why not?'

'He wasn't at all who I had hoped he was.'

'This court requires more explanation, Lady Penhurst. In what ways was the accused a bad husband?' He'd had an inkling. More than an inkling, if he was honest, especially as he had lived in a house where a marriage had become a legal prison, but as the Crown Prosecutor his job was to present the government's case as best he could. The jury deserved the whole truth about the man in the dock, no matter how unpalatable it was. Or how intrusive.

'He was violent, Lord Hadleigh.' His friend Leatham had said as much. Violent and depraved and his heart wept for her suffering. She reminded him of another woman in another time. One who had also endured stoically because she had had no option to do otherwise and had not wanted to burden him with her troubles. The bitter taste of bile stung his throat at the awful memory so long buried.

'He beat you?'

Her eyes nervously flicked to her husband's again because she knew that if he was acquitted, she would pay for her disloyalty today and there was nothing in law to stop that happening. But her spine stiffened again with resolve and she slowly inhaled as if to calm herself and find inner strength. He knew how much that small act of defiance cost her. 'If I was lucky, only weekly.' Her gloved index finger touched the bridge of her nose where the bone slightly protruded. 'He broke my nose. Cracked a rib—'

'Objection!' The defence lawyer shot to his feet. 'My learned friend knows what happens between a husband and a wife in the privacy of *his* house is not pertinent to this case.'

Hadleigh addressed the judge. 'I believe it is pertinent m'lud. It gives the jury an insight into Viscount Penhurst's character.' Because a man who used his wife as a battering ram was rarely a good man, as his own mother had learned to her cost.

'We have debated this many times before, Lord Hadleigh, therefore I know you are well aware the law clearly has no objections to a husband disciplining his wife.' The judge had the temerity to look affronted that it had been brought up in the first place, seemingly perfectly happy that a husband had the right to beat his wife senseless and the courts who supposedly stood for justice would do nothing. 'You will desist this line of questioning immediately and the witness's answers will be struck from the proceedings.'

Hadleigh nodded, his teeth practically gnashing, consoling himself that while the law was an ass as far as the rights of married women were concerned, at least the seeds had been sown. You could strike words from the record, but once said, they took root in the mind. A few of the jurors had looked appalled. That would have to do. 'My apologies.' Hadleigh made no attempt to sound sincere before he turned back to her and the job in hand. 'Lady Penhurst—you lived predominantly in Penhurst Hall in Sussex during your marriage, did you not?'

'I did.'

'Then do you expect this court to believe that you lived in that house and never suspected what was going on in the cellars right beneath your feet?' Her husband had run part of a vast smuggling operation, utilising his estate's close proximity to the sea to receive and sell on thousands of gallons of brandy in exchange for guns. Guns destined for France, and more specifically to the supporters of the imprisoned Napoleon who were desperate to see their great leader restored to power.

'I have eyes, Lord Hadleigh. And ears. Therefore, I knew he was up to something but, to my shame, I had no idea what and nor did I truly attempt to find out.'

'Why to your shame?'

'Because my life was easier if I asked no questions. It is hard being married to a man who answers them with his fists.' Another thing he had learned through bitter experience. 'But with hindsight, I wish I had confided in someone.'

Then, unprompted and in a tumbled rush, she had begun to reel off what she had seen and heard which she had thought suspicious. Things she had neglected to mention the first time he had interrogated her fresh from her husband's arrest, doubtless because she didn't dare say a word against him then in fear of his retribution. Hadleigh had had no intention of calling her to the stand for precisely that reason—wives, even grossly abused ones, rarely turned against their husbands or even testified at all—so her sudden extensive and embellished testimony surprised him.

The guards in the cellars, the menacing servants who watched her every move and reported it back to her spouse, the odd messages which arrived at the house at odder hours which Penhurst always burned after reading, the new and endless supply of money that he spent like water. Most significant were the dates she freely shared. Dates when her husband had been home which coincided with the same dates the Excise Men had recorded sightings of smuggling ships on the Sussex coastline. Dates Hadleigh had already appraised the court of during this significant and well-discussed trial. All in all, it had been a damning testimony, an incredibly detailed and courageous one, and one he was of the opinion she had come to the court room determined to share despite being a named from the outset as a witness for the defence.

Lady Penhurst was a very brave woman.

As a reward, she was subjected to the most spiteful rebuttal from both her vile husband and the defence that Hadleigh had ever heard in all his years in the courtroom. Horrendous mudslinging which highlighted the gross disparity between the law for men and the law for women. He had been reprimanded by the judge for bringing up the way she was beaten by her husband, but that same judge had blithely ignored all Hadleigh's objections to her haranguing because the court deserved to know what sort of a woman the witness was before they chose to believe her.

She was a liar. Who had lain with a succession of men for money. Deranged. Cold and frigid. A drunkard. Unfit to be a mother. Throughout the litany, she had stood proudly, her clasped hands shaking slightly, her expression pained but defiant. Grace in the face of the contemptible. He admired that, too.

By the end, Hadleigh hated his profession and himself more for not adequately defending her, even though it was neither his place nor his job to do so. But as it had been his intrusive questions she had answered with more detail than he could have possibly dreamed of, he knew she was suffering this contemptible onslaught thanks to him. Knew, too, that she had helped him by hammering the last few nails into Penhurst's already rotten coffin regardless of the inevitable cost to herself.

As she left the witness box, she held her head high, but her eyes had dimmed. He knew it wasn't the first time she had been whittled down and belittled by his sex. He'd seen that same expression many times and, while he could never ignore it, he had played along with his mother and pretended he hadn't seen it. That nothing was amiss. That all would be well. A flimsy lie that had never come to fruition. Oh! To be able to turn back time and do things differently...

Hadleigh couldn't shift his immense sense of guilt and shame throughout his closing arguments, although bizarrely that painful, niggling, unprofessional emotion made them sound stronger than any closing speech he had ever made before. Perhaps because he had argued for her. Used his voice in an arena where she had none. Treason aside, more than anything he now wanted Penhurst to pay for what he had done to the quietly proud and stoic woman sat all alone in the gallery.

Then the jury were sent to huddle in a private room to discuss their verdict, away from the circus in the gallery. They came back unanimous in less than ten short minutes.

Guilty.

Of high treason.

Her face had blanched then. Her blue eyes filling with tears and for the first time she stared down at her lap as her husband was dragged screaming from the court. He had hoped she didn't regret her part in the verdict. It had been small, but largely insignificant, because Hadleigh had done his job well. But then he had no emotional attachment to Penhurst, so could regard the man's inevitable demise through a detached and pragmatic lens. For her, there would be complicated ramifications as well as the release from her suffering. Penhurst had fathered her child and been her husband. There were many in society who would judge her unfairly and she was unlikely to ever be welcomed within its hypocritical ranks again thanks to the sins she had not committed but which branded her nevertheless.

While the judge retired for the night to consider the punishment, she had left the court alone as always and gone who knew where, not realising that more machinations far out of his sphere of control would occur before morning which would make her future life undeservedly more impossible than it already was.

Hadleigh learned it had been a reporter for one of the scandal sheets who had blithely informed her that her husband's title and estate had been transferred back to the Crown, his ill-gotten fortune and all his assets seized. It was a petty act of revenge as far as Hadleigh was concerned, designed to put the fear of God into his yet unknown co-conspirators. A stark reminder of what a traitor could expect for his crimes against England and its King even in this enlightened day and age. But Penhurst's infant son was no traitor and nor was the child's abused mother, yet now both of them would also pay for his crimes and for much longer than the crooked Viscount would. Their entire lives had been ruined with one vengeful stroke of a pen.

That was not his concern.

Or at least it shouldn't be. But looking at her

now, sat all alone in the gallery waiting to hear her violent and odious husband's fate, he found he couldn't seem to take his eyes off her or not feel partly responsible for all she was about to suffer. Not a single family member had accompanied her on her daily trips to the court. Nor had a single family member leapt to her defence in any of the hundreds of newspaper stories that made outrageous and wild accusations. Was that because they had disowned her or because she had wanted to do this alone? Or perhaps she was alone? And why the blazes should he care about this woman when he had brought many a criminal to justice and not given two figs about any of their family, when the family were ultimately irrelevant when justice needed to be done?

While pretending to study a document in front of him, he found his gaze wandering back to her hands. As usual, they were buried in her dull skirt, out of sight. Her outfit today was austere, as they all had been this last week, but he noticed that, even though she was seated, the brown spencer hung from her frame. She had lost weight. Rapidly, if he was any judge, and the dark circles beneath her eyes were testament to the insomnia she had clearly suffered in the few scant weeks since her husband's arrest. How would she sleep after today? Would she ever sleep again?

That was not his concern!

She wasn't his responsibility and neither was

her child. Doubtless someone would crawl out of the woodwork and take them in. If she had any sense, she would move to the opposite end of the country and change her name. Perhaps he should tell her as much once this was all over?

He sensed her looking at him and realised he had been openly staring. He schooled his features into the bland, emotionless mask he always wore and allowed his eyes to meet hers unrepentant. There was something about Lady Penhurst's eyes which disarmed him and called to him in equal measure. He found he wanted to keep looking at them, as if within their sapphire-blue depths was something he needed, except the inexplicable guilt which had sat heavily on his shoulders for days got the better of him and he hastily looked away.

Not that he had anything in this instance to be guilty about. Penhurst was a traitor. He had robbed the Crown of taxes, as a minion of the infamous and still-unidentified mastermind known only as The Boss, he had willingly consorted with England's worst enemies and had blood on his hands. Lots of blood. Too many innocent men had died thanks to that smuggling ring and it was hardly his fault the evidence had been so plentiful and compelling the man had got his rightful comeuppance. Hadleigh had no earthly reason to feel guilty at doing his job well. None whatsoever. So why did he? Those eyes perhaps?

'All rise.'

Putting his misplaced guilt and odd mood aside, he stood with the rest of the chamber and forced his gaze to remain fixed on the judge as he entered. The judge sat and so did the rest of the chamber, while Penhurst was brought in to hear the sentence. He appeared terrified and rightly so, his eyes darting around the room nervously while the whole indictment was read. Then, as Hadleigh and most of the baying crowd had expected, the clerk placed the black-silk square atop his wig as an eerie hush settled over the room.

Hadleigh's gaze flicked to her and she was ashen, those lovely eyes swirling with emotion, his heart lurching painfully at the sight. All he could think of was what she might be thinking and what in God's name was to become of her. No husband. No home. No money. None of it her fault.

Professional detachment be damned! Once the judge was done he would offer some help. He wouldn't leave her all alone to be fed to the wolves today. He would escort her home. Give her money. A chance to start afresh. Something— anything—to make his misguided conscience feel better.

'William Henry Ashley, formally the Viscount Penhurst and the Baron of Scarsdale, the court doth order you to be taken from hence to the place from whence you came, and thence to the place of execution, and that you be hanged by the neck until you are dead, and that your body be afterward buried within the precincts of the prison in which you shall be confined after your conviction. And may the Lord have mercy upon your soul.'

'No!' Penhurst broke free of his guards, scrambled over the dock and lunged at the bench. Instinctively, Hadleigh stepped forward to stop him and the Viscount's fingers gripped his robe with all his might. 'I'll tell you everything I know. Everything!' The genuine fear in the man's expression was visceral. 'You have the power to appeal! To respite my sentence! Transport me. Imprison me. Flog me. Do whatever you see fit, but surely I am more use to you alive than I am dead?'

Around them, the gallery had jumped to their feet and surged forward to get a better view. It took two clerks and four men to restrain the panicked Penhurst and several minutes to drag him kicking and howling from the melee of the court room before order was resumed. By the time it was, her chair was empty. The ruined, twisted handkerchief lying crumpled on the floor, still damp from her tears.

Chapter One

Cheapside—five months later

'You are mistaken, Mr Palmer. I promise you I haven't yet paid the account. I came in here today specifically *to* pay the account.' Penny once again held out the money the pawnbroker had given her for her mother's jade brooch only minutes before.

The shopkeeper smiled kindly, but made no attempt to take it. ''Tis all paid, Mrs Henley. In full.' He turned around the ledger and pointed to the balance. 'There is no mistake, I can assure you.' His eyes wandered over to another woman in the corner who seemed perfectly content examining the rolls of ribbon all by herself. 'If there's nothing else I can help you with, Mrs Henley, I'd best see to my other customers.'

'But I didn't pay you, Mr Palmer!'

'Somebody did, because it's been noted down and I shan't be taking the money twice. That wouldn't be honest now, would it? And I pride myself on my honesty. Spend it on that little lad of yours, eh? I dare say he needs something. Growing boys always need something.' He closed his ledger decisively. 'Will there be anything else you need, Mrs Henley?'

He didn't strike her as a stupid man, but it was obvious he was a stubborn one and too proud to admit his error. Perhaps his wife would be more accommodating? 'Please send my regards to Mrs Palmer. I had hoped to see her today.' She cast a glance over his shoulder to the little anteroom beyond the counter. 'Unless she's here so I can do so in person?' The shopkeeper's wife was meticulous and would find a way to gently correct her husband's blatant accounting mistake.

'She's gone off to visit our daughter and the grandchildren, I'm afraid. I shall pass on your regards when she returns next week.'

Not wanting to argue further in public, Penny decided to come back then and attempt to pay her debt to the Palmers' shop. She said her goodbyes and, mindful of the time, walked briskly up King Street to the home of her landlord, Mr Cohen, fully intending to pay in advance for her next month's rent, only to find that, too, had been paid. Unlike the cheerful shopkeeper, Mr Cohen was a humourless individual who didn't like to waste words.

'I tell you it's been paid, Mrs Henley. A full twelve months' rent!'

'But that is impossible! I haven't paid you.' But the coincidence was not lost on her and she found her teeth grinding at the suspicion as to who might have. 'Who paid it?'

'That I can't say. Nor will I, as much as I don't like it. Your benefactor wants to remain anonymous.'

'Benefactor?'

The old man scowled and shook his head. His rheumy eyes burning with accusation. 'That's what I'll call him for now, Mrs Henley—because he assured me he wasn't your fancy man and I choose to think the best of my tenants, no matter how new they are to me or how implausible their stories.'

'Fancy man?' Penny didn't need to hide her outrage at the suggestion. 'I can assure you…' The old man rudely held up his hand.

'And I can assure you, rent or no rent, I'll toss you out on your ear if I get so much as one whiff that he is. I won't tolerate any scandal in one of my buildings, Mrs Henley—if indeed you are or have ever been a Mrs. If you hadn't been vouched for personally by Mr Leatham, I never would have accepted you in the first place. I wonder what he'd have to say about a strange man paying a year's worth of rent?'

An interesting question indeed. Exactly what

would Seb Leatham have to say? He was a man of few words, but one used to blending into the background and doing covert things behind the scenes. Never mind that he would walk on hot coals if Clarissa asked him to.

Suddenly, a nasty suspicion began to bloom in her mind. This was all a little too contrived and convenient. Less than twenty-four hours before she had had a disagreement with Clarissa, the only friend she had left in the world and wife to the aforementioned Seb Leatham. It had been about her decision to seek employment somewhere as a governess or housekeeper or some such to make ends meet which had so thoroughly outraged Clarissa. She had been very vocal on the subject before she had backed down. Her friend had claimed she respected Penny's decision even if she did not agree with it. Yet now, by some miracle, her rent and her household accounts were miraculously all settled by a mysterious benefactor. Twelve months gratis in Cheapside kept her close enough so her well-meaning friend could continue to keep an eye on her and Penny would have no need to sully her poor, pathetic hands with work in the interim.

'I insist you give the money back whence it came, Mr Cohen! I'll pay my own rent, thank you very much.' She wasn't that pathetic woman any longer. As much as she had grown to hate her husband, she had hated the woman she had

been during their marriage more. A scared, spine-
less and stupid girl who had ignored everyone's
cautionary words about the man she had set her
heart on marrying who had lived to rue the day.
Oh! How she had hated being powerless and sub-
servient, and because it went against the grain of
her character she was determined to be a different woman now. She was neither worthless nor
useless. Nor would she be beholden.

Because accepting charity and feeling beholden allowed others the opportunity to control her life and she was done with all that. How
was keeping her in Cheapside any different from
keeping her in Penhurst Hall? And just because
her friends meant well, that didn't give them the
right to use their wealth secretively to get their
own way. After three interminable years of being
powerless and controlled, the only person who
had any say about her life now was her son, Freddie. As he was still unable to talk, there was nobody else who held that power.

To prove her point, Penny began rummaging
in her reticule for the money. What was the matter with working for a living anyway? Perhaps
such a prospect daunted an aristocratic woman
like Clarissa, but it didn't faze Penny. She had
come from trade, spent her formative years working within it and had enjoyed every second. Her
mother and father had worked all their lives with
her on their knee. Why, her father had built his

business from scratch, from the ground up, and those same principles of hard work and honest enterprise were as ingrained in her as good manners. There was no shame in honest labour and she wouldn't be deterred from finding a way to stand on her own two feet after everything she had endured. After three years she was finally free and intended to remain so. Making her own living, living her own life, was something she was looking forward to rather than dreading and just as her dear parents had, she would find a way to make it work around Freddie. A fresh, clean slate that left her shameful past firmly in the past.

'*He* made me promise not to allow that—and paid me over the odds to ensure I complied.' Old Cohen crossed his arms. 'But if I find out there's any funny business going on between you and him...'

'For any funny business to be going on, *Mr Cohen*, I would first have to know who *he* is, don't you think?' Although whoever he was, he was linked to Seb Leatham somehow. The man was a high-ranking government spy, one who had a legion of subordinate spies to do his dirty work for him. She was going to strangle Clarissa. How dared she?

How dared she?

Not caring that she was being rude to her mean-spirited landlord, Penny turned on her heel and began to march home, imbued with the determination and outrage of the self-righteous. How dare Clarissa use her husband to go behind her back like that? When her friend had explicitly promised to support her in her endeavours and claimed she understood why Penny wanted to leave her old life and all its horrid memories well behind.

What other choice did she have? Her parents, God rest them, were dead and the distant relatives who still lived had disowned her before the trial had even started. Either she earned her own living or she lived on Clarissa's charity again as she had during the humiliating trial. Because Lord alone knew there wasn't enough of her mother's old jewellery to pawn to keep her head above water for more than a few months at most. There certainly wasn't enough of it yet to buy Freddie and her a cottage of their own in the wilds of the country.

And *yet* was the operative word, because one day she would have one. That was her dream. The only thing which had sustained her these past months. A pretty place to call her own where she could finally put the past three years behind her. Of that she was determined. If those dreadful years married to Penhurst had taught her nothing, it had taught her that it was long past time she needed to stop being dictated to by others and take control of her own destiny in whatever shape she chose to make it.

Her respectable lodgings in Cheapside were only ever meant to be temporary. A place to lick her wounds in private while she considered all her options. She had happily taken Seb Leatham's advice on that. Aside from the fact she had spent the first fourteen years of her life living here before her father could afford Mayfair and had always loved it. It was a busy area of the city which allowed a person to hide in plain sight. With all the businesses, merchants and transient visitors from far and wide, nobody looked twice at a well-heeled woman with a child in Cheapside. Nor did any of the upper crust of society venture here. They might send their servants, but they would never be seen dead on the same streets as those in trade.

Heaven forbid!

Any more than they would consider continuing their acquaintance with the widow of a traitor.

She stopped dead outside her building and sucked in a calming breath. Perhaps she shouldn't be too hard on Clarissa? Her friend had stalwartly stood by her throughout everything. Quite openly. She would have sat with her through every minute of the trial if Penny hadn't stopped her. She had claimed at the time she wanted Freddie to be with someone he knew, someone who cared for him, rather than admitting she didn't want to taint or ruin her friend's good reputation by well-meant association. Even now, months after

Penhurst's death, Penny refused point blank to darken Clarissa's door in Grosvenor Square. That wouldn't be fair, no matter what her friend said to the contrary. That hadn't stopped her coming here and stepping into the breach when Penny needed somebody to watch her son and for that, she was in Clarissa's debt.

This wasn't worth losing her only true friend in the world for.

Wearily, she took the two flights of stairs slowly and tried to think of a more tactful way of voicing her annoyance at what was obviously meant to be a kindness. Especially as her life had been devoid of such niceness for so long.

She found Clarissa in the tiny parlour sat cross-legged on the floor helping Freddie build a lop-sided tower with his wooden blocks, his current favourite toy. 'You're back early. I thought you had heaps of errands to run.'

Penny hadn't confided to her friend that she was visiting the pawn shop and didn't intend to. 'I did—but something peculiar happened and I thought I'd better come back.'

'Peculiar? You weren't recognised, were you?' Her only friend looked concerned at the prospect. People had been quite cruel during the trial. The press had positively hounded her.

'No. Nothing so terrible.' She untied her bonnet and placed it on the table with her gloves, then stalled for more time by carefully hanging up her cloak on the peg by the door, needing to give herself a stern talking to in order to be that better, stronger, independent version of herself.

Be tactful. But be assertive. This is your life and you can now live it exactly as you choose. Something you have yearned for. For three long years. 'However, I did learn something niggling. Something probably best discussed over a cup of tea.' More stalling, which irritated, although was annoyingly typical when one considered she had always shied away from conflict—even before Penhurst. It didn't matter. All this self-flagellation at her supposed flaws was misplaced and pointless. One could still be fundamentally nice and assertive at the same time. It was not as if Clarissa would punch her.

She kissed her son noisily on the cheek before walking to the fireplace to grab the kettle and prepare the teapot. The lack of servants was another thing Clarissa worried about, but Penny genuinely rather liked her new privacy. It wasn't that much work to clean up after herself and her son. Preparing meals was getting easier, but was certainly not her forte, yet a small price to pay for proper privacy. Besides, she still wasn't completely over the sheer joy of being able to spend unrationed and unmonitored time with her boy. Proper time where she could be his mother rather than the scant few minutes her husband had allowed each day before her little cherub was taken back up to the nursery to the paid sneak, Nanny Francis, and out of her control. Penhurst's servants had been her gaolers. Good riddance to the lot of them. She wouldn't mourn their loss any more than she mourned his.

Clarissa took charge of pouring the tea a few minutes later, while Penny settled down with Freddie in her lap. Once done, her friend placed the steaming cup in front of her, then stared at Penny intently. 'What's happened?'

Best to get straight to the point. 'I know you *mean* well, but you shouldn't have paid my rent.'

Her friend blinked, then frowned. 'I didn't.'

'Perhaps not in person, you're far too clever for that, but you arranged for it to be paid behind my back and you settled my account at the shop as well.' She smiled, softening the admonishment, but was quietly pleased that she had given it.

'I didn't. I wish I had…because heaven only knows you need someone to help you and I can well afford it. But honestly, Penny, I didn't. I value our friendship too much to go against your express wishes and I meant it when I said I *would* respect your wishes. After everything, you of all people deserve to be mistress of your own life.'

'Then Seb arranged for those bills to be paid without your knowledge.'

'He wouldn't do such a thing behind my back. Or yours for that matter. I know you have a justifiably jaded view of men and marriage, but Seb is an honourable man and he would never do anything without my knowing. He loves me.'

Penny picked up her tea and tried not to be irritated at her friend's naivety. Men always did what they thought was best irrespective of the woman's feelings. 'Then how else do you explain twelve months' worth of rent miraculously paid on my behalf?'

'Twelve months!' Her friend seemed genuinely shocked. 'Someone has paid an *entire* year of rent? Who? And, more importantly, why?'

'Oh, for goodness sake, Clarissa—let's not play games.' She wouldn't feel bad for losing her temper. A line had to be drawn somewhere and her overprotective friend had pushed the boundary between concern and downright interference too far. 'I appreciate I've been the biggest of fools, that I married a man you had the measure of from the outset and cautioned me against, that I put up with Penhurst and did his bidding like a quaking dolt for three years! I am walking proof of how stupidly trusting, misguided and downtrodden a woman can be! But I'm not an idiot. Not any more, at any rate. You directly or indirectly paid my rent without my consent or knowledge to stop me applying for work.'

'No. I didn't. I swear it. I had every intention of having another long chat with you about the topic today in the hope you might reconsider. That I will freely admit. I see no earthly reason why you continue to isolate yourself here in this tiny apartment in Cheapside when you could live with us comfortably in Grosvenor Square. And I was jolly well prepared to shake you by the shoulders if you continued to be stubborn, but I respect the fact that only *you* can make the decisions concerning you and Freddie. After Penhurst, and all the dire and wicked things he did to you, I would never dream of robbing you of free will.' Her friend leaned forward and clasped her hand, looking worried. 'I swear to you, Penny, I did not pay your rent.'

'Then who did?' It didn't make sense. She had two distant cousins left, neither of whom wanted anything to do with her. They had been very specific on the subject in their final letter to her during the trial. No other friends. They had all been shamefully quick to desert her, too. Rats hurling themselves from a scuppered and sinking ship. It had hurt, but she understood it. Aside from Clarissa and her husband, she had no one.

'You don't suppose one of Penhurst's old *friends* paid it for you?'

A cold chill skittered down Penny's spine at the thought. 'Why would they?' Surely those cutthroats hated her? 'I testified against him...' Before those same cutthroats had violently murdered her husband in his cell. 'And they've all been rounded up. Haven't they?' The ringleaders were all in gaol—but what if the government

had missed someone? Would they wish her, a
woman who knew nothing outside of what had
happed within her own four walls, harm or malice? By the look on Clarissa's suddenly pale face
she suspected they did. 'I thought nobody bar
you, Seb and the authorities knew my new name
and address.' If her new lodgings and identity
had leaked outside the safety of her minuscule
intimate circle, to people who could feasibly perhaps want her dead, then she would have to take
Freddie and leave tonight. Lord only knew where
or how. She was down to her last five guineas—
thanks, bizarrely, to the money she had not been
allowed to pay to those to whom she owed it, six
pieces of her mother's jewellery and the clothes
on her back.

Clarissa saw the fear and her tone instantly
became reassuring. 'Believe me, if those people
wanted to punish you and knew where you were,
they would have done so. Swiftly and mercilessly.
It makes no sense they would offer you charity. Besides, they've arrested the leaders. Those
crooks beneath them would have long fled if they
have any sense. Staying in the capital is tanta-
mount to a death sentence if they are caught.
Whoever paid your rent doesn't mean you harm,
Penny. We can be certain of that. On the contrary, I suspect. They want to see you safe and
well cared for.'

'I don't want anyone else's money or their help.

Especially if they are linked to my husband in some way.' And even if they weren't, she only had two friends left in the world and Freddie. Being beholden to a complete stranger, no matter how benevolent, made her feel uneasy. 'But what if it *is* one of his criminal contacts?' All manner of dire scenarios flitted through her mind, making her unconsciously tighten her hold on her son.

'There's nobody of importance left, dearest. All the authorities are convinced of it. What if I talk to Lord Fennimore or get Seb to investigate it? I'm sure he'll get to the bottom of your mystery benefactor in no time and then we'll set them straight as well as put your mind at ease. As soon as they realise their well-meaning interference is unwelcome, I'm sure they'll leave well alone.'

Chapter Two

Hadleigh placed the little jade brooch in his desk drawer alongside the dented gold locket, well-worn cameo and the delicate ruby earrings, then locked it and pocketed the key. He was no expert on woman's jewellery—or women's anything, for that matter—but he doubted they were worth a great deal. They lacked the sparkle of the gems he saw glittering beneath the chandeliers at the few society events he was forced to attend when he couldn't find the right excuse to get out of them. If anything, they were a sad, meagre collection of jewellery as far as he was concerned, but they were of great personal value to her. He had witnessed that with his own eyes this time as he had watched her dither outside the pawnbroker's, staring at the brooch for the longest time lovingly before swapping it for a few coins.

Thanks to the Bow Street Runner he had assigned to watch her since she had moved to

Cheapside three months ago, the detailed weekly reports had made it easy to see there was a pattern to those heart-wrenching visits. On the first of the month, every month, she pawned a trinket and used the proceeds to pay her bills. Today, he had paid them all before she left the house and retrieved the latest item within minutes of her leaving the pawnbroker's shop, supremely thankful that she had not noticed him loitering in that convenient doorway as she had briskly bustled past within a hair's breadth of him. A little too close for comfort, truth be told, when a man in his position shouldn't be anywhere near a witness from a prior case.

But the same thought processes which had kept him up at night since the Penhurst verdict still plagued him. Continually worrying about her had compelled him to see her for himself today for the first time since the trial. He had needed to see with his own eyes exactly what was going on in her world and if her situation was as dire as the Runner had intimated it was. Solvent people, he had said in last week's report, didn't sell off the family silver.

For a gently bred lady to stoop that low, things had to be dire. She must be at her wits' end with worrying about how to pay for things. He sincerely hoped she would sleep easier tonight knowing she no longer ran the risk of being evicted. Hadleigh certainly hoped he would sleep sounder.

He also hoped that single act of benevolent charity would appease his niggling conscience. A conscience which bothered him the most in the dead of night when he should have been snatching enough hours of rest to keep his legal mind fresh. He was plagued with insomnia and desperately needed proper sleep. And now unburdened, would grab some—just as soon as he finished today's mountain of paperwork.

He cast a glance at the stack of case notes and witness statements on his desk, next to yet another cold and unappealing candlelit supper his valet had left out for him and allowed himself a pitying groan. There was at least another hour's work there, perhaps two, before he could even consider heading to his bed.

There was no doubt this was the biggest case of his career. For over a year, the King's Elite had been seeking the criminal mastermind behind a dangerous smuggling ring. A few weeks ago, they had finally found the person and, as the appointed Crown Prosecutor, Hadleigh's current and enormous quest for justice had truly started. The infamous, well-connected and dangerous Boss, who had been the scourge of the hallowed halls of Westminster as well as turning more peers than the odious Viscount Penhurst traitor, had finally been unmasked and arrested. And to everyone's shock, including Hadleigh's, the man they had been seeking was in fact a woman.

Viscountess Gislingham was now safely under lock and key in the most secure prison in the country—the Tower of London. Six other peers were similarly incarcerated in Newgate. It was Hadleigh's job to build a watertight case against her and her fellow traitors so they could crush that evil smuggling ring once and for all. Months of painstaking work lay ahead of him, work that would need his full attention. Already Lady Penhurst had occupied far too much of it, when he desperately needed his rest and was tired of mulling over and fretting about her situation. Paying her debts had been an act of charity to himself as well as to her. How was he supposed to be on top form when he spent night after night tossing and turning? Dreaming of knotted handkerchiefs, proudly set shoulders and pretty blue eyes swirling with heart-wrenching emotion.

The question brought her image starkly into view and he ruthlessly banished it as he sat down.

Enough! She was not his problem!

This case was.

He tore a chunk of bread from the half-loaf near his elbow, sawed off a slice of ham and chewed both dispassionately as he reread the meticulous interrogation notes he had made only this morning during another interminable stint with the traitors at Newgate. Five were still pleading their innocence. One had broken and was blabbing everything he knew. Whether or not the information he had given was enough to justify lessening the man's sentence was still in doubt. But in his experience, once a criminal committed to turning King's evidence, they committed wholeheartedly. Tomorrow could be interesting, but he needed to be fully prepared.

Within minutes, Hadleigh was so engrossed, the sound of a fist pummelling his front door had him jumping out of his skin. People didn't bang on his door. Especially not this close to midnight. One of the main reasons he continued to live in bachelor lodgings at the Albany, rather than his own house less than an hour's carriage drive from the capital, was that there was always a porter at the main entrance to dissuade unwelcome visitors from calling at unsociable hours—or any hours, for that matter—and bothering him. That was his excuse and he was sticking to it. He was a solitary beast by nature, partly because his work made it difficult to have unguarded conversations with most people and partly because he had been on his own for so long he was used to it. The Albany, close to his work, made perfect sense. That haunted house down the road didn't.

The fist bashed the door again, reminding him that Prescott, his valet, always took Thursday afternoons off and rarely returned before Friday morning. It also told him whoever was pummelling his woodwork with such vigour was probably known to the porter, hence he had been let in.

Something important must have happened since he left chambers. 'I'm coming!'

He had expected it to have something to do with the government, so was not surprised when he flung open the door and Seb Leatham strode in, looking furious.

'What's happened?' Immediately his mind went to the prisoners and his case. Experience had taught them that The Boss's smuggling gang had no respect for the law or its institutions. Viscount Penhurst and another conspirator, the Marquis of Deal, had been brutally murdered in their cells in Newgate a few days after their sentences had been issued in case they made any final confessions. The bloodthirsty crew of assassins had also ruthlessly sent three prison guards to meet their maker that same night. It had been a grim and stark reminder of exactly how powerful the group of criminals they were dealing with were. 'Please tell me nobody else is dead!'

'Not yet. But the night is young and as I'm royally furious I shan't rule it out.' His friend barged past him and stalked into the only room with a light burning—Hadleigh's study. He tossed his hat on the desk, folded his meaty arms across his chest and glared.

'I am not entirely sure I follow...'

'I made allowances for the Bow Street Runner.' Seb's eyes bored into his, his tautly controlled stance quietly terrifying. 'After everything she has suffered, and in light of the dangerous people her husband dealt with, I reasoned the more people who had eyes on her the better.'

He knew about the Bow Street Runner?

Oh, dear. All ideas of anonymously appeasing his niggling conscience with a secret act of charity swiftly disappeared. 'This is about Lady Penhurst?'

'You're damn right this is about Penny!' One pointed finger prodded him right in the breast bone. 'What the hell were you thinking, paying her debts off like that?'

Confused that Seb had so swiftly traced it back to him and even more confused that the man was angry about his obvious thoughtful and noble generosity, Hadleigh grabbed the still-prodding digit and made a point of pushing it away. 'Not that it's any of your business, but *I reasoned* she would be pleased not to have to struggle to make ends meet after the Runner informed me she was struggling.'

'Then clearly you don't know Penny very well. And clearly you know nothing whatsoever about my wife!' Seb began to pace, his hands waving in annoyance. 'Good grief, man! Talk about taking a mallet to crack a nut! What were you thinking?'

'After the Crown abandoned her, I was trying to help.'

'Well, you've gone and made a splendid hash of it. What the hell am I going to tell Clarissa?'

'As it was meant to be an anonymous gesture, you will tell her nothing, because it has nothing to do with her either.'

At that, Seb finally sat down with a huff in Hadleigh's chair and shook his head. 'Spoken like a true bachelor. Unfortunately, as it was Clarissa who expressly asked me to investigate her *best friend's* mystery benefactor, and because your ham-fisted attempt at being a Good Samaritan has spectacularly served to scare the living daylights out of both women, I have no choice but to tell her.'

'Why would they be scared?'

'You really have no clue, do you? Which is exactly the reason why you should leave the spying and covert machinations to us trained spies and stick to barristering.'

'I don't think barristering is an actual word.'

'And still you fiddle while Rome burns!'

'The Devil is in the detail...' Words he lived by. He was good with details, although clearly he had missed one here.

'Shall I spell it out to you in simple terms?' Seb did not wait for a response. 'Firstly, think about the particular circumstances of your good deed. Only a few months ago, that poor woman's vile husband was arrested on charges of treason. Your own investigation linked him to a whole host of unsavoury characters. Cutthroats. Smugglers. Cold-blooded murderers. When Penny testified against him, she testified against them, too. We assume we've rounded them all up now that we've captured the ringleader—but what if we haven't? It is entirely reasonable to assume any stragglers might have an axe to grind with her. It is one of the main reasons I actively encouraged her to assume an alias!' He stood then and began to pace. 'Furthermore, in paying those debts covertly, you have also alerted a very proud and determined woman to the fact she is under close watch at all times.'

'A gross exaggeration. The Bow Street Runner does not watch her at all times. He has quite specific instructions as I do not want to alert her to his presence.'

'That I am well aware of. Fortunately, my Invisibles have had her on continuous watch since the moment her husband was first arrested.' And hence the reason, no doubt, that Hadleigh's generosity had been quickly traced back to him despite his best intentions of keeping his guilty secret. The Invisible branch of the King's Elite specialised in blending into the background and watching unseen. Worse, the angry man in front of him had personally trained every last one of them. 'However pragmatic, logical and well meaning it was meant to be, Penny is not going to take the news well. Not when we've had the devil of a job keeping her near us in London and not when she was constantly watched for years on her husband's instruction. She is adamant she is entirely done with all that nonsense going forward. And who can blame her? You should have consulted with me!'

'I do not answer to you, Leatham. Or Lord Fennimore. I answer to the Attorney General.'

'Did you consult the Attorney General?'

Of course not. Had he have done, he would have been reprimanded for even considering helping a traitor's wife. A barrister was supposed to keep his professional life entirely separate from his personal one. They wore wigs and gowns to avoid being recognised out of court by disgruntled receivers of justice or their families or being tracked down by the press and goaded into discussing cases. The Attorney General would take a very dim view of Hadleigh's overwhelming urge to rescue the woman they had callously ruined with one stroke of a pen. 'I wanted to help her.'

'Then you went about it in a very poor manner and have undone months of work. I am actually tempted to strangle you!'

'What work?'

'For the first time in years, she has proper freedom and independence—and even though we know that independence comes courtesy of the pawn shop every month, it is still an achievement. A point of honour and pride. One that we will destroy the second she learns a whole host of people have been working behind the scenes to create the illusion she is coping perfectly well all on her own.'

'She isn't?'

'I think she puts on a good front. She's a good mother and seems to enjoy being mistress of her own house, but it worries Clarissa that she's all alone. That bastard knocked all the confidence out of her and such things take a long time to heal, but that aside, she has nothing. She is nowhere near ready for the harsh realities of life yet, especially one she will be forced to start from scratch. Not that she'll hear it. It's almost as if she's embarrassed by the situation she has been placed in and blames herself a great deal for it, when we all know she was a victim of cruel circumstance. Clarissa has been trying to support her to no avail. Penny point-blank refuses to live with us and is unbelievably stubborn about accepting what she sees as charity.

'She has two perfectly good feet, apparently, and thinks it's long past time she stood on them, regardless of her empty purse. London is expensive and she has a mind to move somewhere cheaper and far away from the *ton* before she is recognised. I can't deny the risk of her true identity being revealed is greater here than anywhere else in the country. That worries me, of course, but if nothing else, here I can ensure she is safe and my wife can be there for her. Recently, she's even started talking about seeking employment,

for heaven's sake, in a big house or school somewhere, so she's clearly concerned about her future. Yet she is so proud she prefers to sell her
mother's jewellery to make ends meet. Again,
something she has no idea we know or have blatantly interfered with. Thanks to you, she might
discover Clarissa and I have surreptitiously been
giving her money all along.'

'You have?'

'Of course we have! We couldn't see her struggle! Penhurst sold everything her parents left her
of value. Those trinkets she sells every month are
pinchbeck and paste at best and all of them in
total would barely have raised enough to scrape
six months' rent. I've been bribing the pawnbroker to give her an excellent price for them to keep
her from leaving any time soon.'

'Ah.' Hadleigh would not mention he had paid
more than market worth to buy them back each
month. He was going to have stern words with
that wily, conniving pawnbroker on the morrow.

'Ah, indeed. I dread to think how she will react
if she ever finds out how Clarissa and I have been
quietly interfering.' Seb let out a long, laboured
breath. 'That's not true. I know exactly what she'll
do. She'll feel betrayed and she'll leave. To go
and stand on her own two feet. One lone, proud
woman with nothing bar a small child, no money
and a past that could come back to bite her at
every turn. Believe me, the world is a hard place

for a woman like that…' Seb's broad shoulders seemed to deflate as he exhaled.

'Which brings me to my final point, the most sensitive and delicate of all the points, and one which a sad bachelor like yourself will have little experience of—my wife *trusted* me to find Penny's mystery benefactor.' Seb slapped his own chest hard. 'She trusted me! Knowing that I would sort it quickly and make it right. Put poor Penny's mind at ease and stop her fleeing out of the sphere of our covert and careful protection. Your actions could destroy months of our good work, a lifelong friendship and ultimately leave Penny vulnerable. So, you see, I *have* to report it all back to Clarissa tonight. I made a promise.'

Yes, perhaps Hadleigh had unintentionally made a delicate situation worse, but Seb was being overdramatic about it. 'Surely you don't have to report everything back to Clarissa? Be selective. Lie if need be. Isn't that what spies excel at? You lie for a living.'

Seb smiled winsomely, his eyes softening for the first time since he had stormed into the place uninvited. 'That I do—but I would never lie to my wife. She is my everything.'

Hadleigh wanted to roll his eyes, but didn't. Seb was newly married and still head over heels in love. It was all a bit bizarre and he didn't understand it. Apart from his mother growing up, he had managed to sidestep any emotional attachments or strong bonds in his life. Largely because emotions in general made him uncomfortable, especially his own. He kept friends at a polite distance, too, preferring the reassuring company of his work more. He could socialise and enjoy it, he didn't suffer from a lack of confidence or shyness around people as Seb did, yet he was still always oddly relieved when a gathering came to an end so he could retreat back into his own space again. Even his sporadic and discreet affairs were with women who were wedded to their independence. Getting too close to anyone made him uncomfortable.

He had always been the same. A little detached. Naturally solitary. A typical only child, he supposed. *Lonely.* Where had that thought come from? Good grief, he needed some proper sleep. 'Then tell Clarissa the truth and have *her* lie to her friend. I meant well and I have no intention of taking the money back when she obviously needs it.' That route would only lead to more tossing and turning and vivid dreams involving soulful blue eyes, when he needed to be on top form till this trial was over.

'You have placed me in an impossible position.' His friend raked his hand through his hair in agitation. 'I'll be honest and say, I cannot promise Clarissa will not unmask you. She and Penny are very close and Penny is *very* upset. Ultimately, we will do what is best for Penny and continue to do whatever it takes to keep her close by.'

'I understand.' At least he thought he did. Seb didn't want Lady Penhurst to know he was protecting her. Hadleigh could sleep better knowing that someone was. 'If you think it would help, I am happy to tell her it was all down to me if it comes to it.' Which he sincerely hoped it wouldn't. Her poignant expression and sorrowful eyes outside the pawnshop this morning had haunted all his waking thoughts since. Given the strange hold the woman seemed to have over him, meeting her again, actually conversing with her, was exceedingly unwise.

'That should keep your own machinations on the lady's behalf out of it.' Not ideal, but he could see he had rather put Seb in an awkward and potentially untenable situation. And he didn't want to be the cause of Lady Penhurst either fleeing the safety of their care or taking menial work which was beneath her. That, certainly, had never been his intention. But then, neither had he intended to ever have to speak to her. A conversation which was bound to be awkward, all things considered. Definitely unprofessional in the extreme. He had prosecuted her husband, for pity's sake! 'Perhaps once I explain my actions were borne out of genuine concern, based on irrefutable fact—' alongside an unhealthy and guilt-fuelled obsession with her '—I am hopeful she will see sense and accept the gift in the spirit in which it was intended. Clearly the woman needs help.'

He used reason for a living. If it came to it, once he stated his case, plainly, and backed it with logical evidence, the truth would become apparent. Failing that, he would use the quick wits he had been blessed with and his innate ability to read people to convince her to accept his financial help. She shouldn't have to struggle alone. Not when he could easily right that wrong at the very least.

'And clearly, my learned friend, you don't know much about women if you think that will be the outcome.' Seb appeared amused as well as appeased as he walked to the door. 'But I shall pass all this on to Clarissa and see what she thinks. As long as it keeps both of us above suspicion and still allows me to keep a vigilant eye on Penny, I am more than happy for you to suffer all the consequences.'

Chapter Three

'Try not to be nervous. Now that we know who the culprit is and that it was meant well, there really is nothing to worry about.' Clarissa offered another one of her reassuring smiles of encouragement which Penny returned half-heartedly when the truth was she was still reeling from the revelation hours later.

While it was a relief to know that she wasn't in any immediate danger, to learn that the man responsible for paying all her debts was the same man who had doggedly pursued her husband through the courts was bizarre. Why would he do that? It made absolutely no sense.

She was nothing to him. Just another face in an ever-changing sea of faces on the busy witness stand of the Old Bailey. Their interactions had been brief and impersonal. Or at least his interactions with her had been impersonal. He never once showed an ounce of human emotion in all the many long hours of the trial. For her, those hours had been deeply personal and life-changing. One minute she had been unhappily married to a brute and the next unwittingly married to a traitor who had been sentenced to death. Now, suddenly, out of the blue, the prosecution lawyer decided he needed to pay all her rent… Why? And more importantly, what the blazes was she supposed to say to him on the subject when he imminently arrived at her small apartment.

'It is peculiar though…isn't it? Why would he do it?' Penny asked. Clarissa had asked the same question at least sixty times since Seb had told her the news just after dawn. What exactly had motivated him to be so unwelcomely generous? Guilt? Penny sincerely hoped not. 'And what possessed him to set a Bow Street Runner on me to watch my every move?' Knowing she had been under surveillance when she had assumed she was safe—completely incognito—really bothered her. Aside from the unpalatable fact that it was reminiscent of her years under watch during her awful marriage, if the Runner had easily found her, would the press? Or her horrid husband's criminal friends? That was the trouble with London. In a vastly overcrowded capital, it was too easy to hide in plain sight. She had become complacent and, in so doing, had stayed far longer than she had originally intended. A situation she needed to quickly remedy for Freddie's sake.

'I don't think he did that for anything other than noble reasons. In many ways, I would actually find it a comfort that somebody cared enough to want to ensure my safety and...' Clarissa's voice petered off as Penny glared and the fraught silence settled between them once again.

They had spoken about this most of the morning. While Clarissa seemed of the opinion it was perfectly acceptable to take the man's money now that they knew who it came from, because it made her life considerably easier, Penny found the idea of his or anyone's charity abhorrent. Again, it felt uncomfortably familiar. Penhurst had made her jump through hoops for every farthing she dared ask for and then used it to his advantage afterwards. You need a new dress? Wear this one... Freddie needs toys? He can have them if you stop bothering Nanny Francis... Your mother is dying and you need to take the post to visit her? If you do as you are told for the next week, and beg convincingly, I might give you the fare...

Such experiences scarred a person.

Besides, never a lender or a borrower be. Her father's old motto rung in her ears and was too ingrained to shift. She had marched blindly into a marriage with a shameless borrower and her life had been both miserable and embarrassing as a result. Before he began his career as a criminal, it had been Penny who had had to deal with the debt collectors and the awkward conversations with friends who had lent him money in good faith when Penhurst knew full well he was in no position to pay it back.

Just thinking about how her life had been made her muscles tense and her toes curl inside her shoes. She would not start her new life beholden to anyone.

How did one explain all that to Clarissa?

Nor could Clarissa possibly empathise, particularly as their perspectives were so at odds. But then Clarissa had not had every aspect of her life controlled and Penny had. What she had initially assumed was her besotted groom's eagerness to have her in his life had quickly turned into a rigid and oppressive life which his penchant for ruthless violence ensured she adhered to. Simple, everyday activities like walking to the village to buy ribbons were restricted unless expressly sanctioned by him. Not that she ever did buy ribbons. To buy ribbons, one needed pin money and despite bringing a significant dowry to the marriage, Penhurst never gave her a farthing unless it had many strings attached.

Control like that made you crave the opposite. Freedom and independence like she used to have. Which was why Penny was eager to start afresh. A new life. A new place. A new, improved and better her, shaped by her past certainly, but not tied to it. Rightly or wrongly, she saw her current situation as a second chance and one she refused to squander. Well before his arrest, her life shackled to Penhurst had become a wretched existence. That that had ended, regardless of the circumstances, had to be viewed as a blessing and she was not inclined to mourn its loss.

Her friend wanted to anchor her here where the past hovered ominously to haunt her for her own well-meant but ultimately insulting reasons. Poor, mistreated, misguided and fragile Penny. A label which was probably well deserved, but now galled, because it reminded her too much of the woman she had temporarily been, but now loathed. Much as she loved Clarissa and would be forever grateful to her, her overprotectiveness now was stifling and, when they clashed on any topics involving Penny's future, felt alarmingly like control once again and instinctively that made her chafe against it. Like her awful husband and her oppressive sham of a marriage, the green, anxiously compliant and tragic Lady Penelope Penhurst was dead and good riddance to her. Long live Penny Henley! Whoever Penny Henley was.

They had both lapsed back into their own quiet thoughts, the brittle peace broken only by the ominous ticking of the second-hand clock on the tiny mantel, until the polite tap on the door had her practically jumping out of her seat.

'Finally!' Clarissa stood with the innate grace her plainer friend had always envied and smoothed down her dress, the action highlighting the first beginnings of the tiny baby bump forming in her normally perfectly flat tummy. The bump which she had yet to formally appraise Penny of, no doubt not to give her another excuse to want to stop being a needy burden on her generous friend's time. 'Sit straighter. Pull your shoulders back. Don't smile. Remember, you want to keep the upper hand.'

Clarissa had staged the room to put the lawyer at a distinct disadvantage. Penny sat in the tallest and most regal chair, one which her friend had had delivered from her own house less than an hour ago to give the illusion of a gravitas she did not feel. Both Clarissa and Seb were to sit on the small sofa near the room's only window, there for moral support and to ensure Penny did not allow herself to be walked over. This was well meant, but it galled. As if she would continue being a doormat after all the times Penhurst had metaphorically wiped his muddy feet on her back!

Lord Hadleigh got to sit in the short, hard chair next to the roaring fireplace. Being mild by October standards, the unnecessary fire would also serve to make the interfering lawyer feel uncomfortable. Clarissa intended the man to bake like a crusty loaf while he sweated out his apology. While Penny thought all her friend's staging was taking things a bit too far, she did hope the searing heat would encourage him to leave swiftly. Hopefully with a polite flea in his ear, put there by the new, assertive, improved version of herself and after promising to acquire a refund from Mr Cohen for the rent. Because Lord only knew Penny stood no chance of scrabbling together a year's worth of rent any time soon to repay him.

Clarissa opened the door and the lawyer positively filled the frame. An unpleasant surprise, when she had worked hard to convince herself he had only seemed imposing in the courtroom because of his austere barrister's attire, and she had been entirely intimidated by the proceedings and the intentional, dramatic theatre of the Old Bailey.

He stepped in, his sharp eyes taking in the whole room, and only then did she notice Clarissa's enormous husband behind him. Heavens, the barrister really was tall! And handsome, in an aristocratic and detached sort of way. She hadn't noticed that before—probably because of the wig and gown. The intimidating staging of the legal system.

'We shan't beat around the bush...' Clarissa gestured specifically to the tiny chair '...seeing that you clearly have some explaining to do and we are keen to hear it.'

He walked straight past the chair and stopped in front of Penny, inclining his golden head politely and taking her hand. 'Lady Penhurst—my humblest of apologies. Leatham here tells me my clumsy gesture caused you angst and for that I shall never forgive myself.'

For some reason, she had not expected an outright apology straight away. Nor such a pretty one. Nor had she expected his gloveless hand to be so warm or his touch so reassuring. As if he had read her mind, his other hand came to rest on top of hers in what she assumed was meant as a friendly gesture, but in actuality made her feel a little odd. Not in an unpleasant way, but those large, gentle hands, combined with the way his unusual burnt-amber eyes locked and held with hers, set her pulse jumping.

She recognised the sensation from long ago. That frisson of awareness and excitement she remembered only too well from those initial heady days of her first and only Season, when a dashing new suitor showed an interest and flirted. Her former hopelessly romantic heart would begin to race as her vivid, naive imagination began to conjure up scenarios of a future with him. Because then, despite all the teachings of her sensible and hard-working parents, she had abandoned good sense for unrealistic dreams of romance and love. What a foolish girl she had been then!

Instinctively, she disentangled her hand and buried it with the other safely within the folds of her skirt. She watched his eyes dip to them before he smiled and her stupid pulse quickened further.

She had never seen him smile. It suited him. 'It was not my intention to cause you concern.'

'What exactly was your intention?' Annoyance at her own body's reaction made her tone irritated and for that, at least, she was glad. She had fallen for pretty words once before and look where that had got her. Annoyed was decisive. Penny Henley was decisive.

He took a step back, but appeared perfectly content to stand. Uncharitably, Penny decided he was avoiding the chair on purpose to deny her the chance to take control and she instantly bristled. 'I imagine, given our limited and professional acquaintance, my actions do seem a trifle odd, but believe me, they truly were well meant. After the Crown saw fit to render you homeless, I could not in all good conscience allow you and your innocent son to struggle.'

He considered Freddie? That was nice... *Good grief, girl, grow a backbone! You used to have such a fine one. He took it upon himself to make a decision for you when he had no right. None whatsoever.* She wasn't a wife any longer. Not a chattel nor a charity case.

'Do prosecution barristers regularly pay the household bills of defence witnesses?' He blinked, the only sign her forthright words had been unexpected.

'Under normal circumstances, the Crown would not take the archaic decision to strip a family of their title and assets.' They agreed on that at least. Losing her home had ripped the floor from under her feet, hurting far more than losing her distasteful husband. 'I was merely attempting to make some small amends for that travesty in my own ham-fisted and clumsy way.'

A plausible answer. A charming and disarming one. But not to her direct question and Penny felt her hackles rise further. He was being the unfazed and convincing lawyer she had seen every day at the Old Bailey, attempting to play her like a violin. She had seen him in action. He was charming and decisive. Used to commanding the ears and then the thoughts of those who found themselves listening to his clever arguments and well-chosen words. A man who had reluctantly come here today with one purpose. To justify having her put under surveillance for months and then anonymously settling her debts—apparently for her own good.

Despite all of Clarissa's careful staging, he now thoroughly commanded the room. He had ignored the tiny chair. Avoided the sweltering fire. And instead of regally looking down her nose at him, Penny was forced to look up. A long way up. Another professional trick he had clearly done on purpose. She stood, hoping she appeared partially regal despite the vast difference in their heights, and allowed her irritation to show plainly on her face. Money aside, no matter which way one looked at it, having her followed was a gross invasion of her privacy, one she had every right to feel angry about.

'Did the Crown also sanction the Runner you had spy on me?'

He blinked again, frowning slightly. 'No. Of course they didn't. My actions have nothing to do with the government or the Crown in any way.'

'But you are such a noble man, such a seeker of justice, that you simply decided to right a wrong regardless? Or do you merely have a guilty conscience about what transpired?'

'Not at all.' He took another step back and his normally inscrutable expression dissolved briefly into one of outrage. 'I had no part in their decision.' The bland barrister's mask slipped back in place. 'If you must know, I petitioned the Attorney General on your behalf.'

That she knew. Clarissa and Seb had told her as much that dreadful night in their house in Grosvenor Square once she realised she no longer had a home to go back to. Those had been the darkest and most hopeless days of her life. The press had huddled outside the house like vultures, doing whatever they could to catch a glimpse of the traitor's wife—soon to be traitor's widow. No peer of the realm had been stripped of his title *and* his estates in decades. Neither had any peer been sentenced to death for any crime—let alone treason—since Lord Lovat after the Battle of Culloden two generations previously. Meanwhile, inside her friend's house Penny had been too stunned, too broken down after years of her oppressive marriage, to do anything other than weep or stare, catatonic.

What was she going to do? What was to become of her son? *Oh, woe is me!*

When news came days later that her husband had escaped the hangman's noose only because his criminal associates had decided it was safer to have him murdered in Newgate than risk having him make any deathbed confessions which might implicate them, an intrepid reporter had broken into Seb's house. The intruder had successfully climbed three stairs before he was tackled and removed by the guards. Those had been three stairs too many for Penny and strangely galvanised her into action, awaking a part of her which had lain dormant for too many years. She was so tired of being the helpless victim.

Weeping and lamenting *Oh, woe is me* was not going to change a single thing and it certainly wasn't going to protect her son. Only she could do both—yet could do neither while feeling pathetically sorry for herself when she only had herself to blame. The signs had been there from the outset. Clarissa had warned her. Even her father had offered to help her flee the church on the morning of her marriage despite spending a king's ransom on the gown, the elaborate wedding breakfast and the marriage settlements, and despite knowing her mother would also be devastated to have encouraged the match. But blinded by the belief she was madly in love and madly loved in return by her handsome, titled, ardent suitor, she had positively floated down the aisle towards her groom, regardless of the niggling voice in her head which cautioned she was making a huge mistake.

It had been a revelation to finally accept the fact she had made her own bed, through her own foolish weaknesses, and now had to lie in it—and just because her new bed was hard and uncomfortable, it didn't make it a bad bed. If anything, it was a significantly superior bed to the one she had been lying in. Only this time, she could make it exactly as she wanted.

The next day she had gone into hiding, in plain sight at Seb's suggestion, to live independently for the first time in her twenty-four years and she had not looked back or wallowed in one drop of pointless self-pity since. Her new life had started and she found she rather enjoyed it. The past was the past. Done. Dead. She had come to terms with it all and was well shot of it. Didn't allow herself to think upon it any more.

Yet now the past was back in the most unexpected and unforeseen way. Not from the press. Not from being recognised. But from the man still stood proudly in front of her. Too proudly when he was the one clearly in the wrong here. What gave him the right to assert change on her life when he'd had a professional hand in creating her current situation? Did he feel guilt at proving her husband guilty?

Perhaps that was the problem? That awful possibility had been niggling since she had learned the truth this morning. What if his guilt about the trial ran deeper than he was letting on? If so, then it kicked a veritable hornets' nest she was only too content to leave well alone.

For five months, there had been no doubt in her mind that Penhurst had been guilty of all the charges levelled against him and probably more. Penny had realised as much the moment the King's Men had stormed into her house and arrested him. Later, the lawyer's case had been convincing and thorough, and while she felt stupid at her own ignorance and ashamed of her own cowardice to question that ignorance, so many things she had seen or heard during the final year of her marriage suddenly made perfect sense once all the pieces of the puzzle were finally slotted together.

Lord Hadleigh had done that. So much so, it had given her the confidence to stand up to her husband by telling the truth and she had resigned herself to hearing a guilty verdict.

Resigned was the wrong word.

It suggested she was dreading the verdict, when the opposite was true. While she had not expected a peer of the realm to receive the death penalty, she had anticipated a guilty verdict and a life blessedly free from Penhurst afterwards. Looked forward to it eagerly—something which caused her guilt late at night when sleep eluded her. Whatever Penhurst had done, he was still the father of her son. Something she knew she would one day have to explain to her little boy.

Was it wrong to be completely relieved to be free of him? Or to have helped him on his way by testifying against him the moment fate had given her the chance? For five months, she had consoled herself that she had done the right thing for Freddie's sake so that he could grow into the man he was meant to be rather than one tainted and poisoned by his sire's warped morals.

The lawyer's guilty conscience suddenly made her question the validity of the trial. Had Lord Hadleigh embellished the truth or lied? Covered important and pertinent details up? Fabricated evidence? She sincerely hoped not. Penny did not want to have any of her relief at the tumultuous end of her marriage dampened. She had hated Penhurst and was glad he was dead. Felt no guilt at his violent passing whatsoever. But guilt might well explain why the lawyer had paid her rent for an entire year.

'I don't want your blood money!'

'Blood money?' Her harsh words took him

aback. 'I can assure you, madam, my gift was nothing of the sort.' Hadleigh raked an agitated hand through his hair and began to pace. The very idea was as preposterous as it was insulting and he wanted to loudly proclaim his utter disgust at the suggestion. He was a principled man who believed in right and wrong. Good and evil. Justice and truth. A man who righted wrongs, not caused them. How dare she even suggest his motives were fuelled by...what? Malpractice? Deceit? Wrongdoing? And on what evidence was his good reputation so unfairly besmirched?

But as he paced the worn old rug on the hard, scuffed wooden floor, took in the mismatched furniture, the cramped and basic surroundings alongside the proud and clearly frightened woman stood before him, he couldn't help but remember a similar scene years ago. And another time when he had attempted to rescue a woman who flatly refused to be rescued because there was nothing she needed to be rescued from.

Absolutely nothing.

Hadleigh realised that losing his temper now, just as it had done then, would not help her at all. Better to stick to reason, logic and the truth and keep emotion well out of it.

'I can see why you would jump to that conclusion, so please allow me to reassure you. My actions had nothing to do with guilt regarding your husband or the way his trial was carried out. I am sorry if you find that difficult to hear, but on that score I am remorseless...' Good grief! Hardly the best way to win her over and accept his benevolence in the spirit it was intended. 'I acted as I did more out of a sense of regret that you had to suffer more than was necessary and completely unjustly. If the Crown refused to see you right, then someone needed to. I am a wealthy man, so it was no hardship for me to help. Consider it my penance for failing to get the Crown to see sense.' He was righting a wrong. It was that simple.

'That does not explain why you saw fit to have me spied upon these past months.'

'I didn't have you spied upon.' So much for sticking to reason, logic and the truth. Hadleigh found himself wincing. She had a perfectly valid reason to be angry with him and now that he was seeing it all through her eyes, he had made a royal hash of it. 'All right... I suppose in a manner of speaking I did, but again it was not done with any malice. After you had been left with nothing—through no fault of your own, I might add—I needed to reassure myself you and your child were coping all alone. When the Runner informed me you were selling your jewellery...'

'Insignificant pieces to which I had no attachment.' Her pretty face flushed as she resolutely avoided her friends' sympathetic eyes and he realised he had inadvertently put his big, fat foot in it again. Like his mother, she was too ashamed of her situation to accept help despite none of it being her fault. 'Things given to me by a husband which I would prefer to forget and mine to dispose of as I see fit.' Despite the fact that both her friends, and he, knew she was pawning her mother's jewellery to pay her monthly bills, she was still labouring under the misapprehension that her friends, at least, didn't. 'I no longer wanted any reminders of him in *my* house.'

She was proud in the face of defeat and his heart wept for her. His hands wanted to touch her, tug her into his arms and hold her close. What was that about, aside from the bone-deep exhaustion which came from weeks of sleeplessness? No wonder his emotions were a tad frayed and close to the surface. 'A perfectly understandable reason to sell them and one which makes me sorrier my heavy-handed and unnecessary response has caused you both worry and embarrassment.'

'I am not in need of charity, Lord Hadleigh.'

'That I can plainly see, my lady.' Blast it all to hell, he had gone about this all wrong. Pride always came before a fall and, like his mother, this one would rather suffer in silence than allow the world to see her pain. He, of all people, should have pre-empted such a reaction. 'And once again, I humbly apologise for insulting you. It was well intentioned, although, I concede, highly inappropriate and misguided.'

It was time to make a hasty retreat before he was backed into a corner of his own making and forced into rescinding his gift before she had had time to mull over the many benefits of it. Given a little time, and the obvious easing of her financial burdens, she might be convinced to keep it.

'I really meant no offence, or to cause you worry of any kind. Although I can see that my ham-fisted, overbearing and overzealous attempt at helping you has done exactly that, and for that I am sorry. This has most definitely not been my finest hour. But know that I am on your side whether you want me to be or not.' From his pocket he produced a calling card which he gently pressed into her hand, making it impossible for her to refuse it. For some reason, his fingers longed to linger so he quickly snatched them away.

'What I should have done all those months ago, rather than put a watch on you, was simply this. Should you need anything…anything at all…money, help…a ham-fisted but well-meaning friend…all you need do is ask. Whatever it is, whenever it is, send word to this address and I will move heaven and earth to see it done.' Before she could respond he bowed. 'Good day to you, Lady Penhurst. Thank you for allowing me the chance to explain and to see for myself the error of my ways. You have been most gracious.'

Then, with the swiftest and politest of nods to the room in general, he promptly turned and marched swiftly out the door.

Chapter Four

Three days of silence lulled him into a false sense of security, so Hadleigh wasn't expecting his clerk to inform him she had turned up at his chambers unannounced, wishing to speak to him. While the clerk went to fetch her, he braced himself for another difficult conversation and was not disappointed. She arrived ramrod straight and proud, only her eyes giving him any indication she was nowhere near as confident as she wanted to portray. They were wide and restless, darting every which way before finally settling on him stood politely behind his paper-strewn desk.

'Please forgive the intrusion, Lord Hadleigh, but I needed to speak with you.'

The gaunt, pale woman from the courtroom was gone and clearly her appetite had improved in the intervening months, as the same dull spencer which had once hung from her frame was now filled with gloriously feminine curves. She might be petite in stature, but there was no disguising she was all woman. Something he had no right noticing considering the circumstances.

'It is no intrusion at all.' He gestured to the chair opposite and she sat daintily on the edge, gripping her reticule for all she was worth. Her errant hands, once again, saying much more of the truth than he was likely to get out of her pretty mouth. 'What did you wish to speak to me about, Lady Penhurst?'

Her dark brows drew together in an expression of what he thought might be distaste as her fingers toyed with the ribbon handle of her bag. 'I am not Lady Penhurst any longer and, if you don't mind, I would prefer not to be addressed as such. I go by Mrs Henley now, which was my mother's maiden name.' Her troubled blue eyes flicked to his briefly as she shrugged an apology. He found himself drowning in their intense, stormy depths. 'There is less chance of my being recognised with a run-of-the-mill name and I would prefer not to use my real married name any more…for obvious reasons.' And there it was again, that flash of distaste, although whether it was at the thought of her husband or her situation, he had no idea.

'Of course…very wise.' He settled back in his chair, hoping his posture would help her to relax, calmly waiting for her to proceed. It didn't. Only the smallest fraction of her bottom was on the chair, her knuckles quite white as she continued to nervously fiddle and twist the ribbons further.

After a few seconds ticked by awkwardly, she sat up straighter. 'The thing is, I went to visit my landlord, Mr Cohen, this morning…and was informed you have made no attempt to contact him since our last meeting…to retrieve your money.'

'Mrs Henley, might I speak plainly?' She nodded, eyes widening once again as if fearing his words. 'I think we would both agree our last meeting was a little awkward. I believe we both left a great deal unsaid.' How to frame these next words in the most gentle and appeasing way and leave her dignity intact? 'For my part, I realised that neither Clarissa nor Seb knew you were selling your jewellery, so I quickly backtracked to avoid further embarrassing you.'

'I explained about the jewellery, Lord Hadleigh.' Two charming pink spots began to appear on her cheeks which called her a liar. 'They were gifts from my husband and I no longer wanted them.'

Pride always came before a fall. 'I beg to differ. I saw you that morning outside the pawnshop.' It had done odd things to his heart.

'You did?' That seemed to surprise her and set her expressive eyes blinking. She had lovely long lashes. Dark and thick. The sort that waylaid a man's thoughts from the important task at hand, much like the way she filled out that spencer.

'Indeed I did, so I saw for myself how difficult you found it to part with them.' Should he
tell her he had the brooch? That it was safe with
all the other trinkets necessity had forced her to
sell and hers again whenever she wanted? Probably not. It would make her feel more beholden,
when clearly beholden was the state which caused
her the greatest discomfort. 'I also went in and
questioned the pawnbroker who showed me the
piece. It was old and well-worn. You were married only three years, were you not? Hardly long
enough to cause the deterioration I witnessed
in that brooch. Which lead me to believe it was
hardly the sort of piece of jewellery a husband
would give to his wife.'

'My husband was not a generous man...'

'Mrs Henley, we both know that was your
mother's brooch or your grandmother's. It was a
sentimental item. Worth more to the heart than
the purse.' He had similar items himself. The
handkerchiefs his mother had embroidered for
him. Her letters sent while he was away studying. The last one filled with no hint of the nightmare she was living or the absolute fear she must
have been feeling in the days before her death. If
only he could turn back time.

'And what if it was?' The sudden affected bravado was brittle and unconvincing. Eerily familiar. 'It was still mine to do with as I wished.'

He mentally took a step away from those old

emotions which had suddenly decided to plague him to focus on the here and now. An unfair wrong he could easily right and the woman his soul appeared to demand he rescue. 'The Runner said you took the money from the jewellery each month directly to the shops and used it to pay your accounts.' Hadleigh decided to present her with irrefutable evidence in the hope she might realise further lies were pointless. 'You always go to Palmer's Shop of All Things first because it is closest to the pawnshop. Then you walk to your landlord Mr Cohen's place next, followed by Shank's the butcher and Mrs Writtle's bakery. I can even tell you how much you paid to each of these merchants and how much you received for each precious piece of your mother's jewellery that was sold.'

She blinked rapidly, her mouth opening to speak before she closed it firmly. For several moments, she seemed smaller and he realised now might be the best chance he had of appealing to her logic. 'You see, I had a very clear picture of your finances, Mrs Henley, before I took it upon myself to assist you with them.' He exhaled slowly and waited for her dipped eyes to pluck up the courage to rise back up to meet his. 'You were barely making ends meet and unless you have a jewellery box stuffed full of old earrings and brooches to sell, I also knew your reserves would likely soon run out. That is why I stepped in…or stomped in more like.' He smiled to soften the blows he had just dealt her. 'I wanted to take that worry away from you. I still do. That is why I have not, nor will I make any attempt to get the rent money back from Mr Cohen. Allow me to help you.'

She was silent for an age, sat perfectly still. Only the occasional movement of the fingers now buried within the folds of her skirt made her appear less like an inanimate statue. 'Your Runner really was thorough, wasn't he?'

'I made sure I engaged the best.'

'Except he didn't know everything, did he?' Her head tilted and she gazed at him down her nose, her slim shoulders rising proudly. For some reason, he liked that version of her more. She wasn't broken. She had gumption. 'I am leaving Cheapside soon to take employment elsewhere. That has always been my intention. So you see, Lord Hadleigh, your decision to pay a year's worth of my rent was quite pointless.'

He didn't believe her. 'Perhaps—but at least it gives you the option to decide whether or not now is the right time to take employment. You have a young son, do you not? Is he old enough for you to leave him?'

'I shan't be leaving him. He will be coming with me.' Her nose rose a notch higher. 'Therefore, you have wasted a great deal of money.'

'It is mine to waste, my lady.'

She briefly chewed on her bottom lip, drawing his eyes to it, before she caught herself and feigned nonchalance. 'Have it your own way.' She stood quickly, looking as though she was about to break into a run, then surprised him by rifling in her reticule. 'I anticipated your refusal.' She placed six guineas in a neat stack on his desk. 'I believe that covers half of the debt I owe you. I will begin reimbursing you for the rest as soon as I receive my first month's wages.'

He hadn't been expecting that, she could see, because he stiffened and frowned at the coins. Finally, after what felt like an age, his penetrating gaze fixed on her. He had unusual eyes. Golden brown, almost amber in colour. Unnerving and perceptive. They matched his hair which was a tad too long and curling above his collar and austere, simply tied cravat. Pompous and handsome. The all-too-familiar combination. His prolonged scrutiny unnerved her, but she stood proudly. She had made a plan, a good one, and all she had to do was stick to it.

'There is no way I will accept it.' To prove his point, he slid the column of coins back towards her. She ignored them.

'As our business is now concluded, I shall bid you a good day, Lord Hadleigh.' She had hoped to appear formidable as she said this before turning and striding decisively towards the door.

'Oh, for goodness sake! Stop being so stubborn when it is patently obvious you need it!' He stood, his palms flat and braced on his desk as he quashed the brief flash of temper and replaced it with an expression which was irritatingly reasonable. 'The Crown, in its lack of wisdom, did you wrong and I am simply making it a little bit right.'

'That is your opinion and you are entitled to it, just as I am entitled to be stubbornly opposed to your unwelcome interference in my life.' An awkward silence hung and she let it. There was no point in arguing with the man. He was used to getting his own way, as men were, and she needed to get used to being the new improved Penny who was mistress of her own destiny. Besides, it felt empowering to take a little control back from this man who was clearly used to owning it.

The overbearing lawyer stared, then for the first time since she had encountered him he appeared awkward in his own skin. He glanced down at his feet, then raked a hand through his hair before those unusual eyes locked on hers, the emotion in them unfathomable. But there *was* emotion. And it wasn't anger at her rude behaviour. 'Why won't you allow me to help you?'

'I have no need of anyone's help, my lord.'

'I think you do. The life you now have is no life for either you or your son.'

That was insulting. It might well not be much of a life yet, but it was infinitely better than the one she had had and she was committed to making it better. What right did he have to judge her? To do what *he* thought best and enforce *his* will? 'My life is none of your business.' Another rude outburst which she wasn't the least bit sorry for. Clearly, a tiny bit of her spine had already grown back to so plainly voice her outrage.

'I cannot, in all good conscience, allow you and your son to continue living like that when I have the means and the desire to help you. Is a life of poverty, pawnshops, scrimping and saving...' he scowled again as if the cosy little oasis she had lovingly made was somehow abhorrent '...truly the life you want for your son?'

'Was it your intention to insult me and the life I have worked hard to make for myself? For if it was, you have succeeded, sir.'

'I meant no offence. I am merely trying to help to make your lot in life better after the grievous injustice you have been made to suffer.'

'By bullying me into your way of thinking? By accepting your money to make yourself feel better about whatever it is that has put a bee in your bonnet?' She watched his golden eyebrows draw together a second before his eyes dropped to stare at the ground. 'If you really want to help me improve my lot, my lord, then you can start by sparing me the continued ordeal of your presence or interference.' Realising her feet had taken her back towards his desk during her impassioned speech, Penny briskly walked back to the door, strangely enjoying the sensation of being angry at a man and not fearing his retribution, although bewildered as to why she didn't fear it with him when he was so annoyingly overbearing.

It made no difference that his broad shoulders were slumped or that his normally piercing gaze was rooted to the floor as if he was miraculously unsure of himself. As if a man like him would ever know what it truly felt to be uncertain about anything. He deserved one more parting shot and so did she. 'I have spent three miserable years being dictated to by a man. Three years being bullied and lectured.'

'You cannot compare my actions to his.' He appeared hurt at the suggestion.

'Can I not? You had me spied upon, just like him. You are trying to enforce your will upon me—just like him. And ultimately, whatever your intentions, noble or otherwise, you are using my weaknesses to control me. You just belittled me to my face. Just…like…him.' She sounded like her old self, the one before Penhurst she still liked. It was a heady feeling and she was proud of herself. This was the Penny she wanted to be again. Brave and undaunted. Unapologetically marching to the beat of her own drum.

'You are not my master, sir. I cannot begin to tell you how relieved I am that nobody is any longer nor will anyone ever be again. Nor do I need a benefactor. What you see as for my own good to right a wrong, I see as unwarranted and insulting interference now that I finally have my freedom back. If I want money, I will earn it. My labour in return for wages! Because that is an equal transaction, one I am entirely familiar with. One both parties can terminate whenever they see fit.'

Head still bent, his eyes lifted, seeking hers almost tentatively. 'I find myself again in the awkward position of having to offer you another heartfelt apology, for if you misconstrued any of my actions as bullying then I am mortified. I abhor bullies and it is humbling to realise that in attempting to enforce my will, I inadvertently became one. You are quite correct—you have every right to be angry at me. If it is any consolation at all, I am furious at myself.' He looked pained and awkward as he slowly picked up the six guineas from the desk and placed them in the drawer. Only once he had pushed it closed did those unusual perceptive eyes lock with hers again. They were swirling with an emotion she couldn't quite fathom. Regret? Sadness? Shame? Whatever it was it made him seem more human. 'But for the record, despite all the mounting evidence to the contrary, I swear to you on my life I am nothing like *him*.'

Chapter Five

The pews in St George's in Hanover Square weren't meant for big men, yet for some inexplicable reason the ushers at Lord Fennimore's wedding had decided to seat the two biggest together in the middle of a row. Seb Leatham's ridiculously burly shoulders were encroaching into his space on one side and a strange woman's ludicrously large bonnet inhabited the other. In silent, tacit agreement, both men were twisted at the same obtuse angle to try to make the best of it.

'Dear God, I hope the bride arrives soon!' Leatham hated social occasions and was already getting twitchy.

'It's the bride's prerogative to be late, so please try to sit still.'

'My leg is going to sleep. My backside is already numb!'

'Then it shouldn't be long till your leg joins it and you won't feel the pain any more.' If only all pain could be so easily desensitised. The dull, constant one in his conscience had taken permanent root since she had held a mirror up to his face. What had he been thinking? Acting like the Admiral of the fleet, snapping out orders and expecting them to be followed, when any fool with half a brain would know a woman who had suffered at the hands of a dictatorial, brutish husband was never going to respond well to such behaviour. Common sense would tell them that the reaction would either be cowering fear or bristling outrage. He was heartened that her response to his I-know-better-than-you tactics had been to fight back. He doubted he could live with himself if he had caused a woman's fear. No matter how much he worried that the man in the mirror that day might be a little too much like his father for comfort, to be that much like his father made him feel physically sick.

'The bride is certainly milking her prerogative to be late! There is late and then there is just plain self-indulgence.'

A scowling society matron offered them a pointed look, one which clearly said shut up. Hadleigh lowered his voice further, because he couldn't pretend even to himself any longer that he didn't need to know. 'How is she?' A very touchy subject, seeing as Leatham had threatened to break his idiotic, ham-fisted and worthless neck over the guineas incident three weeks ago.

'How the blazes do you think she is?' Seb offered him his most withering of glances. 'Applying for every blasted housekeeper or governess
job from here to John O'Groats to no avail to pay
you back what she owes you. Hell-bent on leaving
London as soon as possible regardless. Scrimping on food for herself to make the last pennies
she has stretch further. Clarissa is beside herself
with worry! I hope you are pleased with yourself.
If she ends up working for some robbing scoundrel for farthings in the back of beyond, I give
you fair warning, I've promised my wife I'll give
her your *jewels* as earrings.' His friend threw up
his hands despite the confined space. 'I just don't
understand it. You are normally such an affable
fellow. Charming, even. Upright, upstanding—
normally annoyingly very sensible. Yet in all your
dealings with poor Penny you have been a total
oafish idiot!'

Hadleigh couldn't argue with that description.
'Surely I can do something to help? I could try
talking to her again…' Something he had desperately wanted to do since she had given back
his now-tainted six guineas and left him with
a heavy heart and his tail between his legs. He
only wanted to make things right and it was driving him mad that he had been thwarted in that
noble quest.

'Stay away from her!' Seb's elbow jabbed him
hard in the ribs. 'Unless you know some gener-

ous toff with an estate that needs a very well-paid housekeeper, you've caused more than enough trouble already!' Hadleigh had an estate… She wanted to trade her labour for honest wages… *that* might just work…

No! Bad idea… A very bad idea. For so many reasons.

'Hallelujah!' Seb's cry had the stern matron frowning again. 'I do believe it's finally time for the off.'

Hadleigh settled back in the pew as the organ began to play and fixed his gaze firmly on Lord Fennimore waiting nervously at the altar in an attempt to stop his mind whirring. There was no point in attempting to meddle again. She wouldn't take well to it and Seb would kill him. Clarissa, too. Lady Penhurst probably hated him. Another depressing thought. Not that he wanted her to like him, but still…she thought him a bully. No better than her awful husband. He felt an ache form between his eyebrows and realised he was scowling, something which was hardly fair on the bride, so he stalwartly banished all thoughts of saving the proud and exasperating woman who didn't want rescuing to focus on the unlikely wedding about to take place in front of him.

The Commander of the King's Elite was close to sixty and, up until recently, had been a confirmed bachelor wedded solely to his profession. Yet, like Warriner, Leatham, Flint and Gray, he had also fallen victim to the parson's trap. All five men—Hadleigh's friends and comrades—had succumbed in quick succession this past year. Like dominoes, lined up just to fall, there had also been an inevitability about it. The ladies they had fallen for were all perfect for them. But out of the five of them, only Lord Fennimore's impending nuptials had surprised him. Not because his choice of bride was wrong—Hadleigh had developed a soft spot for the indomitable Harriet and wished them all the happiness in the world—but because he saw a great deal of himself in old Fennimore. More, he hoped, than he saw of his father.

They shared the same set of values, had a defined and unwavering moral compass and the same determination to see things through no matter what. It was a solitary path, but a noble one. A vocation even. Nothing was more important than getting the job finished and seeing justice done.

Righting wrongs.

That single-minded, driven determination was what made them the men they were and why they had climbed so quickly to the pinnacle of their careers. Nothing else was more important.

Except, apparently, now the soon-to-be Lady Fennimore was equally as important, or perhaps more so, and that was a state of affairs Hadleigh simply couldn't fathom. He had never been in love. Never come close to it and couldn't imagine why he would want to be. Despite knowing he was capable of experiencing powerful emotions, because Lord only knew they had plagued him since the blasted trial, they had never been something he had been comfortable with. He buried them, hid them and, if the situation warranted it, hot-footed it as fast as he could to escape them. Anger was destructive. Fear knotted the gut. Grief was too painful and shame gnawed at you from the inside as it was right now.

He'd had indigestion for a week thanks to his spectacular error of judgement and his insomnia concerning a certain former witness had got so bad, he rarely managed a few hours of broken sleep before his troubled conscience woke him up. The strange nightmare was cyclical and went nowhere. Stormy, proud blue eyes with ridiculously long lashes haunted his dreams. Fevered dreams where her expressive, elegant hands kept trying to hide the truth in his tangled sheets as his own tried frantically to hold one again. Or hold her. But she was always out of reach. It was driving him mad and he hated all the foggy-headed confusion which inevitably followed for hours afterwards.

If shame and his initial misplaced guilt was capable of doing all that, one didn't need to experience romantic love to know that its power could be unbelievably destructive and he knew enough about it from observation to be certain it required far more effort and time than he was prepared to spend on it any time soon.

The old man saw his bride in the entrance to St George's and visibly relaxed, his permanently scowling expression softening into a smile for once at just the sight of her. When the ceremony was over he proudly stood with her on his arm, basking in the congratulations of the guests and later in her company during the interminable wedding breakfast.

Interminable because, despite the crush, the laughter and the presence of good friends, Hadleigh felt alone. As if something was missing. An odd thought when he always preferred his own company and, being an only child, had lived like that for as long as he could remember. Both self-reliant and usually contentedly solitary. Yet that alien feeling refused to go away no matter how much small talk he exchanged with the other wedding guests at the wedding breakfast or how many times he reminded himself he was perfectly at ease with his life exactly as it was as the party whirled on around him.

Alongside that was the annoyingly persistent melancholy which he was usually very adept at burying in work, but which had bothered him unrelentingly since the Penhurst trial first began. Probably because Lady Penhurst's situation reminded him too much of his mother's. That, and the enormous hash he had made in trying to help her.

Rationally, he knew that. He dealt in evidence and truths, so it was impossible to ignore the stack of eerie coincidences piling inside his troubled conscience. Like his mother, Lady Penhurst had been subjected to both physical and mental abuse during her marriage. Exactly like his mother, she was an innocent suffering thanks to an overbearing man. And because history enjoyed repeating itself, both women were destined to suffer for ever for their spouses' sins when they had had no hand in them themselves. The law gave no rights to wives. While Hadleigh was determined to uphold the law until his dying breath, he was also prepared to concede that as far as women were concerned the law was an ass, too, and desperately needed changing.

On this occasion it had been the biggest ass of all. A big, fat, clumsy, vengeful ass which he hadn't been able to prevent or overturn despite his being entirely in the right. Which, in turn, had led him to be a big, fat, clumsy, ultimately domineering ass himself. Just like his father and her foul husband. History repeating itself again, yet that still didn't make the truth any easier to swallow.

Logically, his legal brain also recognised it was no coincidence that the timing was significant, too. The Penhurst trial had taken place exactly one decade since his mother's tragic death.

Ten years was a significant anniversary and one which had lurked darkly for months long before the blasted Penhurst trial. It had been the first thing he had thought of when he had awoken on New Year's Day and would doubtless lurk until the bells signalled the turning of another year in a few months' time. Yet, exactly like that year, this one was a defining one in his life. This year, he would try the biggest case of his career. Back then, the year had culminated with his call to the bar.

He should have deferred that year. As his health declined, so too had his father's temper become more erratic and explosive than it had ever been before. Irrefutable evidence he had witnessed with his own eyes ten years ago, yet he had preferred to listen to the untruths his ears had heard come from his selfless mother's lips.

Everything was fine. She could cope.

Good grief! All this pointless pondering on his own befuddled emotions created by the past twisting and tangling and confusing with the present was exhausting. No wonder he couldn't sleep!

'How is the case coming along?' Lord Fennimore's voice snapped him blessedly back to the present. 'Is it as cut and dried as we'd hoped?'

'Perhaps not cut and dried.' Because in a British court of law anything could, and did, happen. 'But certainly promising. Now that we have the ringleader, I've been able to dig up all manner of things.' Lady Gislingham's co-conspirators were beginning to panic. 'Unsurprisingly, already two of her former associates have felt compelled to turn King's evidence to save their own sorry skins and each day more damning evidence spews out of their mouths.' The two had pleaded guilty and accepted a lesser sentence of life imprisonment in exchange for their testimony. 'Although the circumstances by which it comes still galls me.'

'Irritating—but we must sacrifice a few minnows for the shark. Though I dare say after a few years in that stinking gaol they'll regret saving themselves. If they avoid the diseases for that long...' Lord Fennimore cast a quick glance to his new wife who was holding court in the corner. Harriet was a vivacious and entertaining woman. An unlikely match for his serious and brusque superior. 'I promised my wife I wouldn't talk shop till tomorrow. Do you have a date yet?'

The dedicated commander of the King's Elite was postponing his own honeymoon until the case was over. 'The Crown want it done and dusted quickly—however, to put forward a thorough and conclusive case I'm tabling the first week of January.'

'Capital. Two months is a good buffer. I shall be sure to speak to the Attorney General and the King's advisors, endorsing your suggestion.

Like you, I want to be sure that woman and her minions get exactly what's coming to them. As keen as the government are to get this over and done with, a hasty trial may well backfire. However, Flint won't like the extra delay. He's understandably reluctant to bring his wife to London after the circus of the Penhurst trial…and just in case there are a few wrong 'uns still at large who we've missed.' The old man rolled his eyes.

Flint's new wife was Hadleigh's key prosecution witness. Not only had she been forced to work with the Comte de Saint-Aubin-de-Scellon, the crazed leader of the French side of the smuggling ring, she had also written encoded messages to all the British traitors, which categorically implicated them in the treachery. She knew each one by name.

'Do you think she is still in danger?'

'I don't—but then she's not *my* wife. If it was Harriet, I'm not sure I'd want her in the capital either until absolutely necessary. Too much risk… what with the press and all.' His eyes drifted to his new spouse again and his serious, professional expression curiously disappeared for a split second before he scowled again. 'But I suppose you need her here for the good of the trial.'

'I need to go through everything she knows again with a fine toothcomb. Every day turns up something new which will need corroborating.

I want to leave no stone unturned and no loop-hole open.'

'A fair point. I'll strap on some armour and put it to Flint. Although I dare say he'll insist on using all the resources of the King's Elite and perhaps all the King's cavalry regiments to guard her, too, if I demand she has to venture out of his castle. Have you seen how many people he has guarding this wedding? I had the devil of a job convincing him to leave Cornwall to come today—and I was his father's oldest and dearest friend. But he is a man besotted and there is no reasoning with such a man.'

'Perhaps he'd find it more palatable if we hid Jessamine somewhere not too far from London?' The idea was forming again. No doubt a fool-hardy one, but his emotions had apparently taken hold of his reason and no matter how much he tried, he still couldn't shift his misplaced guilt or his ridiculous need to rescue that woman who had been wronged so grievously on his watch. 'Somewhere private enough to avoid any sus-picion and easily secured. A place owned by an honorary member of the King's Elite...'

'I'm listening...'

'Well, I have an estate in Essex which would work perfectly if the government would care to borrow it.'

Don't open Pandora's box!

'You do? You've never mentioned it.'

That's because he preferred not to remember it and all the bad memories within it. 'My work here keeps me too busy. I rarely go there.' Around nine years ago had been the last time—to put his father in the ground. He'd had it boarded up four years ago when the butler, the last-standing indoor retainer, had finally acknowledged Hadleigh was never coming home and had taken his pension and his wife to move closer to their son. 'It's spacious. Walled and sits on a hill in the centre of its five hundred acres. Flint, his wife and all the guards he can muster could live there until the trial. It wouldn't take much to make it habitable.' Aside from removing four years' worth of dust and cobwebs, ripping off the dust sheets and hiring a whole host of new servants to bring it back to life. Nothing a small fortune and a good housekeeper who could start immediately couldn't sort out—

If he could find a way to convince her—because he had the small fortune a hundred times over. She did want to work for wages, after all.

He could lie, he supposed. Pretend the house was Flint's... As soon as that thought popped into his head, he sent it swiftly packing. No more well-meaning deceptions and schemes as far as Lady Penhurst was concerned. An offer of genuine employment wasn't charity, so she could hardly refuse it on that score. She either took the job above board, knowing who the real owner was, or she didn't. And perhaps this time he should allow her to meet the real Hadleigh, too. The charming one who had a way with people, not the self-righteous oaf who used a mallet to crack a nut and behaved like a cretin. Either way, at least he would have tried everything within his power to help her rise above the government's unjust punishment and his prickled conscience would have to find a way to cope with that.

There were other benefits to having her take charge of his unwanted house. Genuine benefits which had nothing to do with his own need to right a wrong. Firstly, as a good friend to Clarissa and by default Seb, she knew about the King's Elite so they would not have to creep around covertly in case she overheard something. She was bound to have been kept abreast of developments, even if the Leathams had been sketchy on the details and so far nothing had leaked. Therefore, it stood to reason she was trustworthy. That was a practical consideration. As was the fact she knew what it was like to be a witness in a high-profile case. She could help better prepare Jessamine for the ordeal ahead. Most practical of all, was that it was far enough outside of London to allow Flint and his bride to hide from any perceived danger, but close enough that Hadleigh could travel back and forth in a day, therefore never having to sleep in the damned place.

Two birds. One fat stone. *And Pandora's blasted box!*

'That might work, Hadleigh.'

He could see that Lord Fennimore was already enthused by the prospect because he wasn't scowling, yet instead of feeling the elation at having convinced him, dread settled like lead in the pit of his stomach. He would have to go home. *Good grief! He would have to go home!*

'It would certainly keep the blasted press away.'

'A blessing indeed, as they have already started to pester me.' Bands of panic had already began to wrap themselves around Hadleigh's neck. Squeezing. Why was he doing this? He knew the answer, but didn't quite understand it. *Her.* And his ongoing and debilitating insomnia.

'Then let's make it so and I'll give Flint no choice in the matter. He's never been very good at disobeying direct orders. Besides, we want you to build a conclusive case, Hadleigh, and this timely solution allows us to do it. After all the effort and lives it took to stop The Boss, we cannot allow anything to get in the way of seeing proper justice served.'

Chapter Six

She pulled open the door impatiently. 'I didn't expect to see you again.' Although bizarrely Penny was not surprised to find him on the other side of it when all hell had just broken loose in her apartment. When she had heard the knock, she didn't dither. Didn't bother asking who it was, because she knew it was him. She could sense it.

'Yes, I know. But I have a proposition.' As she glared he raised both hands, palms up in surrender. 'Not from me—I wouldn't dare—but from the government.'

'The government?' She hadn't expected him to say that and wasn't entirely sure she believed him. 'And pray what do *the government* want with me tonight?'

'An important service which they will happily pay you handsomely for—if you can spare them a few months.' His eyes wandered from her suspicious face to the utter carnage beyond. How typical he would turn up now when she was at a distinct disadvantage, looking exactly like a woman who couldn't cope. She had turned her back for two minutes to make herself a well-earned cup of tea after a taxing day and her son had found the small sack of flour she had bought on the romantic and foolish whim of baking biscuits. All by herself. To cheer herself up after receiving yet another rejection letter. The third this week. Nobody wanted to employ a woman with a child in tow, so she would never be able to pay this man back.

Now, all that flour which her son wasn't currently wearing coated the entire floor. Instead of looking aristocratically appalled at the mess, he smiled sympathetically. 'Although I see I have called at a bad time.'

'A very bad time.' But for some reason, she didn't slam the door in his face as she should have. 'Since Freddie started toddling, I apparently have to nail everything down. Even things locked away in a cupboard.' She didn't need to justify herself to him, except her nerves were frazzled and after a day spent trying to soothe an unreasonable baby who flatly refused to be soothed or give her any indication as to why he was so fractious, she was pathetically pleased to see someone. Even if that someone happened to be the sanctimonious, self-righteous lawyer. Parenting alone was hard work. Especially at the end of a long day when she hadn't spoken to a single other human being over the age of one.

'I looked away for a second…perhaps a whole minute…and he has wreaked complete destruction.' Suddenly she wanted to cry. Crumple to a heap on the floor, roll herself up into a ball and wail in complete, impotent frustration. When the hideous trial or the imminent prospect of financial ruin hadn't beaten her spirit, clearly another stupid rejection letter and a bag of spilled flour could. She must have looked as utterly miserable and fed up as she felt because he immediately stepped over the threshold and reassuringly squeezed her arm.

'Then allow me to help before you dismiss me again.' Once again, she found his warm touch strangely reassuring, except this time, although only the lightest and briefest of touches, she could still feel it after he took his hand away. 'It is the least I can do after everything. Besides, I am exceedingly good in a crisis. It is one of my strengths.'

'There is no need for you to help me. I can manage…'

'Perfectly well on your own. Yes, I believe I have heard that speech.' He was still smiling. It was a nice smile. An extremely human and genuine one. 'And while I am prepared to concede that under perfectly normal circumstances you can—without my overbearing interference—this hardly constitutes a normal circumstance and helping you to clean up a bit of flour hardly leaves you for ever in my debt, now, does it? If it squares things up in that proud head of yours, I shall have flour strewn all over my office on the morrow and you can come and help clear it up to make us even.'

Not waiting for her response, he headed straight to her tiny kitchen and began to look about. 'Do you own a broom? A dust pan, perhaps?' She hadn't expected that and pointed ineffectually to where they were kept in the furthest corner as she closed the door. Before Freddie caused more chaos, she picked him up. Something which didn't please him because he struggled and whined, smearing flour all over the front of her dullest, most shapeless house dress.

Not that she should be ashamed of that, when she had not expected visitors and certainly never him again, but up against his fine clothing she did. His outfit today was more suited to a fancy dinner party than an official visit to Cheapside.

'Have you ever had cause to use a broom?'

'I've brushed down a horse and mucked out a few stables in my time.' From the amusement radiating from his unusual eyes, he was plainly not insulted by her lack of faith in his domestic abilities. 'I'm sure the principal is similar, but I'm happy for you to give me pointers.'

He swiftly shrugged out of his greatcoat and tossed it over the sofa, then stalked back towards the kitchen to retrieve the tools. Then, in a surreal spectacle she had never dreamed of witnessing, she stood by stunned as he began to wield the broom with economic precision. The wretch had clearly used a broom before. Of course he had. 'Really, I can manage well enough and you are hardly dressed for the occasion.' Freddie chose that moment to begin to howl, push and twist his back over the cage of her arms. His small, angry handprints making a haphazard pattern across her bosom.

'Why don't you sit down and try to distract your son from his ill temper while I remove the worst of it?' His amber eyes were kind for once and out of frazzled necessity she found herself complying, despite not wanting him to witness her continued current ineptitude. Doubtless he would enjoy seeing stark evidence of her inability to cope all on her own.

He picked up her smothered embroidery hoop and frowned as he handed it to her. 'I fear your sewing might be ruined.'

'Believe me, it was ruined long before the flour got to it.'

As Freddie's fidgets became less enthusiastic, she could do little else but watch her rescuer. Lord Hadleigh didn't look much like a lawyer now, nor did he seem half as intimidating. He did well to tame most of the flour into a tiny heap in the middle of the parlour, but puffs of it floated around regardless, clinging to his highly polished boots from heel to shin. Something he either didn't appear to mind or even be aware of when they were clearly expensive boots. She had never seen him without a billowing greatcoat or barrister's gown before, so the sight of him in boots and breeches was unexpected. Without those extra layers he was still a large specimen of the male species. Tall and surprisingly broad, he would have topped Penhurst by several inches in height and significantly more in width. There had to be at least two feet of man between his arm sockets, maybe more.

As he knelt to sweep the pile of flour into a pan, she got to study the sight of those breeches in profile unwatched. He wore them well. Because of his height, she had assumed his legs would be thin and gangly. However, the thighs which perfectly filled out the buff kerseymere stretched taut around them had been honed on horseback rather than by sitting behind a desk. They had to be. A gentleman might pad his jackets as her husband always had, but never his breeches. That would only look silly... Why was she thinking about a man's breeches? Not that she needed to feel guilty about contemplating an impressive pair of thighs now that she was a delightedly unmarried and independent woman. But *his* thighs! When she hadn't shown a single jot of interest in any man's anything in years! Clearly, she was overtired and overwrought this evening to be so befuddled. An unanticipated flour storm could do that. 'Really, thank you... I can clean up the rest once I put Freddie to bed. It's late and he is tired.' Polite code for leave. Now.

'I suspect your little man could do with a bath before bed. Why don't you see to that while I finish up with the mess? Then we can talk business unhindered.' Making it plain he had no intention of leaving any time soon, he went to the heavy kettle and grabbed a nearby rag to test its weight before topping it up from the jug as if he had spent his life in tiny kitchens. 'Where do you keep the tub?'

In her bedchamber. A place Lord Hadleigh was most definitely even less welcome in than her parlour. 'I will fetch it.' She bustled off with her grumpy son balanced on one hip and closed the door firmly behind her. No sooner has she deposited him on the rug, an unwelcome tap on the door made her realise the lawyer had no respect for boundaries.

'What?' She practically snarled the word at the wood and felt instantly guilty for her tone when he genuinely was only trying to help.

'It seems silly dragging the bath out here when there is still flour everywhere and I can just as easily bring in all the water. Then I'll have everything spick and span before you finish.'

While his suggestion made sense, she still did

not want him setting one foot into her most private of spaces, nor did she feel particularly gracious. 'Kindly leave the water outside the door once it's ready. I don't want Freddie accidentally scalding himself.'

'Ah...yes. I never thought of that. My experience with children is limited.' She heard his boots retreat over the hard, wooden floor, heard the sound of flour being swept into the dust pan and sighed with relief. If he wasn't leaving, then seeing to Freddie in private gave her pause enough to compose herself properly. Clearly, he had pondered their last interactions and decided he was unhappy with losing. She had seen his technique in court—whittle away until there was nothing left to whittle. Whatever he was intent on *proposing* needed to be digested with a level head, not a frayed one. The lawyer had a fundamental problem with the word 'no' and her nerves were too close to the surface to have his clever arguments wrap her in knots designed to encourage her to comply. Besides, making him wait would make her feel a tad more in command of the situation.

Penny took her time preparing everything she needed. Soap, towels, Freddie's nightgown. She stripped her son and hugged his adorable, wriggling cherub's body while she dusted as much of the flour as she could out of his hair. Finally, she placed the half-bath near the glowing fireplace in time to hear the water arrive outside.

He had taken himself back to the kitchen out of sight by the time she opened the door, so she set about filling the tub with all the boiling kettle water and a generous amount of the cold water he had also left in a large pail. The warm bath seemed to improve Freddie's mood and he allowed her to wash him from head to toe while he splashed about giggling.

His eyes were drooping as she gently towelled him off, brushed his damp, brown curls and bundled him into his bedclothes. Some warm milk and he would be out like a light for the rest of the night. She left him lying on his back on the rug, examining his small feet as they shamelessly waved up in the air, while she tried to repair the damage done to herself. It was little more than Clarissa's staging again, but it would make her feel better. When the dampened edge of the towel failed to remove the flour handprints from her bosom, she quickly retrieved another dress from her limited selection in the wardrobe and hastily put it on in case the man beyond the door decided to barge through it.

The silence beyond suggested Lord Hadleigh had finished bringing order to floury chaos and the time for avoiding him was now past. Hopefully projecting a confidence she didn't feel, she scooped her child up and decisively opened the door, only to find the current bane of her life not in her now-spotless parlour at all. No evidence of the flour explosion remained anywhere. He must have beaten the rug as well as washed down the floor. A few wet smears on the dull polished floorboards bore testament to the latter.

He poked his golden head out of the kitchen and smiled. 'Perfect timing. I've just made an entire pot of tea...*all by myself.*' Was he mocking her lack of faith in him or being self-effacing? Penny was too jittery to tell. 'I thought you might need it.' To prove it, he held a laden tray aloft. It ominously held two cups. 'Everything is better after a cup of tea.'

'I need to warm some milk for my son.' She couldn't quite bring herself to say thank you just yet, although a thank you was deserved regardless of her belligerent mood. He had restored her life to calm order at a time when her nerves had taken about as much as they could. Penny lowered Freddie to sit with his now neatly tidied blocks and bustled past Lord Hadleigh as he carried the tea over to the table, mentally rehearsing exactly how she could thank him while still appearing as if she had not needed his help at all.

Like her parlour, the kitchen was also as neat as a pin, so he hadn't only managed to make a pot of tea all by himself—he'd cleaned up after himself as well. Uncharitably, his thoughtfulness irritated her. She didn't want him to be thoughtful and helpful. She wanted him gone. Put in his place. As she sloshed some milk into a pan and set it to heat, she listened to the china clatter beyond. 'Do you take milk and sugar?' Now he was apparently pouring the tea, too. There was no end to his domestic talents or his thoughtfulness tonight.

'One spoon, please.' The *please* came out reluctantly through gritted teeth. 'With just a splash of milk.'

This would be the first time any male not a servant had ever made her tea. Penhurst would never have done such a thing. Nor would her dear father, come to that. Pouring tea was women's work. Childishly, she hoped the brew was either pathetically weak or so strong you could stand a spoon up in it. Just something she could feel slightly superior over, seeing as the dratted man was clearly good at everything and this evening he had found her on the back foot.

The milk began to hiss a little as it frilled against the edge of the pan, so she tested it with her finger and, satisfied, poured it into Freddie's nursing bottle. She should begin to train him with a proper cup, she knew, but as one of the last things the horrid Nanny Francis had tried to do, much to her darling boy's distress, she couldn't bring herself to do it yet. Not when he was six months away from two and still really a babe. The dour and judgemental nanny Penhurst had grown up with was all about sparing the rod and spoiling the child. If Penhurst was the end result of her heartless attitude, then Penny could think of no good reasons to pick up the rod and much preferred to continue spoiling her darling boy and smothering him in love. And she didn't care what anybody else thought of it.

She snatched up the bottle and turned, then stood frozen to the spot at the sight of her little boy stood holding the barrister's knee with one chubby hand and offering him a block with the other. Bemused, but friendly, he lowered his face to Freddie's and took it, ruffled the boy's curls gently, then added it to the tower which the pair of them had begun building next to his chair. It was a strangely arresting sight and one she was not entirely sure what she felt about. When she sensed her heart softening a little, she decided it was likely a ploy to disarm her, so she decided to double her efforts to remain righteously peeved at him.

Lord Hadleigh looked up as Freddie clumsily dashed to retrieve another wooden block, completely unfazed by the overfamiliarity of her child. 'He seems to be in better spirits now. I bet you had the devil of a job getting all that flour out of his hair.'

She had. The flour and water had made a paste which took three separate lots of lathering and rinsing to shift. But unwilling to make small talk, because small talk was friendly, Penny simply nodded, then intercepted her son and took him to the sofa. Something Freddie made sure she knew he wasn't particularly happy about when he had a new building playmate. 'Drink your milk, darling.' She snuggled him next to her and began to stroke his head, something which never failed to make him drowsy. Knowing that, her son decided to fight her all the way. Something that made her feel inadequate once more.

A steaming cup of perfectly brewed tea appeared at her elbow.

'Thank you for your kind assistance this evening, my lord.' Continued avoidance of basic good manners was petulant. Her eyes finally lifted to meet his and she immediately regretted it. It was as if he could see right through her, past the determined and proud façade, to the uncertain and lost woman beneath. 'It is much appreciated.'

'No, it isn't.' He grinned, his intuitive eyes dancing, and the sight did funny things to her insides. Why couldn't he be wearing his bland and inscrutable expression tonight? She knew where she stood with that. 'You would have rather walked over hot coals than have me help you and I cannot say I blame you. I behaved poorly on both our last encounters. Boorish, high-handed and arrogant with a healthy dose of sanctimonious mixed in. I had no right to attempt to force my will upon you or to assume I knew what was best. I've mulled it over long and hard since and chastised myself repeatedly for my crassness.'

Another pretty apology. Why did he have to be so good at apologies when she wanted to remain annoyed at him? Being righteously annoyed justified overt formality.

'You have flour on your face.'

'I do?' Her free hand swiped at her chin.

'Here...allow me.' His fingers brushed her cheek and Penny swore she felt it all the way down to her toes. She found her breath hitching as he dusted it from her skin, not daring to breathe out in case it came out sounding scandalously erratic. Which it suddenly was. As if sensing the new, potent atmosphere between them, his unusual, insightful amber eyes locked with hers and held. They both blinked at each other before he severed the contact and took several steps back.

Did he realise that the dormant female part of her body had suddenly just sprung to life? That her pulse had quickened or her lips tingled? Damn him and his well-fitting breeches and perfect cups of tea!

'You are now here on the behest of the government—*apparently.*' Better to keep things polite but distant. Matter of fact.

'Indeed I am. With a proposition.' He settled himself back into his chosen chair, the large one left by Clarissa which only served to make him seem bigger and more in command, crossing one long, booted leg over the other as he reached for his own tea. 'I'll get to the point, as I can see you want to be rid of me...' To her shame, Penny's cheeks instantly flushed at his perceptiveness, followed swiftly by embarrassment with his next, damning statement. 'I know you have been actively seeking decent employment with little luck.'

'I have been offered positions, my lord. None have suited.'

'I should imagine it is hard to find a decent position with a little boy.' His eyes drifted to where Freddie was now finally beginning to relax, then seemed to soften before returning to hers. 'Which is why I immediately thought of you when this opportunity presented itself—because in this case, your unique skills outweigh the fact they come with a child in tow.' He leaned forward, his gaze holding hers intently. 'Would you accept a position as a housekeeper if Freddie was allowed to come with you? Only the government and I find ourselves in a bit of an unusual situation.'

Suspicion made her frown. He had neglected to mention thus far that he was also involved in the proposition. 'What sort of a situation?'

'I assume you are aware of the case I am working on?'

'The Gislingham case.' Much as she had tried to avoid it, it had been hard to miss and she was too inextricably linked to it all to avoid it with the necessary detachment such avoidance took. Her husband's shameful involvement aside, both

Clarissa and Seb were also part of the proceedings. Both would be witnesses again. 'I think every man, woman and child in Christendom knows about that case.' Much as they had known about Penhurst's scandalous trial and aftermath. 'What has that to do with me? Apart from the obvious connection, I mean…'

Chapter Seven

She was already bristling, patently ready to decline whatever he was about to suggest. How he worded this next bit was crucial, especially as he was still a little unsettled at his body's peculiar reaction to one brief and innocent touch. His fingers still itched to caress her skin again—properly. Despite the lack of floury smudges decorating her bosom in the new dress, it took a great deal of effort not to allow his eyes to drift back to that magnificent area and feast. Or picture her peeling off that previously soiled garment mere feet away from where he had been when she had removed it and imagining what lay beneath it. Was every inch if her skin as soft and velvety as her cheek? Probably.

What the hell was he doing lusting after a woman while she was rocking her child to sleep? 'May I speak plainly?'

'I wish you would.'

'Do I have your word that anything I tell you now never leaves this room?' He watched her dark brows furrow as suspicion gave way to curiosity.

'Of course.'

'The key prosecution witness in the case is a woman. Lady Jessamine is now the Baroness of Penmor, but she used to be the proxy daughter of the Comte de Saint-Aubin-de-Scellon, the man almost entirely responsible for running the French side of the smuggling operation. When her mother died, Jessamine was imprisoned and forced to write and translate the coded messages which passed back and forth across the channel between the Viscountess Gislingham and her co-conspirators. She holds within her head a vast wealth of damning evidence. Perhaps unsurprisingly, that has made her a target once she escaped to England. My friend and King's Elite agent Lord Peter Flint was tasked with protecting her. The Comte hired assassins to silence her and when they failed he came himself. I cannot deny it was a near-run thing at one point.'

There was no need to tell her that it had been his bullet which had dispatched the evil Saint-Aubin. He didn't want to scare her by appraising her of the fact he had killed a man in cold blood despite his conscience being entirely clear on the matter. Saint-Aubin had been a murderer and tormentor of women. Had Hadleigh's bullet not hit its mark, then his friend Flint would be dead and Jessamine would have been dragged back to a life of cruelty and imprisonment in France.

His only regret was that he had failed to be as decisive all those years ago when similar opportunities had presented themselves—a memory long forgotten, one of the first consigned to the sealed box in his mind. Yet since saving Jessamine, that buried memory had resurfaced and plagued him constantly since. Why had he been able to pull the trigger for a woman he barely knew, yet not for the one who had birthed him?

Clearly both the rattling skeletons in the dark recesses of his mind and the inappropriate lust were symptomatic of how hard he was working.

That had to explain it.

'Suffice to say, good triumphed over evil as it always should and the Comte de Saint-Aubin is now dead. However, even though the Viscountess Gislingham and the rest of her accomplices are safely under lock and key, Jessamine's new husband—the aforementioned Flint—is over-protective. He is reluctant to bring her to London because he still fears for her safety. While I am confident the spectre of further assassination attempts are highly unlikely, I cannot deny I share his reservations about dragging her here to the capital until it is absolutely necessary. As I am sure you can entirely empathise, the press will have a field day.'

'An understatement, Lord Hadleigh.' Her face clouded as she nodded. 'They will make her life unbearable.'

'I knew you would understand...' How to broach the next part delicately? Because he suspected it would all hinge on this. 'In many ways, Lady Jessamine's situation tragically mirrors your own. Saint-Aubin was a violent man and she suffered horrendously while he forced her to do his bidding.' He doubted he would ever erase the haunting and shocking image of Jessamine's scars from his mind. 'Like you, she was an innocent victim of a callous monster and, like you, I fear she will suffer the petty and harsh judgement of the society which abandoned her.'

'He beat her?' Her eyes were wide, awash with pity, and he had to lock his fingers together tightly in his lap to prevent reaching out to comfort her.

'Among other things.' His eyes drifted to the tiny bump on her otherwise perfect nose. The perfect nose she had stated under oath Penhurst had broken and felt anger bubble at both of the men who had used pain and cruel mental manipulations to subdue Jessamine and the brave, stoic woman in front of him. If Penhurst wasn't dead, he might have been tempted to visit him and give him a taste of his own medicine. Except he wouldn't stop at the bastard's nose. 'Her life was not her own for many years well before her imprisonment. He used the health of her dying mother as a tool to blackmail her.' Injustices which made his blood boil. 'Hardly a surprise her devoted new husband is keen to protect her still. But this presents the Crown with a challenge. We need her here while the case is prepared.'

Hadleigh found himself rising to his feet and pacing. To her it might appear he was doing so because he was agitated about the case, when in fact it was all the wrongs he couldn't right which gnawed at him. 'I need Lady Jessamine close. As each day passes, I learn more and more from the suspects. A couple seem eager to spill everything. Others sling mud, hoping to save their own skins. Corroborating what they are saying and separating the fact from the lies is becoming increasingly arduous—especially when Lady Jessamine is the only witness who can categorically confirm or dismiss the majority of their claims.'

'I still do not understand what this has to do with me?'

'We have found a compromise which Flint is willing to agree to. A way to have his wife at hand when I need to consult with her and a way for him to be able to guard her privacy. I have an estate just a few miles from London to the east— less than an hour's ride away...' *Pandora's box.* Fear of revisiting it warred with his overwhelming desire to help her.

'Your estate?' She didn't look happy with that

detail. He waved it away as if it was inconsequential, when it wasn't. For either of them.

'Who the estate belongs to is by the by because I have lent it to the state for the duration. It is the location which has led to us selecting it. I've not used it in almost a decade because my work keeps me here.' And he loathed the place and all its ghosts. Would have sold it had it not been entailed. 'It's been boarded up for years and will be boarded up again once this is over. However, its situation and design make it the perfect place for Flint and Jessamine to live while we await the trial. In view of your own unique *experience,* and no doubt the many sympathetic insights you might be able to add, combined with your close connection to Leatham and his wife and this case, the government wondered if you would be willing to run the house in the interim.'

'The *government* wondered?'

'At my suggestion, I cannot deny—because you instantly sprang to mind when I discussed it with my superiors. Who better to ensure the privacy and care of a witness than one who has lived through the experience?' She didn't appear convinced. 'This is a state matter, my lady. The Gislingham trial is the single biggest treason trial in England in a century. Justice not only needs to be done, that goes without saying, but it also needs to be *seen* to be done properly. We cannot afford any speculation or criticism on a job completed poorly, nor do we want any misinformed sympathy for the traitors involved—especially as the ringleader is a woman. And we need to learn from our previous mistakes. I would not wish the way you were treated by the press on anyone. You can help us do that.'

'I suppose I am familiar with all their tricks...'

'Indeed you are, alongside all of the pressure and concerns Lady Jessamine will have to endure. You and she have a great deal in common.'

Her scepticism had given way to thoughtfulness, which in turn meant he had argued his corner well and convinced her that this was about more than her. Or at least that is what he had told himself when he had concocted this complicated and uncomfortable justification for offering her a job. He had almost convinced himself the undeniable benefits also justified him having to face the house again.

'I only have a few months to construct a conclusive case. With time of the essence and the house barely habitable, we need someone trustworthy who can start straight away. Instinctively, I thought of you because I know you are actively seeking such a position, but by no means do you need to feel you have to take it. It is a temporary offer of employment. But as I said, in view of the gravitas of this case, and the unusual circumstances and particular duties such an important position will entail, you will be compensated generously. We suggest an amount of ten guineas per month and a further hundred guineas at the end of the tenure as a bonus for your sacrifice and eternal silence.'

A staggering amount no matter which way she looked at it. Enough, he hoped, to lure her into accepting without questioning the tiny lie he had just told her.

'One hundred guineas!' Hadleigh saw her eyes widen and her lips part in shock. His gaze was apparently magnetically drawn to those lips until he caught himself staring.

'And obviously, you will leave here with glowing and unquestionable references from myself, the Attorney General and Lord Fennimore, which will ensure a lifetime of similar employment should you need it and firmly establishing *Mrs Henley* as the *crème de la crème* of housekeepers.' Now he was in danger of over-egging it. 'You will manage a small staff which we will recruit the bulk of, however, because of the delicate and secretive nature of the conversations which will inevitably have to take place—only you will be privy to some of the rooms in which those sensitive discussions will occur. The fewer people who overhear, the less chance there is of those conversations being repeated outside the house. We cannot risk anything leaking to the defence or, heaven forbid, the press, before the trial. Therefore, recruiting from scratch is, as I am sure you can see, problematic.'

'But you want *me* to be the housekeeper? A convicted traitor's wife?' She sounded incredulous.

'He was the traitor, my lady. Not you. To my mind, you have proven to be an asset to the Crown before and we have been impressed with the way you composed yourself both during and after your own ordeal in the courtroom. You are discreet and honourable. Leatham and Clarissa have always vouched for your good character.' Thank goodness he had had the good sense to discuss things with them in front of Lord Fennimore at the wedding party.

Both were all for it if it meant keeping their friend close and safe from the sort of vultures who preyed on single young mothers left all alone in the world, or the key defence witness who also happened to be married to one of their closest friends. 'What better choice than a person who already knows of the government's covert machinations? Or the ridiculous lengths the press will go to in order to get their story? You might seem an unconventional choice in the first instance, but your recent experiences actually lend themselves perfectly to such a sensitive task.' He almost had her. He could practically see the cogs spinning in her mind as she digested everything he said. His instincts warned him not to give her too much time to ruminate or himself any more time to act upon his unwanted and inappropriate impulses. He had come here to rescue her, not stare at her lips with longing, although he had no earthly idea why he was suddenly so consumed with the latter, other than something about her called to the man as well as his conscience. Something that transcended his noble quest and had absolutely nothing to do with pity or guilt or righting wrongs.

'Everything to do with the running of the inside of the house will be down to you. Unhindered. There will be only essential staff. I see no need for a butler as he would interfere with your decisions. Neither I, nor Lord Fennimore, will have the time or the inclination to attempt to interfere either. The grounds and security will be overseen by the King's Elite as you would expect. You will liaise with them on how the security is organised within the house or how to deal effectively with any potential breaches...not that we envisage any. The location of Flint and Jessamine will be of the utmost secrecy, known only to a select few who need to know. That is Flint's express stipulation.'

'Only Lord Flint and Lady Jessamine would live there?'

'As I have said, my work necessitates me staying here. But I will make regular trips to meet with Jessamine, although I have no plans to stay overnight.' The mere thought made his gut

clench. Nothing short of an earth-shattering ca-
tastrophe would ever have him sleeping under
that godforsaken roof again. 'So you will barely
have to suffer my presence. Which, alas, I fear
you might have suffered quite enough of already
this evening.'

He unfolded himself from the chair and
grabbed his coat, making his intention to leave
crystal clear, despite not having yet received her
answer. Years of courtroom experience taught
him that sometimes it was best to assume rather
than ask. Seeking forgiveness was always easier than asking permission. And, it went without
saying, he really didn't want to have to properly
clarify anything, knowing that the whole truth
and nothing but the truth would likely result in a
firm no. There was a sharp and clever brain behind those beautiful blue eyes and he had learned
to his cost how blunt and cutting those enticing
lips could become when given just cause. 'If you
could begin some time next week, that would
be marvellous. I'd like the house to be ready for
Flint and Jessamine to move in by the first week
of November.'

Penny's definition of barely habitable and Lord
Hadleigh's were poles apart. An hour after arriving at Chafford Grange, and despite the icy
chill created by the cold walls and the myriad
eerie cobwebs, she could see it was a grand

and sumptuous house. It wouldn't take much to bring it back to life. The gardens were immaculate and had obviously always been tended, while the house had been lovingly put to bed. Before it had been closed all those years ago, the former servants had taken great pains to protect it. Heavy dust sheets covered every stick of furniture and were wrapped carefully around the curtains draping each window. She had lifted a few on her solitary tour of the house and been pleasantly surprised by what lay underneath.

Comfortable brocade sofas, glossy marquetry end tables, ormolu clocks, Sèvres vases, enormous Venetian mirrors, a huge and imposing mahogany dining table which would not look out of place in a royal palace—it was a veritable treasure trove of exquisite taste and ultimate luxury. Oddly incongruous with the professional government servant who spoke with such assured and convincing eloquence in the Old Bailey or the perplexing man who had swept her parlour clean before making her the perfect cup of tea.

Because it was calling to her, she used her foot to roll open a large rug in what she assumed might be a sunny morning room, as its floor-to-ceiling arched windows overlooked the garden and undulating parkland beyond. It was stunning. The bold turquoise base was woven with a wide band of gold interspersed with subtle colourful flowers. Similar yet larger flowers swirled with golden leaves in the centre of the carpet. It was a beautiful piece that oozed class, one that would make a statement in this otherwise sedate and plain room. Although in this case, plain did not mean stark. The walls had been kept white, but covered in the most subtly patterned silk damask to bring texture and warmth, a luxurious touch so subtle it served to showcase the magnificent Persian. The only other splashes of colour came from the curtains. Turquoise again, the exact same shade as the carpet, held back with chunky golden-rope tiebacks. Understated, yet in being so made far more of a statement than anything fussy and patterned.

Class was a commodity no amount of money could buy. Something Penny knew only too well, having learned it at her mother's knee. She had never understood Penhurst's taste at all. He had been of the school that the more gilded and ostentatious the item, the more he coveted it.

All flash and no class.

A statement her mother would often utter in disdain when a merchant attempted to sell their emporium crass and showy furniture, but which summed up her former husband perfectly. He had no class. Ironic, really, when he had always lamented at marrying so far beneath him. Had she been allowed to decorate her former home, it would have resembled something like this rather than the tawdry monstrosity her husband had created.

Her mother would have approved of *this* carpet. Her eye for such things had been impeccable, one of the main reasons she and Penny's father had made such a success of their business. He had dealt with the financial side while her mother had hand-picked the stock. A match made in heaven in more ways than one.

Unable to help herself, Penny knelt and ran the flat of her hand over the thick pile. As she had suspected it was densely woven from the finest gauge of the softest wool mixed with just enough silk to give the fibres a lustre.

Class.

And clearly very expensive. The very best quality Persia was capable of creating. Superior craftsmanship, elegant, timeless... Words she would have used to describe it had it been on sale at Ridley's. Clearly once a shopkeeper's daughter, always a shopkeeper's daughter.

That thought made her smile. It was the sort of high-quality rug her father had imported for his well-heeled clientele many moons ago, back when their emporium and catalogue had been thriving before he sold it and retired on the proceeds.

She missed those days, the hours spent with her beloved parents in their fancy Bond Street shop learning the trade, or years before that in their larger emporium in Cheapside or the original draper's shop in Clerkenwell. But like all the most precious things, she had not appreciated them properly until they were gone. As her father's fortunes had rapidly increased, so too had their standing in the community. They might well have come from the wrong end of trade, but with an impressive dowry like the one her parents had accumulated for her, Penny had been destined for a life within the aristocracy they had once served. That was her mother's dream and she had allowed herself to become swept away in it. Once upon a time, she had foolishly thought life would only get better and had spent far too much time dreaming about her future than living in the now.

More regrets.

Another classic example of what she would change if she could turn back time. Yet there was no point in harking back to those halcyon days of her girlhood or lamenting them at the same time. That route only led to dissatisfaction when she found herself quietly satisfied with the way things were turning out in the here and now. Ten guineas a month for at least the next three months and one hundred more thereafter! Good heavens, that felt like a fortune. Enough money certainly for her to lease somewhere decent in the home counties. A nice little cottage with a garden for Freddie to play in… If only she could clear her mind of the reasons it had come about and her nagging doubts as to the validity of it all.

But she had a contract, therefore it did all seem to be exactly as he had outlined. The meticulous and thorough document had arrived the morning after Lord Hadleigh's impromptu visit alongside six guineas and a note from Mr Cohen, her old landlord, acknowledging he had refunded a portion of the year's rent money. The very legal language in the contract stated her exact duties and stipulated the *government's* precise terms. In a nutshell, it was Penny's job to see to the smooth running of the house while ensuring the strict privacy of its important inhabitants—Lord Flint and his wife Lady Jessamine alongside whichever high-ranking government or King's Elite official might also be involved in the Gislingham trial.

Any breach in the strict secrecy clause on her part would result in making the agreement null and void, with instant dismissal without payment or references. Not that she ever would talk to the press or confide the details to anyone outside the clearly defined inner circle. The only two friends she had left in the world were part of that circle and beyond that Penny was determined to remain entirely Mrs Henley. A young widow who had lost her husband at sea and who had never been tainted by a speck of scandal in her entire life—although she still wasn't entirely comfortable with that version of her because it felt like an ill-fitting suit. But she would make it fit in time and then there would be no stopping her.

No, indeed. This temporary stint as a housekeeper meant she could and would strike a line through the last three miserable years and truly start afresh. Why else invoke such a strict clause unless the deal was entirely genuine?

Something she really had to thank Lord Hadleigh for. Whatever his initial motives, he had given her the chance to earn her own living and do so without having to leave Freddie. For that alone, she would make more of an effort with the man. Perhaps she was even starting to like him a little? Or at least the version of him who made tea and wasn't too proud to hold a broom. The inscrutable, emotionless lawyer was a separate entity entirely. She doubted she would ever warm to that Hadleigh at all.

One hundred and thirty guineas! And all for relatively light organisational duties she could do in her sleep and all with a household budget so vast she could spend with impunity every day for a year and barely make a dent in it. Not that she would, nor would she let such a budget allow her to overspend when she could haggle for cheaper prices. Once a shopkeeper's daughter and all that. Organising and management had been her forte, not that Penhurst had allowed her to do much of it. But her parents had. Accounting, negotiating prices for services, arranging staff and planning events. All the things which had made their business run like clockwork all those years were akin, in many ways, to the skills necessary to run a great house.

However, Penhurst had never allowed her to run his house and was very secretive about his household accounts, chose staff not for their ability to do the job but to spy on his wife or keep any outsiders from poking their noses into his business. The only leeway he had allowed her to be mistress of the house was in the planning of the frequent parties.

Penhurst had loved a house party and, as his fortunes mysteriously improved, loved hosting regular soirées to show off his wealth. Penny had organised the entire events, especially fun entertainments for the ladies, knowing that those unfortunate women would need something to take their minds off the debauchery which her horrid husband would inevitably lead them into from almost the first moment they arrived at Penhurst Hall. That was, after all, the main reason those men came…

'The staff are arriving, Mrs Henley.' The King's Elite agent who had brought her to Chafford Grange seemed to appear out of nowhere, giving her a start. Something she supposed she needed to quickly get used to in this house of government secrets and government spies.

'Thank you. Have them gather in my sitting room and I will be there shortly.' Part of Penny's contract had stated she had her own contained apartment within this grand house. It had been the first suite of rooms she had elected to see and was still amazed by their sheer size and situation. A cosy first-floor sitting room-cum-study leading to a staggeringly large bedchamber for her and a smaller bedchamber for Freddie. It was nearly twice the size of her rented lodgings in Cheapside, lighter, brighter and certainly more cheerful, although she would need to replace the fine-quality rug in the main room with something more robust for her son. And throws for the lovely furniture, too. If he spilled something on any of those fine pieces she would never forgive herself and did not want to live on permanent tenterhooks that he might.

For now, her darling boy was staying with Clarissa and Seb in Mayfair, no doubt having a whale of a time being spoiled rotten as the pair of them practised being parents. Not that they had confessed that detail to her still, but to Penny it was obvious and she was delighted for them. Perhaps now that she was earning her own money doing something they approved of they might cease attempting to mollycoddle her and entrust her with their secret. It would be so nice to have Clarissa as just her friend again, rather than her self-appointed nursemaid. These past months had been trying on their friendship.

But all that was behind her now. This was exactly the kind of fresh new start she had wanted. A few months here and then the world was her oyster! How marvellous that was. Her best friends were bringing Freddie to join her in five days, which meant she had four days to get this beautiful house shipshape and shining like a new pin. A stocked kitchen, decent spirits in the cellar, fresh linens, a thorough spring clean and airing, roaring fires in every fireplace to take the chill out of the walls. They would need a veritable forest of chopped wood, candles, flowers... As she ticked off each thing on her extensive mental list of things to do, she couldn't help but notice that for the first time in for ever she was walking with an excited, almost giddy spring in her step. Almost like the old Penny.

Chapter Eight

There was no getting away from it, Hadleigh felt nauseous. The queasiness had started before he turned his horse on to the drive and had increased with every yard he had travelled. Now, still sat in the saddle and staring at the house, his head was spinning, his chest so tight it made breathing an effort and the last remnants of the breakfast he had choked down was roiling in his stomach. He was intentionally opening that securely sealed box.

What had he been thinking? What had started as a means to help a woman who refused to be helped had spiralled out of control to become his worst nightmare. Aside from being a handy hideaway for the main prosecution witness, Lord Fennimore and his team were determined to use it as their base. Which in turn meant Hadleigh had to spend much more time here than he had originally bargained for and was certainly unprepared for—if his body's tumultuous reaction was any gauge. The temptation to turn his horse around and gallop away was overwhelming. Typical, really, when he had always preferred to run from the demons of his past like a worthless coward rather than face them.

Hell, he'd been running for days already. She had been there for three whole days and he'd made a plethora of pathetic excuses not to visit, until he had realised sometime around three this morning as he had awoken in another cold sweat that he needed to do so before Flint and the others arrived. He didn't want them to see that mere bricks and mortar could render him so sick and panicked he could barely function. He needed to harden himself to the place before he was in any fit state to work collaboratively with others within its haunted walls. This *had* been *his* idea.

One of his stupidest.

In the distance, someone stepped out of the stables and waved. There could be no turning back now. That simple wave would start a flurry of activity within the house. Servants would be warned, scurrying to welcome him. The new housekeeper, the woman who had prompted him to make this foolhardy decision in the first place, would be at the front door to greet him.

A cold trickle of fresh perspiration made its way down his spine. He didn't want her to see how much this place panicked him either. Perhaps if he kept this first visit short and sweet, he could wear his detached lawyer's mask for the duration?

And perhaps pigs might fly.

The second he stepped into that cavernous marbled hallway he would be confronted with the staircase. Then the events of that dreadful day a decade ago would all come rushing back. The anger, then the numbness which still shamed him. That caused the oppressive guilt he always carried with him but buried in work. He'd buried it so well with so much work, he had barely thought about it in years.

There would be no burying it today because there was no way of avoiding that blasted staircase. Even if he blindfolded himself he would sense it. Picture her last moments before she plunged helplessly to her death.

'Good morning, my lord.' Closer, he recognised the new groom as one of Lord Fennimore's agents and raised his hand quickly in an approximation of a cheery wave. A little too quickly because it made him instantly bilious.

This was nonsense! A man halfway through his thirtieth year shouldn't be so petrified of visiting an empty house. And it was an empty house and not Pandora's actual blasted box, so he needed to stop thinking about it in those terms. What was done was done. Dusted.

Buried.

Hadleigh gave himself a stern talking-to as

the agent took his horse and he walked on alone the short distance to the house. Near the entrance he dithered, considering if for this first visit he shouldn't ease himself in by entering through the back via the kitchens or, if by some miracle they were unlocked, the French doors leading into the morning room. That had been his mother's favourite room and the place they had spent many a happy hour. Just the two of them. Avoiding talking about his father or the increase in his erratic behaviour because it was easier to pretend everything was fine...

'Lord Hadleigh!' Her voice stopped him staring resolutely at the gravel and made the distasteful decision for him. 'I wondered when you might make an appearance.'

Reluctantly he looked up. She was stood at the top of the colonnaded steps which led to the enormous front door, smiling. Wearing a pretty blue dress unlike any of the dour dresses he had seen her in before. The colour suited her. The style suited her more. The demure, long-sleeved bodice fitted her trim figure perfectly, showing off her splendid bosom to perfection. A bosom, which to his shame, he had contemplated a great deal since he had seen it dusted enticingly with flour. The blustery autumn breeze plastered the skirt to her body, giving him a tantalising hint of the rest of her figure properly for the first time. A petite hourglass finished off with a very shapely and surprisingly long pair of legs. For a split second the sight made him forget where he was.

Then reality came crushing back like a tempest.

'My lady... I mean, Mrs...' Good grief, with all the stress of being here he had completely forgotten her new alias. *Hendon? Henry?* It began with an 'H', he was certain. She must have seen him floundering.

'Under the circumstances, with the lines between my old life and my new still so blurred, maybe it would be easier to simply call me Penny.' She was smiling again, attempting to stand still, but practically bouncing with a suppressed energy he had never seen in her before that warmed his heart. She was happy. He might be in hell because of it, but he had made her happy. 'Come in! I've been itching to show someone. I think you'll be delighted with our progress.'

Like a man headed to his own execution, he slowly took the short steps to the threshold of the house and then took a deep breath. Penny—he liked that name, liked the sound of it on his lips—had skipped on ahead and was stood in the centre of the cavernous atrium. Behind her, on either side, were the stairs. Two unyielding marble flights, flanked with the intricately carved ebony banisters his mother had once helped him slide down, curved around in a sweeping arc before meeting at the landing above.

She was everywhere, his mother. He could hear her echoing laughter in the walls, picture her dashing down those stairs to greet him. Arms wide, smile wider. Picture the grisly scene of her body broken on the hard marble floor at the base. Neck broken. Dead eyes staring lifeless.

He shivered.

'It's still a tad cold in here, isn't it? I think it will take another couple of days at least to heat the walls properly.' She touched his arm and that anchored him to the present. He wanted to grab her hand, absorb her strength and stay there. 'Especially here in this vast space. Marble is notoriously cold and unforgiving.' Indeed it was. Catastrophically unforgiving. 'Would you like some tea or some refreshments before we take the tour or after?' Despite standing next to him, she sounded so far away.

'After.'

Best to get the hideous experience over and done with before he did part ways with his breakfast.

She led him down the hallway and he waited for more hideous memories to batter him, but bizarrely none came. His arms and legs felt leaden, his breathing shallow, his emotions numb. Something which bothered him more than anything. In all these years, he hadn't grieved. Hadn't shed a single tear. The tragedy had happened, he had calmly dealt with the aftermath in what he would later realise was a detached haze, then he had focused on his studies. Just like his callous father he felt nothing whatsoever. Neither of them had mourned his mother properly.

As if she sensed his disquiet, Penny never said a word or, to her credit, expected him to say anything. They stopped at the door to the drawing room and, before he could remember his manners, she opened it for him. 'We have focused on what we presume will be the most used rooms first.' The old ormolu clock on the mantel was ticking loudly. The familiar, but long forgotten, noise sounded hollow to his ears. Other than that, Hadleigh had no visceral reaction to the space. He was able to glance dispassionately over it as was expected.

It smelled of fresh beeswax mixed with the faintest whiff of lavender. The windows shone, letting in the crisp early November sunshine and making the room feel bright and airy. He recognised every stick of furniture, but perhaps not their exact position. She must have moved things around, he supposed, although to his eye, it all now appeared to be in exactly the correct space.

He found his gaze fixated on the thick woollen blanket draped neatly over the arm of a chair and decided he had no recollection of it ever being there. As if reading his mind, she explained its presence. 'Big rooms like this can get chilly even when the fire is roaring. I thought Lord and Lady

Flint might appreciate a few cosy, homely touches while they are residing here. I hope you don't mind.'

Mind? Why would he? He had no opinions regarding this house other than complete abhorrence. He wouldn't be here now if it weren't for her. His eyes listlessly lifted to meet hers and he saw her confusion. He'd allowed the silence to stretch too long when she was clearly seeking his approval. 'Everything looks perfect.' And he couldn't wait to leave.

She beamed then and the numbness lifted.

She had dimples. Two adorable matching indents which framed a smile that turned her quietly pretty face into something quite beautiful. 'Oh, I am so glad! On the one hand, I didn't want to tamper with what was here when this house is *so* lovely, but on the other, I couldn't resist gilding the lily with a few tweaks here and there... Come—I bet you are dying to see the rest.'

He was slowly dying inside, more like.

Everything he was, everything he enjoyed about life, was being slowly sucked out of him just by standing within these walls. Leaving a vacuum...of numbness. Odd, really, that he should feel so detached when everything that had happened here was so intensely personal—or at least should have been.

The next few minutes passed painfully slowly as she led him from room to room, pointing out her subtle changes or appraising him of how much work it had taken to bring the space back to its former glory. He managed to grunt one or two responses and hoped they were appropriate. Speech was hard when dread was strangling his vocal cords.

But, in truth, the rapid progress she had made surprised him, as did his reaction to it all. Hadleigh had expected to feel horror at everything, as the sights and smells of his childhood home conjured up all manner of uncomfortable memories. His calm detachment came as a relief. They were just rooms after all. Just furniture. Aside from his first glimpse of the staircase, the ghosts of his past remained blessedly silent and the lid remained firmly closed on the terrifying box of unpleasantness in his mind. To such an extent that the queasiness he had suffered since setting out at the crack of dawn began to wane and he started to believe he *could* do this after all.

'This is my favourite room...' She flung open the door to the morning room, then stood aside so he could enter first. 'There was no need to tweak anything in here. Just a good dust and an airing...' Every thus-far silent ghost suddenly bombarded him as they screamed and exploded out of the woodwork, so swiftly they caught him off guard. The pain was instantaneous and all-encompassing. 'And of course these magnificent windows needed a significant amount of cleaning.'

In his mind's eye he could picture his mother there. Hear every damned word of their last conversation. Stood staring sightlessly out of the window, the weight of the world on her shoulders, her posture shielding the faded, ugly bruise from his gaze. One palm flattened against the glass.

'Leave! Come back with me to London.'

'Out of the question. Your father needs me here.'

'He is becoming dangerous. More dangerous than usual.'

'He's ill, darling—not dangerous.' She had turned then and smiled in reassurance, all hint of the burdened woman banished solely for his benefit, touching the bruise and then brushing it off. 'Let's not confuse my innate clumsiness with anything more dramatic.'

That had always been her answer to every injury and bruise over the years. *'Silly me. I walked straight into an open cupboard door. Would you believe I tripped over my own feet...my skirt...a floorboard?'*

No. He hadn't. Not once. Except while those occasional bouts of violence which occurred only when his father was home could be readily glossed over by his mother and to his shame he had let her, things had taken a more sinister turn and Hadleigh had been scared. 'Besides, he needs me here. The physicians really don't see him lasting long—no more than a year at most.'

There had been no love lost between his mother and his father, nor between father and son. His sire had been a difficult man to love. Dictatorial, aggressive, cold and unfeeling. Free and handy with his fists, especially after a drink. Nothing anyone did was ever good enough, but until his health had declined he had been largely absent from Chafford Grange and their lives.

But then he had spent longer stretches at home and things began to change—more for her than Hadleigh. He had his mother to thank for that. She did a splendid job of keeping the pair of them apart until he had learned fairly late at what cost. He had been fifteen. No longer a child, but nowhere near an adult. He had tried to intervene once he realised the awful truth, planned several ways of permanently stopping his father from raising his hand to her again, but ultimately had always fallen short of succeeding. Just a frightened boy attempting to be the bigger man, but never quite rising to the challenge.

Right and wrong.

Good and evil.

The law and the lawless.

That was the problem with all his solutions. They jarred with his fundamental beliefs, all the things that made him...*him*. With hindsight which came from a decade of seeking justice, he should have shot his father that awful summer of eighteen hundred and five. The man had been all alone on the turnpike which clipped the furthest edge of the estate. Roaring drunk after another night of hedonism. The moon was full. He had a clear line of sight. Thanks to their close proximity to the capital, this busy road was a notorious spot for footpads. And despite practising hundreds of times for this exact opportunity until he could hit anything dead centre the first time with his first shot, squeezing the trigger of his gun to kill a flesh-and-blood man rather than an inert, lifeless target proved to be too difficult.

Instead, he had run, thrown his stolen pistol in the lake and by the time he had come home, his father had taken his drunken anger out on his mother again. He had found her weeping in the kitchen, a cold cloth pressed against her blackening eye.

'I should have lit a candle before I came downstairs...silly me. Would you believe it? I hit my head on a sconce.'

A lie he should have spared her, simply by taking that shot.

Instead, that fateful day had taken his feet down a different path. If he couldn't *break* the law to protect his mother, he would *use* the law to do it. From then on, he had been single-minded in his pursuit of that lofty goal, losing sight of the here and now while he chased the all-consuming promise of the future he intended to shape. That was why he had chosen to be a prosecutor rather than a defending attorney. In the decade since her death, he had used the system to defend other defenceless women, whether that be to seek proper justice after their deaths or to help free them from the prison of a toxic marriage or, at the very least, ensure they received adequate financial compensation for their suffering. Penny wasn't the first woman who had received some of his father's fortune and he sincerely doubted she would be the last. Whatever it took to right the wrongs.

'I cannot leave him to die here all alone. He's scared. It's so sad to watch. The illness is confusing him.' She always called it *the illness*, preferring that to the truth. But then syphilis sounded so distasteful and his mother had not wanted the servants to know why their master could no longer control his own bladder or recall where he was.

'Then I'll stay home. I'll help you.'

'What? Defer your studies? Out of the question. Everything is fine, darling. Or at least as good as can be expected under the circumstances. It's not as if you can do anything which will alter the course of things and most days now he doesn't remember his own name, let alone yours. I promise I will send word as soon as the end is close.'

She had walked to the chair he was sat in, cupped his face with her hands and kissed him on the forehead. 'It was lovely to see you today, Tristan. An unexpected and wonderful surprise.

But it's getting late and you know I hate to think of you riding back to town in the dark. Be a good son and don't add to my worries. Besides, I am sure there is some lovely young lady desirous of your swift return.' There was. There always was. Although the lusty widow who had warmed his bed that year was a good decade older than he had been. 'I am sure she's missing you terribly. And do stop fretting about me and your father. There are servants watching his every move, the physician comes every other day and I am never left alone with him.'

Because it was simpler to accept those lies than deal with the truth and upset with his stubborn mother, he had left and put it out of his mind as he always did. That was the easiest and simplest option. Bury himself in his studies so he could fix things for her and every other voiceless woman properly—legally—for ever once he was qualified.

A week later, he received word of her death. Ostensibly an accident, but he knew in his heart of hearts that his father had pushed her down those stairs because the servants had heard his sire's nonsensical shouting in the small hours shortly before they found her. He also knew that he could have prevented it simply with his presence. An extra pair of eyes and ears to protect her. But he had been too eager to hurry down the path that called to him, when his studies could and *should* have been deferred that year for obvious reasons.

'Is everything all right?' A voice, not his mother's, dragged him out of the pit.

'*Yes*… Yes, of course.'

'I think you do need that cup of tea now. You have had a tiring journey.' Penny was regarding him with confusion. Had his lawyer's mask slipped? Had she witnessed the terror and disgust on his face when he had been trying so hard to keep it bland? 'I'll send for some. Why don't you sit down?'

'No!' The atmosphere and the newly settling numbness were suffocating him. 'Please…don't trouble yourself.' He needed air. Miles of open road. The ability to turn back the clock. Cold settled in his spine while hot perspiration suddenly appeared on his skin.

'It's no trouble at all. And I absolutely insist. A wise man once told me everything is better after a cup of tea.' She threaded her arm through his and, as if realising this room had something to do with his current state, tugged him back into the hallway, closing the door and trapping the ghosts inside. 'I'll have it brought to the drawing room. If you don't mind, I will join you as I have some questions regarding Lord and Lady Flint and the overall organisation for the next few weeks.'

He found himself manoeuvred away, distracted, enveloped in the soft, lilting sound of her voice as she deftly rescued him from his past and delivered him back safely to the present.

Chapter Nine

Penny instantly took to Lady Jessamine. There was so much in her that was like looking in a mirror that they had instantly developed a rapport. They were both survivors in their own way and both only too happy to leave their pasts in the past. Jessamine wanted this trial over with so she could draw a veil over hers. Penny wanted it over so that she could have the funds to bury hers. Only three days in and she felt more like her friend and confidante than her housekeeper. It was so lovely to be able to discuss those things with someone who *knew* exactly what it did to a person. They both suffered from misplaced self-loathing at their supposed weaknesses, yet completely understood why the other had had to conform as they had.

Lord Flint was nice enough, but preoccupied with keeping his new wife safe from whatever imagined threats lay outside the quiet estate's outer wall, so they didn't collide much. The Dowager Baroness of Penmor, his irrepressible mother, was a breath of fresh air in what could have been an oppressive situation. A tad eccentric, a tad overdramatic, nosy to the point of outrageous and absolutely hilarious. She made sure that laughter became part of every day.

'He sounds like an absolute brute!' Penny had brought the ladies some mid-morning tea and now found herself the main topic of their conversation. The Dowager had insisted on a full rundown of her awful marriage which had been strangely cathartic, much as the in-depth recollection of the entire trial yesterday had allowed her to begin to view it with some distance and new perspective. Time was beginning to heal the wounds and purging her soul, as the Dowager was prone to point out whenever Penny tried to sidestep the most awkward questions, and felt so much better than bottling it all inside. 'There must have been one good reason you chose to marry the man? You did *choose*—didn't you?'

'Alas, I did, so I cannot blame anyone for that folly other than myself.' She picked up the pot again to refill the cups seeing as this latest friendly inquisition was bound to last a while. 'I thought myself in love with him and foolishly convinced myself that feeling was mutual.'

'But he only loved your dowry.'

'Mama!' Lady Jessamine quickly interjected

to spare her feelings. 'I am sure he initially saw more in Penny than that.'

'And I am quite sure he didn't.' Penny smiled as she passed the cup back. She had been reconciled with her feelings concerning her hasty and regrettable courtship long ago. 'I was young and naive and quite out of my depth. To be brutally frank with you, ladies, I was also pathetically shallow. I was so delighted a viscount wanted to court me I never took the time to consider why that was, when I wasn't a particularly good catch in the eyes of the *ton*. I came from trade, you see, had no aristocratic connections and had to learn quickly how to behave like a proper lady. What I was, ultimately, was an easy target for a fortune hunter and a desperate fortune hunter found me. Very quickly.'

The Dowager leaned forward conspiratorially. 'How quickly?'

'We were married within three months of our first meeting.'

'A perfectly acceptable amount of time. I met and married mine within two and my son married Jess in just one.'

'Perhaps, but in truth I barely knew Penhurst at all. Before I skipped blindly down the aisle, I do not think we spent more than a few hours in one another's company overall and certainly for no longer than a scant few minutes at a time. I had no clue then that *anyone* can pretend to be somebody else entirely for a few minutes. Over a few hours the first cracks began to show and the true blackguard I had shackled myself to emerged swiftly afterwards. I knew within weeks I had made the worst mistake of my life and by then, of course, it was too late. I should also state for the record, in case you are feeling sorry for me, I had been warned about him from the outset. Clarissa cautioned me not to marry him, as did my own dear father on the wedding day itself.'

'No...'

'Yes. He had discovered Penhurst was up to his neck in debt and had his suspicions as to his motives, but I wouldn't listen. I was too caught up in the romance alongside my ailing mother, who so wanted to leave this mortal coil with the happiest of memories. A viscount wanted to marry *me*. Penny Ridley. A shopkeeper's daughter.'

'Ridley's was hardly a shop, my dear. It was an institution. A fine one. People used to brag about owning a piece of Ridley furniture. I always spent a few hours there perusing its treasures whenever my dear husband, God rest him, dragged me to London. And always such fine quality! Why, I still have a pair of mahogany end tables which I must have bought over a decade ago and they are just as good as when I first bought them. I miss Ridley's.'

'My mother and father would be delighted to know that.' Both ladies already knew her parents had passed. Thankfully, they never got to witness the full extent of the huge mistake Penny had made in marrying her Viscount. 'As am I. Once a shopkeeper's daughter, always a shopkeeper's daughter. I am tremendously proud to have been part of Ridley's.'

'Are you ever tempted to resurrect it? Because that would be marvellous!' The suggestion caused a bubble of unexpected excitement before reality quickly popped it.

'Alas, if I were to open a shop now it would have to be Henley's and it couldn't possibly be in London. For obvious reasons.'

'Damn Penhurst. I've decided I loathe him doubly now, for treating you abominably and for depriving me of good shopping. When did you realise you loathed the brute rather than loved him?' The Dowager had a canny knack of asking the most intrusive questions outright and would not be waylaid from the main topic at hand. There was no point in trying to avoid the question. Three days in the Dowager's company had taught Penny that she could teach the meticulously thorough Crown Prosecutor a thing or two about interrogating a witness.

'Quite quickly.' She had been a delirious bride for almost the whole day and then Penhurst had shown his true colours. It had been their wedding night and he had been drunk. Too drunk to do what her mother had whisperingly promised a wedding night involved. He had stumbled into her bedchamber in the small hours, dropped his trousers, roughly hoisted up her nightgown and then blamed her for his lack of passion. He might, he had castigated in a slurred and spiteful voice as he had attempted to caress his own body into life, have been able to overlook the fact she was a lowly *cit* if she had been a real beauty, but beggars couldn't afford to be choosers. 'Which in some ways I am grateful for as it allowed me to quickly learn to loathe him with a vengeance.'

'I'll wager he was an atrocious lover, too.'

Penny almost choked on her tea.

'Mama, that is none of our business!' Poor Jessamine looked appalled.

'Why ever not? We are all married women here, Jess. It perfectly acceptable for *married* ladies to discuss such things in private.'

'I am *so* sorry, Penny. She is incorrigible. You do not need to answer.'

'She is incorrigible—but we adore her for it.'

'I *knew* he was an atrocious lover! Villains like him always are. Was he selfish? Rough? Lacking in the correct equipment?'

All of the above, alongside repugnant. The only way to endure Penhurst's impersonal and unpleasant intrusions had been to close her eyes and imagine she was somewhere else. Somewhere so far away she could completely detach—like the moon. Fortunately, he only cared about his own gratification, so the act was over quickly and then he always left her bedroom straight after.

'All I will say in response is that I was exceedingly relieved when I learned I was carrying Freddie, so that he stopped visiting my bedchamber and thankfully never bothered to return. I am not sure I could have withstood many more months of *that* chore.' The marital bed had been nothing like her mother had promised, not that she had ever confessed as much to her. Far from it, in fact. Her mother had promised tenderness, passion and pleasure, not a drunken, grunting lecher. In the days and weeks after, Penny had pretended she was ecstatic to be married—solely to please her romantic mother—when the opposite had been true. Straight away she had felt trapped. Straight away she had bitterly regretted her folly. Without thinking, she made a face of disgust. Then, remembering she was trying to keep the tone of the conversation light-hearted, shuddered for effect. 'He was an all-round sorry excuse for a lover...'

'I hope I am not interrupting...' At the sound of Lord Hadleigh's deep voice behind her, Penny did choke on her tea. She made a delicate attempt not to retch out a cough, but when it became apparent she would likely turn purple unless she did, had to suffer the further embarrassment of the Dowager whacking her on the back until the wayward tea finally dislodged itself.

Penny immediately shot to her feet and tried to look more like a housekeeper than a gossiping lady. 'Let me take your coat. Did none of the footman greet you properly at the door?' In her embarrassment, she was babbling. 'We did not expect you till later this afternoon, my lord.'

She hadn't seen hide nor hair of him since last week when she'd practically had to drag him around his own house before he had dashed away. He had been aloof and uninterested, not at all like the charming fellow who had helped her with the flour explosion the week before. At the time she had put the change down to the shift in their statuses. She was no longer a peer's widow and was now a servant and technically, despite it being commandeered by the Crown, this grand house was his so that made her his servant.

But upon reflection, his manner and demeanour on that visit had bothered her to such an extent that he had occupied a great deal of her spare thoughts since. She had never seen him so out of sorts or so…uncommanding. He had been positively monosyllabic for the entire tour. Penny had had to prise every word out of him and, once or twice during that short half-hour visit, when he was not being terminally detached he had even seemed almost vulnerable. Not so now, though. The confident barrister had come visiting today. He stood in the doorway still clutching his hat, looking windswept and handsome. Perhaps, on a second glance, he still seemed a little bit awkward to be there now, too, if she was honest.

Good heavens! Had he heard her discussing intimacies?

'Do not let it trouble you.' He could barely meet her eye, which suggested he *had* heard her. 'I came around the back. Through the kitchens. I didn't mean to startle you.' Although if she had been doing the job she was being paid to do rather than sitting around sipping tea and discussing her disappointing history with marital congress, she wouldn't have choked on it in the first place.

He shrugged out of his greatcoat, sending a waft of something delicious her way as he handed it to her. A subtle, spicy cologne mixed with the crisp autumn air. She took the garment, trying not to be so aware that it was still filled with the warmth of him as he greeted the other ladies with much more affection than she had expected.

'Hadleigh! How are you?' Lady Jessamine smothered him in a hug.

'I am well.' He held her at arm's length and grinned his pleasure at seeing her, something which shouldn't have bothered Penny in the slightest—but did. She wanted him to be the charming man for her again, too. 'But look at you! Marriage clearly suits you.' Then he held his arms open to the Dowager. 'Lady Flint! I had no idea you were coming.'

'As if I would leave dear Jess to suffer *you*

alone.' She kissed his cheek affectionately and then neatened his cravat. 'You have form, young man. Somebody needs to be here to make sure she is allowed to eat at civilised times.'

'I didn't realise you all knew each other so well.' And Penny felt oddly left out despite knowing she had no reason to. She was a servant here, not really one of the ladies and certainly not part of this affectionate reunion.

'Indeed,' said the Dowager, still obviously thrilled to see him, 'Jess endured many *arduous* hours being interrogated by this scoundrel. But he *did* save her life, so we all feel duty-bound to be nice to him.'

'He did?' The man in question appeared discomfited by this admission.

'I can assure you, they are exaggerating my part in it all.' Before anyone could elaborate, he was all business once more. But only to her. 'Is the room readied as I instructed?'

'Of course.' Although why he had insisted setting up a new study in what had been the music room she couldn't fathom when there was a perfectly serviceable study further along the hallway containing everything he had requested she buy again from scratch. But she had purchased a new sturdy desk exactly as he had asked for, a comfortable chair to go with it, paper, quills, ink. Organised the furniture to catch the daylight as well as moving in a few homely touches to make it seem less sparse now that all the instruments apart from the beautiful pianoforte had been relegated to the attic. 'Everything on your list is ready and waiting for you.

'Then if you will excuse me, ladies, I need to head there directly and prepare. And might I have a word, Penny?' As he was already striding purposefully towards the door, she had no choice other than to follow, quietly dreading any potentially awkward conversation about her place in his lovely house or the sort of conversation she had just been having within it.

Chapter Ten

Hadleigh had been mulling over what he should say for days. A brief apology for his odd behaviour the last time they met which would include a tiny, dismissive nod to the painful memories this house had conjured in him, swiftly followed by his heartfelt thanks that she had readied it so quickly. Something he should have done on his last visit before he had fled the estate as if his breeches were on fire. Not his finest hour.

He had been sorely tempted to flee the house again a moment ago—but for entirely different reasons. That would teach him to cowardly sneak into the back of his own house like a thief and then spend several illicit minutes eavesdropping on a conversation that really didn't concern him. In his defence—although blatantly such behaviour was wholly indefensible—he had been intrigued to hear about Penny's marriage. She had been so open to the Dowager and Jessamine, admitting to her own folly in hastily marrying the man and inadvertently appraising him of details he had not known. Like the fact her time with her son was strictly limited or that he used that time to blackmail her with. No wonder she had adhered to all his demands when she had been threatened with banishment if she stepped out of line. Having seen her with her little boy, seen the palpable love she had for him shining in her eyes, being wrenched from his life like that would have destroyed her.

When she had told him that she had lived with a controlling man, he had assumed she had lived with someone like his father. His word had been law—but even he had not attempted to control all aspects of his mother's life. She had been able to come and go as she pleased, visit friends, do exactly what she wanted with the house and bring up Hadleigh in whatever way she saw fit. His father always had more pressing things to do than care two figs about the running of the house or being a parent to his only child. He much preferred spending all his time with his current mistress, or, more often than not, *mistresses*.

Yet Penny had endured more than that—her entire life had been rigidly controlled, which went a long way to explaining why she was so adamantly determined to control her own future without any outside interference now her husband was gone. Aspects of her character now made more sense. The stubborn pride was a sign that Penhurst hadn't broken her spirit—or if he had, it was recovering. Hadleigh was glad he had overheard she felt no inclination to mourn the man because she was well shot of him. He wasn't entirely sure what he felt about overhearing that snippet about what had gone on in the marital bed, though.

Pity had been the first emotion he had experienced, rapidly followed by a whole host of clamouring emotions he had not been the slightest bit prepared for. The anger had been so sudden and explosive it shocked him. He had wanted to pummel Penhurst's smug face with his fist for treating her with such brutish carelessness. Intertwined with the anger had been something which was worryingly akin to jealousy. It had been that surge of irrational, wholly male possessiveness which had prompted him to either make his presence known and put an abrupt end to the confession or storm out of the house again. Because if she had elaborated, with actual specific detail of those lacklustre intimacies, Hadleigh wasn't entirely sure how he would have reacted, truth be told. Not when he had been dreaming about intimacies with her himself since the fateful night with the flour.

He'd had the same dream every night for a week. She stood at the top of the steps in front of the front door, her dress plastered to her body by the wind just as it had been the last time he had come here. Only in his dream, the house beyond didn't bother him because she was there waiting for him, so he had sprinted up those steps and taken her in his arms, kissed her. What happened next in the dreams varied from night to night, depending on how much cheese he had had at the interchangeable, unappetising but reliably cold suppers he had eaten before falling exhausted into bed. But they always reliably ended up in that same bed and he awoke hot and bothered, a little ashamed and a great deal hard.

He had suspected that, on top of everything else currently clouding his mind, he was seriously attracted to her. Now, thanks to the undeniable knot of jealousy he couldn't seem to shift, he knew he was.

He blamed this house. He'd opened Pandora's box to right a wrong when his mind was at its most occupied and the pressure resting on his shoulders was the greatest. And, if he was honest, he blamed himself, too. He could and should have walked away when she had politely sent him packing, heeded Leatham's order to leave her well alone, but something about her called to him and he hadn't been able to resist. He had gone out of his way to find a solution to help her. Gone out of his way to visit her. Allowed his wayward hands to touch her cheek and his wayward eyes to look their fill when he should have been focusing all his energies on the trial.

It was a good thing he hadn't been stupid enough to give the object of his nightly fantasies a job in his own house! Oh, the irony! Of all the stupid decisions he'd made in the last month, that one had to reign as the stupidest. His only consolation was the poor woman had no idea of his raging lust now that she was here. He sincerely doubted she would have taken the job if she had.

He reached the music room and took a deep breath. He had spent hours here growing up. Mostly on his own, but occasionally with his mother. Conscious of Penny waiting behind him made procrastinating impossible, so he gripped the handle and flung open the door.

Nothing. Only numbness.

Splendid. Exactly why he had chosen it as his temporary study for the duration.

'Is everything to your satisfaction?'

Hadleigh instantly regretted his quick glance sideways, because she was worrying her plump bottom lip with her teeth when he really didn't want to have to think about her lips any more than he wanted to think of her in bed with Penhurst. Or the silky, bouncing, dark curl which had dislodged itself from its sensible coiffure in her haste to keep up with him. Dragging his eyes resolutely from temptation, he took in the room.

It was a tableau of ordered perfection. Uncluttered. Simple. Eminently practical. Alongside the excellent, high desk she had chosen to accommodate his long legs and the well-upholstered high-backed chair behind it that could have been crafted with his exact measurements in mind, there were now a row of deep and sturdy bookshelves he had most definitely not requested lining the back wall. All empty. All awaiting his detailed and meticulous notes which would doubtless soon fill them in the precise alphabetical order he found easiest to work with.

How had she known he was incapable of functioning in anything less? Unless she thought him stuffy and staid, which rankled, before he reassured himself that was probably for the best. Better to be seen as a crusty, emotionless, rigidly organised nitpicker than a man who had apparently been suddenly and catastrophically consumed with lust. Hadleigh strode to the desk and practically threw himself into the chair in case that lust decided to immediately show itself.

Good grief, what was the matter with him? Had he become so overly tired that he now no longer had any control over his animal urges? 'It is exactly as I wanted it. Thank you.' Hardly a gushing compliment when he had barked it at her, so he tried to immediately make amends. 'You have a canny eye for good furniture. Your parents taught you well.' And in that single, desperate sentence, he might as well have just told her he had been lurking in the hallway, eavesdropping for a good ten minutes, because they had never had a single conversation about her parents or their blasted emporium. He knew the exact moment she realised because she quickly glanced down at her clasped, busy hands before they buried themselves in the folds on her skirt. A sure sign he had made her feel completely uncomfortable.

'Thank you, my lord.' Her eyes didn't rise, but that only served to give him a better view of those beautiful long eyelashes as she chewed once again on that lush bottom lip to torture him. He needed to stop looking at her lips! 'I take it you overheard my conversation with the Dowager.'

'Well…er…' Perhaps he could still save face? His talent with words was legendary, after all. 'Er…' Clearly, like the unmistakable bulge in his breeches, he had lost control of his vocal cords, too. For that he would blame the new dress. Where had all the dour ones gone?

'Oh! I am *so* sorry!' Her eyes finally lifted to meet his and they were swirling with emotion. It turned the pretty blue irises a deeper, stormier cobalt. 'The Dowager asks a great many personal questions and it is almost impossible to avoid answering them!' He watched a blush stain her cheeks, forcing him to remember that it was those exact cheeks which he held entirely responsible for his current predicament. Alongside another pretty new dress which drew his blasted eyes to the fine bosom encased within them. If he hadn't stupidly brushed those inconsequential specks of flour off those cheeks, then he never would have realised how soft her skin was and he certainly would not have begun to fantasise about its texture beneath her clothes. 'Although I realise it was highly inappropriate in this instance for me to answer all of them with such...candour.'

Good grief! She was alluding to the bedchamber part of the conversation. The part he most definitely did not want to discuss with her at all, because ever since he had overheard what a chore she had found it with Penhurst, God help him, he wanted to show her what it could be like between a man and a woman. Or more specifically what it would be like with him.

'The Dowager was most insistent that it was acceptable for married ladies to talk about such things and I forgot my place and should never have allowed myself to be lured into talking about my husband's—'

'Please!' Hadleigh held his hands up, supremely conscious that the tips of his own ears had begun to redden. 'For both our sakes, I beg you, let us leave it unsaid.' He smiled, or he attempted to smile and feared it might actually be more akin to a weird grimace. 'I should have informed you all of my presence sooner. It's entirely my own fault. And that is not at all what I wanted to talk to you about now.' He needed to stop snapping. The poor woman was stood at his desk like a naughty pupil awaiting punishment. 'Please...take a seat, Penny.'

She did, but once again was perched on the edge of the chair, ramrod straight. Beautiful blue eyes wide. Gloriously soft cheeks still flushed. That distracting coil of hair still dangling, drawing his eyes to her neck now and the acres of alabaster skin on show above the scooped neckline of her forest-green gown. The deep colour suited her. It complimented her pale complexion. Unfortunately, it also gave him the smallest glimpse of a tiny bit of cleavage as her chest rose and fell with her breathing. 'The thing is...' His mouth was suddenly as dry as the Sahara. 'I wanted to apologise to you for last week.'

Her lips parted and stayed that way long enough for his to get entirely inappropriate ideas. 'Apologise? Whatever for?'

Just say it as you rehearsed it. Get it over with. 'My behaviour here last time was...well, a little odd,and I might have come across a tad abrupt. I did not mean to be rude, especially as you had done such a good job. Nor did I mean not to compliment you on a job well done. Being here...' he gestured lamely to the walls and ceiling '...in this house after such a prolonged absence was a little overwhelming.' Not at all what he meant to say, because being overwhelmed made him sound pathetic and despite being entirely pathetic as far as this godforsaken place was concerned, he did not want to appear that way in front of her. 'What I mean is, this house brings back lots of memories... I was not prepared for the full extent of them.' Time to wave it away as if it was of no matter, exactly as he had rehearsed. 'So, how is Freddie settling in?' A safer topic. He even managed to steeple his fingers on the table casually.

'Freddie is doing well. I wanted to thank you for sending Gwendoline.' He'd interviewed fifteen potential nursemaids, all highly recommended, until that kindly old lady had arrived at his chambers armed with a glowing pile of references. References he had diligently and thoroughly checked to ensure they were genuine. 'He already adores her and so do I.'

He brushed that away, too. 'I am glad.' Which rather left him at a loss as to what else to talk to her about, but as he had asked her to sit, realised he needed to think of something. 'How did you know I would want all these neat bookshelves?'

She offered him a half-smile which made her eyes sparkle. 'I have watched you work, remember. You are an organised person by nature. So very *thorough* and *meticulous*.' She gave a little shrug. 'The notes in front of you in court were always neatly arranged and you seemed to know exactly where to find something when you needed it and could immediately put your hand on it. While the defence lawyers were always shuffling papers.'

'And a predictably *thorough* and *meticulous* person needs shelves.'

She seemed very pleased with herself. 'Lots of them. And with all the work you have to do in the next few months, I suspect they will fill quickly. Although I sincerely hope that not all aspects of your life are so rigidly organised. A little noise and chaos enriches life, or so I've found. At least that is how I justify the noise and chaos Freddie brings to mine.' She was smiling, making small talk. Extending the olive branch of friendship.

'I get quite enough noise and chaos in the courtroom.' Why had he said that? It sounded like a criticism when he had intended to grasp the proffered branch with both hands. Now his mouth as well as the bulge in his breeches was refusing to listen to his head.

There was an awkward gap as he racked his brains, trying to think of something, anything, to say to her to make the awkward situation feel better.

Sensing his discomfort, she stood. 'Luncheon is at one and will be served in the dining room.' He nodded and she made to leave, turning at the last moment with a quizzical expression. 'Were they good memories or bad?'

'A bit of both.' As he said it, he realised that was true. Not everything that had happened here had been bad. When his father had been away, in many ways his childhood and youth had been idyllic.

'But it is always the bad our mind presents us with first, isn't it?'

'I suppose it is.' There had been laughter here as well as tears. Good memories lurking in these walls, too long forgotten. His eyes drifted to the pianoforte still sat in its original place near the furthest window. Remembered playing it for his mother all the time. *Mozart*. Always Mozart—her favourite—while she sat on a chair close by embroidering something which would make its way into his bedchamber at some point to hide among his things. Handkerchiefs, his initials woven into a flourishing swirl on all manner of clothes— cravats, shirt tails and, entirely to vex him, his drawers in case he lost them at university. With that recollection his fingers flexed and he had the sudden urge to play a tune. How long had it been since he had done that?

'The good memories will win in the end. They always do, or at least I like to think that is the case. As you say, good should always triumph over bad.' Words he lived by. 'Shall I send in some tea?'

'Yes. Tea would be lovely.' Hadleigh waited till

she had gone to walk to the pianoforte and trace his fingers lovingly over the keys. Glad he had one good memory to treasure again in the swirling sea of bad.

Chapter Eleven

Now that Freddie was fast asleep, Penny left the new nursemaid watching him while she did her final evening round of the house. The Flints and the Dowager were happily settled in the drawing room, dinner had been cleared and the dining room was spotless, and the daytime servants had retired to their own quarters now that the Invisibles had taken their posts for the night. The fact that a group of men known only as the Invisibles now seemed the norm made her smile, because not in a month of Sundays would she ever have imagined in her wildest dreams that one day she would work hand in glove with a whole battalion of government spies. She still had moments where she had to pause and wonder what a bizarre twist in the path her life had taken, when at this time last year she had still been trapped in a loveless union with Penhurst. Yet, despite the bizarre twist, things had settled into a routine over the past two weeks.

Every other day, Lord Hadleigh would turn up through the back of the house after breakfast, take tea in his new study alone which Penny always brought to him. Their exchanges were brief but pleasant. He enquired after Freddie or the Flints, appraised her of his plans for the day so that she could time luncheon and dinner properly, then he would get an odd look in his unusual amber eyes which always signalled it was time for him to bury himself in his work. On these days, he sat with Jessamine for hours upon end, asking questions, meticulously going over her answers. Her new friend came out of these sessions mentally exhausted, but Lord Hadleigh never seemed to stop. After Jessamine, he would always work alone for several hours unless he had someone else lined up to talk to. Flint or the other regular visitors—Seb, Lord Fennimore and Gray.

While those visitors nearly always stayed the night, Hadleigh never so much as stayed for dinner in his own house, preferring instead to leave as it was served at seven to ride his horse alone in the dark for the hour it took him to return to London. That bothered Penny.

Now that the November weather was starting to bite and it was pitch-black outside from four in the afternoon, she had started to worry about him all alone on those deserted roads where anything could happen. Then, of course, it was his health which concerned her. He looked more and more exhausted with each passing day. Dark circles shadowed those perceptive eyes, no doubt from exhaustion. Aside from the unnecessarily long journey he undertook twice each day he was here, the pressure of the case was obviously taking its toll. He worked too hard, cared too much about the case, and if he wasn't careful he was going to make himself ill.

She had discussed both of these worries at great length with Jessamine and the Dowager, but no amount of their talking to him made a jot of difference. Lord Hadleigh was a stubborn man and flatly refused to listen. What she had never discussed with those ladies was the thing about it all which bothered her the most. The case and his heavy workload aside, she was coming to believe his continued stubbornness was not borne out of his belief that he knew best, but fear. There were parts of his house he deftly avoided like the plague—the morning room and anything involving stairs.

When she thought back over his first visit, those had been the places where he had been the most rigid and aloof. How could a man own such a magnificent house so close to the capital and fail to visit it for years? Nearly ten years according to the old gardener who diligently tended the flower beds. Flower beds he had carefully looked after when the rest of the house had been boarded up. However, he flatly refused to elaborate as, apparently, it was not his place to say and he always managed to leave Penny with the impression she should be ashamed of herself for asking.

Yet that only made her more curious.

His obvious reluctance to live under the same roof as his work made no sense, unless she weighed it with Lord Hadleigh's brisk and throwaway apology on his second visit. She had known the second he had said it that he had let on far more than he wanted anyone to know.

This house brings back lots of memories... I was not prepared for the full extent of them.

She had pondered both that sentence and his expression as he said them a great deal since, because for the first time since she had known him, his inscrutable lawyer's mask had developed a crack. One that had allowed her to see, if only for a moment, that those unusual amber eyes were a little lost and sad. Frightened, even. But she might have imagined that. Despite his tired demeanour he had certainly displayed no cracks since, although he quite obviously stayed away from certain rooms and, of course, the front door which he deftly avoided like the plague. Aside from those foibles, he was every inch the determined and tenacious seeker of justice his reputation proclaimed. She dreaded to think how many hours in a week he dedicated to this impending trial, or, more worryingly, how many hours he failed to dedicate to his self instead. He was working himself into the ground.

But if he wouldn't listen to his friends, he certainly wouldn't listen to her. Not that she'd attempted to reason with him. That wasn't her place and since she had commenced her employment here, the dynamic in their relationship had changed significantly since the night of the flour. They maintained a polite distance—or at least he did. Probably because he didn't want to muddy the waters now that she had stepped back down into the class she had been born into.

She headed to the music room to carry out her last duty, one he hadn't asked her to perform, but which she did anyway. He worked so hard, she didn't want him to have to concern himself with time-wasting chores such as refilling his ink pot or replenishing his neat stack of foolscap in the top drawer of his pristine desk. Most days she sharpened his quills, too. If he noticed, he never mentioned it, so she never did either. It was a small and insignificant gesture for a man who grafted so tirelessly and wouldn't be helped.

But as she turned into the long, dim hallway which lead to her destination, she hesitated at the sight of the thin shaft of light bleeding out from under the closed door. As he should have been long gone, she assumed one of the maids had simply forgotten to extinguish the lamps, but knocked just in case before she opened the door.

He was sat hunched at the desk, his dishevelled golden head propped on one hand as he turned and appeared shocked to see her.

'What are you still doing here?' A quick glance at the mantel clock confirmed it was nearly nine. 'I thought you'd left hours ago.' Several documents were strewn across his desk in a manner most unlike him.

'I have some things to finish.'

'Things that couldn't wait until tomorrow?'

'If I left them, they would niggle at me and then I wouldn't sleep. I need to work through this conundrum.' He pointed to the sheet of foolscap in front of him that was divided into two long columns. 'When I cannot see the wood for the trees, I always list things side by side—evidence versus conjecture, motive versus circumstances, pros and cons...' He offered her a half-hearted smile which didn't touch his troubled eyes. 'I'll be done shortly. Just as soon as I work out which column tells me the answer. The one with the majority is always the right course of action.' As if dismissing her, he turned his weary head to stare at his lists. Perhaps it was his posture—usually so straight, it was now slumped. Or the disorganised clutter on his desk, or the bleak, burdened nature of his expression.

Penny hovered instead of leaving.

'Have you eaten?'

'I will eat once I get home.'

'You are home. And if you are determined to continue working then you need something in your stomach.'

'I'm fine… I'll be leaving soon. But I wouldn't say no to some coffee.' He looked up again and he appeared so lost and alone she decided not to take a blind bit of notice. Coffee! He seemed to live on the stuff. Someone had to look after his health and well-being if he was going to continue to neglect them.

'Very well.'

She strode out of the room, leaving the door ajar, and headed directly to the kitchens. On the stove, slowly bubbling away, was the hearty stew that the cook had prepared to sustain the men on watch through the night. She ladled a healthy portion into a bowl. Sawed off two thick slices of bread which she buttered, then retrieved the remains of the apple tart that had been served for dessert which she finished with a huge dollop of cream. In deference to his request for coffee, she poured him a large glass of milk instead, then balanced the whole lot on a tray.

She practically kicked the door open as she marched back into the room and deposited the whole lot noisily on the sideboard. Lord, she was fuming at him! His head had snapped up and he was staring at her confused, but by that time she was in no mood to be trifled with. Like a mother tested to the furthest limits of her patience, she briskly went to his desk and scooped as much of the paperwork to one side where she hastily gathered them up into a pile, then snatched the list from under his fingers. 'You are going to make yourself ill, you silly man!'

'Silly man?' If he was angry at her rude outburst, she neither noticed nor cared.

'Yes! Silly man! You are being so stubbornly *thorough* and so determinedly *meticulous* you are working yourself into the ground. And neglecting yourself horribly in the process!' He went to defend himself, and she found her forceful mother's finger had attached itself to her hand from beyond and started to wag itself in front of his stubborn face. 'You ought to be ashamed of yourself! This is the biggest trial of the century! The government are depending on you! And you risk it all with your own disgraceful carelessness! What good will you be to anyone if you are laid up in bed?' Now that the papers were all gone, she fetched the tray again and dropped in unceremoniously in front of him. 'I was employed to ensure the smooth running of this house and the comfort and safety of all of its occupants. While you are under this roof, that also includes you! There will be no more work until you have eaten a proper meal, Lord Hadleigh.' She folded her arms for good measure. 'So eat!'

He stared down at the food and then back up at her, his expression as unfathomable as it always was. She watched him take a deep breath in and then wondered what had possessed her to be so direct and so loud. She needed this job. Needed the money and the references that came along with it. He was well within his rights to give her a jolly good carpeting for her insubordination. Had she dared speak to Penhurst like that, he'd have hit the roof. But just as she was about to cave in and issue a grovelling apology, he picked up the spoon and sighed.

'Well, that was a well-aimed kick up the backside. One I suppose I deserve.' He dipped the spoon into the bowl and stared at the thick stew. 'I was going around in circles anyway... This case is sending me mad.' Then he took a mouthful and chewed thoughtfully until his eyes locked with hers once more. Amused this time. 'If you are going to keep watch to ensure I comply, you may as well sit while you're doing it.' He gestured to the empty chair with his spoon.

Penny sat, feeling both relief at his reaction and that he was finally putting something wholesome in his belly. When sitting and watching made her feel awkward, she decided to make conversation. 'What has you going around in circles?' It was a bad question and she winced. She had no right to ask about the case. 'What I mean is...'

'It's—how did you put it?—gilding the lily. I

have built the case and as it stands it's a solid one. But because I am doggedly *thorough* and *meticulous*, I'm trying to mitigate against the defence tearing Jessamine's testimony apart. As the main prosecution witness, there is a chance they can call hearsay on some of the details. That's what I would argue in their shoes. The word of one person against another is not conclusive proof of guilt. What I want to establish, and which I am failing to do in the case of some of her co-conspirators, and prove is a direct link between them and Viscountess Gislingham to knock those arguments down with. Three have already laid the blame firmly at her door and have put forward tangible evidence or witnesses who can corroborate their version of events. One was a childhood neighbour, the other two regulars in her... social circle.'

Polite code, she assumed, for the Viscountess's bed.

'The remaining three are refusing to talk at all. Lady Gislingham herself is pleading complete ignorance of any of the charges laid against her. While the state has a great deal of evidence to the contrary, including all the evidence we have been able to glean from the three turncoats, there is a slim chance that with the right counsel, one or two of those other peers will escape justice because the evidence we have is circumstantial. We can prove the smuggling—but not the treason. The long and the short of it is, I wish I had more names on my witness list for Jessamine's sake. That is a heavy burden to rest entirely on her shoulders.'

He spooned up another mouthful, looking despondent. 'Were the other traitors her lovers, too?' Penny asked.

'They could be. She was rather free and easy with her favours and we know for certain she had an affair with Saint-Aubin during her first Season. That was quite the scandal at the time, because of the wars with France and his links to Old Boney. That scandal forced her out of London society then and years later that damning link couldn't be overlooked, seeing that it was Saint-Aubin who provided all the smuggled brandy in the first place. But proving she seduced the other men into treachery won't be easy if they refuse to admit it.' He picked up the milk and frowned at it. 'What made you ask that?'

'Because Penhurst and Lady Gislingham were also lovers—both before we married and after.' One of his earlier indiscretions in their short marriage, back when his affairs had still hurt.

The lawyer's eyebrows rose and he sat forward. 'How do you know they were intimate?'

'He told me.'

Penhurst had found pleasure in parading his virility in front of her while listing her many failings. Usually her prolonged barrenness was his chosen emotional stick to beat her with, when he needed an heir and her womb remained defiantly empty, but he wasn't restricted to just that hurtful barb. Her figure was disappointing, her personality lacklustre. She wasn't pretty enough, enthralling enough, alluring enough. Her breasts weren't anywhere near big enough, she lacked the passion he enjoyed in his other lovers' beds and he had only married her because of her dowry. Never mind that it was hard to feel passion for a man who ruthlessly pursued his own pleasure to the detriment of everything else. From that first night when he had swiftly and roughly taken her innocence at the start of their marriage to the last time he had drunkenly demanded his conjugal rights a few days before she learned she was carrying Freddie, Penny had felt debased and disgusted by her husband's touch.

They had only been wed a few months when she came to welcome his frequent affairs. While he was laying with another woman, he wasn't laying with her. Thankfully, as soon as he had made his heir, he never visited her bedchamber again. 'My husband never saw the point of keeping that sort of secret. Ironic, really, when so much of his life was kept hidden. Beyond his nocturnal relationship with the Viscountess, I am afraid I know nothing more to aid your conundrum.'

'That you have proved there was a link between them is enough for the purposes of my investigation. It does prove a theme…and suggests the Viscountess had a tried-and-tested modus operandi as a seductress. It might be exactly what I need—if I can find witnesses to the infidelities.'

'Have you spoken to the wives of the men who refuse to talk?'

'I confess, I am reluctant to speak to the wives.' He had not spoken to her after Penhurst's initial arrest either.

'Why ever not? Nobody knows better her husband's affairs than the poor little woman left at home.' She watched him look down at his food blandly and then realised exactly why he had left her alone. 'Are you are trying to protect them?' While that was noble, it was also foolhardy for his purpose.

'Legally they are exempt unless they choose to speak out and I am going to be sending their husbands to the gallows—surely that is humiliation enough after all they have endured? If they want to come forward, they know where to…'

'Do they? Have you explicitly offered them the opportunity?' Penny reached across the desk and touched his hand, a huge mistake because she found she didn't particularly want to let go. 'If you had asked me about Penhurst again before the trial, once the shock had worn off and reality had settled in, I would have told you everything I knew. I felt so angry, so betrayed and so terrified he would be released into my life again. Instead, I had to wait and hope his lawyers would call me to the stand to say my piece. And in leaving me—and please do not think I blame you—I was left all alone feeling impotent and aggrieved and ashamed of who I was. My voice was stolen from me during my marriage, but I found it again in the witness stand. Perhaps their husbands weren't monsters at home and perhaps they might refuse to co-operate. But unless you give them the opportunity to speak, how do you know those women don't feel the same?'

Chapter Twelve

She had left him to eat. The stew proved much easier to digest than her insights. The way Penny told it, being part of the proceedings had been the start of the healing process for her, a way to fight back and matter again. With the clarity which only came with hindsight, he realised that perhaps her life during those weeks leading up to and during the trial might well have been easier if she had been named as a witness for the prosecution. A traitor's wife still, but publicly seen to be both brave and honourable herself because she had chosen her side.

Hadleigh had also grossly underestimated her. In blindly honouring the law and allowing her the right not to testify against her husband as was the norm, he had cast her as a victim who needed cosseting rather than giving her the chance to prove her mettle. He should have asked her. Should have granted her a voice sooner.

He was ashamed of himself for not treating Penny with the same rigour as he had treated all the other witnesses during that trial, something he had avoided because he had known beforehand she had suffered Penhurst's violence. Ashamed, too, that part of his reticence came from his own experiences. His mother had not wanted to speak of her turmoil, therefore he had wrongly assumed Penny—and every other abused wife out there—would feel the same. He had assumed they would all be like his mother and deny any wrongdoing from the monsters they had married for fear of what? Judgement? Retribution? Shame?

Did it also follow that he took it upon himself to shield them from having to admit it because he had failed to protect his mother all those years ago? That uncomfortable truth left a sour taste in the mouth, because, whichever way you looked at it, he was tarring every abused woman with the same brush when he prided himself in always seeking the truth—no matter what. Yet he had purposely left stones unturned.

That knowledge was preventing him sleeping.

That knowledge and the fact he had agreed to the unthinkable and was currently attempting to sleep at Chafford Grange.

To be fair, she had ambushed him when his mind was still reeling. She had come back to collect his tray and announced she thought it careless and foolish to ride home so late, especially when he was intent on returning on the morrow. That it made no sense, which of course it didn't unless he confessed to his guilty conscience. She also reminded him that his friends were worried about him and that the Flints had better things to concern themselves with at the moment than his selfish insistence to put himself unnecessarily at risk of footpads. Then she had played her trump card, one which tugged at his emotions more effectively than any other argument possibly could have.

I worry about you, too.

Five words which had done odd things to his heart. Her solemn blue gaze had instantly dipped as soon as she said them, as if she was bearing a little bit of her own heart and was embarrassed by that, yet his soared gratefully at the admission.

So he had said yes. He would stay the night just this once and take better care to leave before dark in the future. Then hastily concocted a series of unbelievable excuses why he couldn't possibly stay in the family wing tonight, when the truth boiled down to two things. Firstly, there was no way he would ever set foot in his father's bedroom which she had readied weeks ago for him as the designated master of the house. Flint and Jessamine were already in his mother's while the Dowager slept in his old bedchamber. There were too many memories in both those rooms, too, so he was relieved they were taken. And secondly, and perhaps most importantly, he wanted to avoid the main staircase. None of those were things he would tell her—or anyone. He might well be a pathetic coward, but hell would have to freeze over before he admitted it out loud.

Perhaps Penny had worked that out, because she hadn't argued and had, of her own accord, led him up the servants' stairs to the row of guest rooms located at the front of the house. Not only did that allow him to avoid the stairs which had killed his mother, they didn't come with walls crammed with ghosts either, so he had assumed he might be able to snatch a few hours of rest.

How wrong he was.

After hours staring hopelessly at the ceiling, he had decided enough was enough. If his mind was whirring from Penny's revelation and the way his body had reacted when she had briefly touched him, he might as well work! He could snatch a few hours before the first servants woke and sneak back up here before Penny was any the wiser. He flung the covers angrily aside and shoved his feet in his breeches. The blasted woman had got under his skin and was making him rest when he had better things to be doing! Like preparing the single biggest case of his career! He grabbed his shirt before he stormed out of the room and tugged it over his head as he retraced his steps down the dimly lit servants' staircase once again.

As he made his way down the narrow corridor to the rear of the house, he noticed a light coming from the kitchen. One he would have ignored had he not heard a child's fractious cry as well.

'Shh, Freddie darling, or you'll wake up the house.'

Hadleigh stopped, then shook his head. It didn't matter that his first instinct was to rush to her, it was none of his business and she probably wouldn't appreciate him barging in on her while she was trying to calm the child. Besides, at this ungodly hour, there was every chance she was in her nightgown and he really didn't need to see that any more than he needed to be willingly alone with her in the cosy intimacy of the kitchen. More distractions in a head already crammed with them!

Furthermore, in his haste to escape his mattress prison, he had neglected to put anything on his feet. Wasn't wearing either a waistcoat or coat. No cravat. He really wasn't decent himself. And what did he know about crying babies?

Nothing.

'Please, darling…try to calm down…shh.'

Penny's voice was soft and soothing, but like a siren's it called to him. Rather than let his bare feet take him to the music room where his overly occupied mind had intended to go, they transported him quietly to her instead.

At his first sight, she had her back to him. The glowing fire at the furthest end of the kitchen gave the room its only light, but that light floated through the gauzy linen of her nightdress and cast the contours of her body into a dark silhouette, forcing him to watch her delectable round bottom undulate as she rhythmically rocked the grumpy child in her arms. Her feet were bare, too, while her dark hair fell between her shoulder blades to the middle of her back in one thick, loose plait. That, too, swayed as she did, giving him alternate views of both sides of her swan-like neck. Beautiful and seductive.

Utter torture. Exactly as he had known it would be.

Yet for several moments he still stood transfixed, simultaneously panicked that she would turn and see him loitering while wondering what the hell he was going to say when she inevitably did. His throat had gone so dry and tight with unexpected longing, he feared whatever he said would come out in a strangled croak and he'd look foolish and guilty at being caught red-handed. Or worse, look utterly charmed and bewitched.

Better to pre-empt the embarrassment. 'Is there anything I can do to help?'

Despite his whisper, her head whipped around

and her expression was alarmed. 'I am so sorry, my lord, I didn't mean to wake you!'

'You didn't.' And his wayward feet were off again, walking directly towards her. His mouth was smiling. His eyes drinking her in. 'Like Freddie there, I couldn't sleep. I'm afraid sleep and I have not been bedfellows for a while.' Bedfellows! What a horrendously appropriate word which hinted at the direction his thoughts were headed.

Her lovely face softened and her body turned around to him. 'Poor you. Insomnia is awful, isn't it?' As she rocked her child innocently in her arms, she had no idea that the firelight gifted him with the willowy shape of her legs, the steep, alluring curve as her trim waist flared to hip. Nor was she aware how the embers added copper and red tones to her dark hair or deepened the colour of her eyes to make them seem more sultry.

'It is.' But it had its benefits. His feet scandalously took him to stand right in front of her. They were clearly marching to their own agenda now and had formed an alliance with his overactive and lusty imagination. 'What's wrong with your little man?'

'I have no idea. The last of his teeth, perhaps? Not that they have shown themselves. He has no temperature either and his appetite is hearty, so he is not ill. I cannot even blame the change in environment for his temper tantrums either, because he was like this a good month before we left Cheapside as you saw the night of the exploded flour.'

Mention of the flour reminded him of the flour on her bodice that night and the womanly breasts that filled that bodice. Breasts that would be unbound tonight in that nightrail. Only one layer of linen separating them from his gaze. His groin tightened at the thought.

'Gwendoline claims that even the most even tempered of children turn into beasts in their second year. According to her that is what ails him regardless of the fact he is not two for five more months.' Penny gave a put-upon shrug, then shifted her son from sitting on one arm to the other. Was Hadleigh a beast for lusting after her when she clearly had her work cut out? Probably. 'I came down here to make him some warm milk, but as you can see, he is stubbornly refusing to allow me to make it. Noise and chaos in action.'

He needed something to focus his mind rather than the inappropriate ideas suddenly racing through his head and in case his hands decided to mutiny like his feet. Under the circumstances, it was best not to watch her. Aside from the fact it was a gross invasion of her privacy, he knew already he would suffer horrendously from this night forward with more fevered dreams. Dreams which would take his mind further away from his work and drive him mad with yet more unslaked lust. How long had it been since he had lain with a woman? Months? A year? A bit longer... Good grief.

Far too long than the male body was designed for if his overwhelming carnal reaction was any indication. 'Then why don't I hold him while you do?' He could have offered to heat the milk for her, but reasoned that dealing with a squalling child was the perfect antidote to all the inappropriate things he was feeling.

'Would you mind?'

'I wouldn't have offered if I minded. Besides, you are clearly in the grip of a crisis and you already know that is when I can be most relied upon. Noise and chaos is my forte.' Hadleigh held out his arms, then wondered what the hell he was supposed to do when the fidgeting boy was placed in them. He had never held a child. Had no idea *how* to hold a child. Instinct had him supporting his bottom with one hand while the other held his back as he had witnessed her do, but conscious his big hands might harm the child, he was undoubtedly holding him far too limply if Freddie's sudden acrobatics were any gauge.

She smiled at his ineptitude. 'He is not made of glass and is certainly much stronger than you could imagine.' He was heavier, too. A positive, wriggling dead weight with no personal boundaries judging by the annoyed little hand which was now pushing hard at his chin in his eagerness to escape. Hadleigh adjusted his hold which lessened the wriggling, but not by much. 'Sometimes, the tighter you hold him, the more likely it is he will give in to Morpheus.' She bent to fetch a pan. 'Although sometimes it just makes him worse.' Pan in hand, she shrugged as she filled it with milk from the jug. 'My best advice is do whatever you think is best. That has worked for me so far. Or hasn't.' Hardly reassuring.

While she heated the milk, he dedicated all his energy into keeping Freddie still. He jiggled him. Rocked him. And when neither worked, dragged the boy's moaning head to his shoulder, stroked his hair and began to pace up and down in the kitchen, whispering encouraging nonsense into the boy's ear. Miraculously, that appeared to work, because the wrestling stopped. Then the squalling became the odd moan and by the time she was filling Freddie's bottle, the child's head lay heavily on his shoulder and his small body was finally limp in his arms.

Mindful that any sudden movements might end the blissful peace, he gingerly lowered himself into a chair and arranged the pair of them so that Freddie could lay across him unhindered with just the lightest support from his arms. The boy's thumb went to his mouth and he snuggled against his chest, almost as if the sound of Hadleigh's heart beating was like a lullaby.

* * *

Penny picked up the bottle and the two steaming mugs of milk and turned, then faltered. The sight of her son sleeping soundly on Lord Hadleigh's chest and Lord Hadleigh cradling him as if he were the most precious thing in the world made her heart stutter. Why hadn't she had the good sense to pick a man like that to father her child? One who was clearly born to be a natural father...

Where had that thought come from?

As if he sensed her errant and romantic imaginings, he looked up, his dark amber eyes flecked with gold in the firelight, smiled, and her silly heart did somersaults against her ribs. Good heavens, he was a handsome man. More handsome tonight, for some reason, than he had ever been before.

Perhaps because he was the most human she had ever seen him? Certainly the most relaxed. Over-long hair mussed from his pillow, his long legs stretched out and crossed at the ankles, big feet bare. The loose linen shirt both untucked at the waist and open at the neck. Even his jaw was informal, shadowed slightly with a day's growth of beard. The overall image he presented made her feel odd and unsettlingly fluttery inside. It also made her supremely conscious of her own body in the most peculiar way and, scandalously, she seemed suddenly very aware she was entirely naked under her sensible nightgown.

'I don't think Freddie wants the milk any more.' His voice was soft and low, the deep, intimate timbre sending a shiver down her spine. 'I think he is out for the count.'

'Never mind.' To her shame, her voice sounded strange. Breathier than normal. 'I made you some milk, too… To help you sleep.'

She placed the mug within his reach on the table and quickly retreated to the opposite end with her own drink which she was clutching tightly as if her life depended upon it. This all felt very naughty. Both of them here in the small hours, all alone. Not properly dressed. Her body humming with what she assumed was need.

How bizarre? She had never experienced it, but knew exactly what it was. Her breasts felt heavier and more sensitive than they ever had. Her skin felt almost on alert, not quite like her own and gloriously alive. Certain parts tingling, longing to be touched. All in all, quite the revelation as she approached her quarter century, as she had never experienced anything vaguely similar with her horrid husband. Not once.

She cradled her own mug and stared into it rather than at him, in case her needy body leaked out clues, hoping she appeared nonchalant as she sipped the warm milk. But she could feel the force of his stare before she risked returning it. It made the tiny hairs on the back of her neck dance with wanton abandon.

'I've been pondering everything you said earlier and you are right. Tomorrow I will approach the wives. I am so sorry I never afforded you that same chance.'

'I didn't tell you so you could castigate yourself over it. In truth, I was so confused and overawed by the whole thing, I didn't realise that saying my piece was exactly what I needed to do. Hindsight is always a wonderful thing.'

'Even so, it was wrong of me. We men are brought up to take care of women.'

'Not all men.'

His face clouded. 'No. Not all.'

'But your father taught you well.'

His expression became bland again, a sure sign he was about to hide something, then he surprised her by shaking his head, allowing bleak sadness to show instead. Gifting her with the truth. 'Alas, my father was a man exactly like your husband… He was violent and cold. If he taught me anything, he taught me the exact sort of man I never wanted to be.'

'He beat you?'

He shook his head, causing a lock of deliciously mussed hair to fall boyishly over his forehead. 'No…never me. I escaped that. To be frank, most of the time he barely noticed me which suited me fine. But he took his temper out on my mother throughout their marriage—although she attempted to shield it from me even when I was old enough to know full well it happened. Denied it flat out as if she were ashamed. Every injury was apparently caused by something other than my father's hand, usually inanimate objects she had walked into or tripped over, when I never knew a person move with more grace than she did. But it was easier if we both accepted the lie she was clumsy, because then we could ignore the awful truth.' He took a thoughtful sip of his milk then stared at her over the rim. 'My bitterest regret is that I allowed her to do that. I should have challenged her and I should have prevented him—but then it was too late.' His irises swirled with emotion. Frustration. Anger. Self-loathing. 'I should have been there.'

'We mothers are brought up to protect our children. Do not be hard on yourself. You *are* far too hard on yourself. In everything.' She wanted to go to him and comfort him, wrap her arms around him. 'How old were you when she passed?'

'I had just turned twenty. I was away when she died. Cambridge…' His voice trailed off and the shutters immediately came down, dimming all those telling emotions like a bucket of iced water on a flame because they had stumbled into territory he did not want to discuss. He gave a dismissive half-smile she didn't believe and his overly cheery voice came out insincere. 'But enough of all this maudlin talk. I think it's time this little man went to bed.'

Penny set aside her mug, not wanting this enlightening conversation to end. 'Here—I'll take him.' Perhaps then he would linger and she could find a way past the defences he had suddenly raised.

'And risk waking him up? Not a chance. I can carry him up to bed just as easily as you can.' He carefully unfolded them both from the chair, ensuring he escaped all further questions or the temptation to answer them. 'You lead the way.'

It was awkward walking ahead of him in her nightrail when her traitorous skin still wanted his touch and her mind was alight with curiosity about his past, but she hoped she feigned serene calm as she slowly took each of the steps on the servants' staircase. She paused outside her door, wondering if he would relinquish his burden, but when he didn't she experienced a rush of nerves at the thought of him entering her private space. A space that, thanks to Freddie, lacked the organised neatness she maintained throughout the rest of the house. What would such a meticulous man make of the clutter? She flicked her gaze towards him and saw his own staring down the long landing towards the guest rooms. 'I see we are neighbours of sorts.'

'Yes.' Why did that suddenly thrill her? 'Perhaps a bad choice on my part, seeing that Freddie is currently so troublesome at night.' She practically flung open the door and scurried across her sitting room, wishing she had had the foresight to pick up the building bricks still littering the carpet, then opened the second door belonging to her son's bedchamber.

Lord Hadleigh carried him in, his big, capable hand gently cradling his neck as soon as Penny pulled back the blankets, before carefully using his entire body to lower Freddie down. Her son murmured, let out a half-hearted cry, then lapsed soundly back to sleep as Lord Hadleigh gently stroked his hair. She carefully covered her son and found her eyes inexplicably drawn to the man opposite. The complicated man who she now knew hid more from the world than he was comfortable with it seeing. His locked with hers as he smiled and her own hearted melted.

All those years she had wasted believing that ardent suitors, bouquets and waltzes were romantic, when the singular most romantic thing she had ever known was this. This simple domestic chore shared with him topped each of those foolish ideals instantly.

One man. One woman. Bent over one sleeping child in his crib. A romantic moment which would have been utterly perfect if the sleeping child were his.

A foolish thought! Penny straightened, alarmed at the way her silly imagination was running away from her. She shouldn't be having romantic thoughts about him, despite her wayward body's current wild ideas to the contrary. They were pointless. She was just his housekeeper. She would always be a traitor's widow.

He followed her to the door and waited for her to softly shut it. Then leaned close to whisper, 'Success! Between us we can conquer a terrible almost two-year-old.' She wished his warm breath hadn't caressed her cheek. Wished her nerve-endings hadn't tingled as a result. Wished he wasn't still smiling. That infectious, handsome smile played havoc with her senses. And his eyes…gracious, they were making her swoon, when she hadn't swooned in years. Nor had she ever swooned with the same ferocity as she was in danger of doing now. Something about him tonight had thoroughly seduced her already and she was powerless to stop it.

Panic made her retrace her steps to the door before she realised she was being impatiently impolite. 'Thank you for helping me. And once again, my apologies for waking you up and dragging you to the kitchen.' Minimise it. Don't allow him to see what a wonderful time you had in that kitchen. Just the pair of them. Being themselves…

'It was naught but a detour to the kitchen.' Another intimate whisper, far too close for comfort. She could smell the faint traces left of his cologne, see every tiny golden whisker on his jaw and his throat. 'I was heading to my study to work. I confess I was hoping to sneak a few more hours in without you knowing.'

As if it had a mind of its own, her hand went to his cheek. 'No work... You need to sleep. You look exhausted.' She made the mistake of locking her gaze with his, then couldn't find the strength needed to tear it away.

'Have you made it your mission to look after me?'

'Somebody needs to.' Her thumb was scandalously tracing one of the shadows under his eyes. They fluttered closed for a second, but when they opened his irises seemed to have changed once more. Gone was the sadness and the regret. Now the golden flecks positively burned.

Then, as if they were both caught under this night's same, all-encompassing, intoxicating spell, they closed the distance between them at the same time. His lips brushed hers softly and Penny sighed, hers opening in response. One of them deepened the kiss, she wasn't sure who. Nor would she later recollect whose arms had wrapped themselves about the other first. All she knew in that loaded moment with any certainty was that their kiss felt right. The passion which rapidly grew out of it felt right also.

Her hands found their way into his hair, anchoring his mouth to hers. His smoothed down her back, her hips, tugged her close so they stood touching from head to toe. Rested possessively on her bottom. She felt his desire through the flimsy barrier of her nightgown and it didn't repulse her. She revelled in it. Revelled that he wanted her and she wanted him. Revelled in the kiss until it was he who dragged his mouth away. Still holding her, his breathing as ragged as hers, his expression confused, they simply stared at one another until he let go. Stepped back.

Raked his hand through his hair.

'Perhaps I should bid you goodnight?'

She didn't want him to go. Wanted to ask him to stay, but had no idea how to. 'Promise me you will try to sleep.'

'After that kiss, Penny, I doubt I shall ever sleep again.' Then he left her hugging herself, bewildered, thinking the exact same thing on the opposite side of the door while he walked the scant few feet to his bed down the hallway.

Chapter Thirteen

He'd kissed her! And, blast it all to hell, it had been a kiss which exceeded all the heated kisses he had imagined nightly in his fevered dreams. He'd kissed her, ran his hands greedily over her body, then practically floated to his bed thoroughly overawed by it all, where he then slept like the dead for hours.

Now he could hear the sounds of the house in full swing beyond the bedchamber door and realised that not only had he slept, it sounded as though he had overslept to boot. He felt clumsily for his pocket watch on the nightstand and glared at the dial. Nine o'clock.

Nine o'clock, for pity's sake, when he should have been up at six! Worse, now he would have to dress, take himself downstairs while breakfast was doubtless in full swing, be sociable with Flint and his family—and face her, too. She'd be there. Diligently doing her job as usual.

What exactly did a man say to a woman in his employ he had shamelessly ravished the night before? One he would have ravished further if his conscience at his own rampant and obvious lust hadn't brought him to his senses, the evidence of the former quite apparent, pointing at him in accusation beneath the blankets. Rock hard and showing no signs of deflating any time soon despite the inappropriateness of his behaviour towards her.

Penny was a woman who under all normal conditions would still be in the midst of mourning!

She was a woman whose entire life had recently been turned upside down. One who was undoubtedly still very vulnerable from her ordeal. A woman who at his insistence now worked in his house!

Had she kissed him back because she feared for her job? He sincerely hoped not, because that made him something he really didn't want to be.

But she hadn't seemed reluctant...

She had kissed him back. He was sure of that. She had burrowed her hands beneath his shirt, run them over his back. He could still feel where her touch had lingered like a brand before she had moaned against his mouth and the last vestiges of his reason had temporarily flown away. Until they had come crashing back and he'd needed her consent to continue and, in so doing, killed the magical moment between them stone dead. Because she had happily bade him goodnight.

What was he going to do?

An apology went without saying. A great big fat grovelling one, explaining he had been… what? Overwrought? Overtired? Overwhelmed? When the truth was it had just felt like the right thing to do in that precise moment despite him being all of those things. And, God help him, if she was similarly inclined, it would be something he would happily do again.

In a heartbeat.

Kissing Penny had been a revelation. She had felt so damn good in his arms. Tasted so damn fine on his lips. That delectable, womanly body of hers fitting against his to perfection, so soft… so seductive. Despite the layer of his shirt and her nightdress, he had enjoyed the way her breasts had flattened against his chest, the way he had known exactly where the tips of her nipples rested against his body, rousing his passions further and driving him mad with need. It had been a miracle he had managed to stop himself from hoisting up her nightgown and filling his greedy hands with those breasts, tracing for himself the hard, pebbled shape of her nipples. Instead, he had made do with dragging her hips to press against his, showing her in no uncertain terms exactly what effect their illicit kiss had had on him.

Recollections which really weren't helping his current state of confusion or arousal one jot.

With a groan, he pushed threw back the covers and stared at it in disgust. Then, when that didn't work, stalked over to the vanity and sloshed the chilled water from the jug into the basin before sluicing it roughly over his face and body.

What was it about Penny that affected him so? Passion aside, he'd allowed her to convince him to stay the night—with very little fight, all things considered—he'd willingly gone to her assistance in the kitchen, stared at her body shamelessly without her knowledge and thoroughly enjoyed being alone with her once the staring was done. Then, told her things about his parents he had never confessed to a living soul. Private things. Intensely personal things which could never be taken back and then he had blithely given in to temptation and kissed her. A whole other and equally as terrifying Pandora's box, except he had practically ripped the lid off this one and had no idea where he had carelessly tossed it.

He stared at his still rampant privates miserably. Lord Fennimore was arriving at ten and would expect a thorough summary of his progress on the case since last week. How was he supposed to do that when his mind was stubbornly lodged elsewhere?

Miserably, he shoved his feet in his breeches and did his best to make his crumpled shirt from yesterday seem more presentable. If only the damn thing didn't still carry the lingering scent of her subtle floral perfume. Or happen to be the same shirt her hands had wandered beneath. Had he not overslept, he would jolly well get on his horse now, ride like the wind back to town, and swap the guilty garment for another. Preferably the stiffest, most starched shirt in his wardrobe. Or a hair shirt, if such a thing existed beyond the annals of history. So he could repent properly.

With leaden feet, he took the servants' staircase down and followed the sounds of the voices. He could hear the Dowager laughing. Then, to his horror, he heard Lord Fennimore's wife, Harriet, laughing and accepted it was probably fitting that his abject mortification should be witnessed by all and sundry. He undoubtedly deserved nothing less—unless fate would take pity on him and present him with Penny before he entered the dining room.

But typically, the hallway was ominously empty as he walked through it, forcing him to stop outside the door and take one last fortifying breath before he stepped inside.

'Good morning, Mr Lazy Bones!' At the Dowager's exclamation, poor Penny sloshed hot chocolate over Lord Fennimore's hand.

'Ouch!'

'Oh, I am so sorry, my lord!' Her lovely face glowed beetroot red as her eyes flicked to meet

Hadleigh's before they hastily looked away. Because the world was cruel, she looked particularly lovely this morning. She had done something different with her hair. A looser, yet more intricate style. Yet another well-fitting new dress he had never seen before did wonders for her figure and, once again, his throat dried at the sight.

'Thank goodness I have another hand I can use now that this one has been burned to a crisp.' Lord Fennimore's curmudgeonly response snapped him back to the present, reminding him that Penny didn't look particularly pleased to see him. If anything she was horrified, which further compounded his shame at taking advantage of her.

'Pay him no mind, Penny,' said Harriet, swatting her husband's arm. 'Cedric is a dreadful grouch in the mornings. Unlike our handsome barrister here, he clearly didn't get a good night's sleep.'

Hadleigh felt the tips of his own ears redden, trying to brazen out his entrance for Penny's sake as well as his own, because, frankly, she was doing a very good job of looking as guilty as sin. Trust him to ravish a woman who was incapable of lying! She might as well be carrying a placard.

'Good morning, everyone. I apologise for my tardiness. Sorry for startling you, Penny.' She nodded, then practically sprinted from the room, still clutching the chocolate pot.

'Did you have a bad night?' the Dowager

asked innocently. 'Or was it a particularly good one?' She and Harriet exchanged a knowing look thanks to Penny's jittery behaviour and he feared the blush might spread to his face, too, branding him as the guilty party responsible for it. Another loaded look passed between her and Harriet, except this time, they included Jessamine and his friend Flint.

'I slept like the dead.' Which was true, but felt like a lie with everyone suddenly watching him. Stalwartly ignoring them in case his guilt gave him away, too, he took himself to the sideboard and began to load a plate, taking his time in the hope they might actually forget about him.

It was only when he had dished up a veritable mountain that he realised he would now have to choke it all down. Something good manners dictated needed to be done with more decorum than panic wanted to allow. Desperately strapping on his lawyer's mask, he decided to grasp the bull by the horns and direct the conversation at the person he reasoned was likely to be the least interested in speculation and gossip. Lord Fennimore.

'I am going to visit all the wives later and see if any of them would be willing to testify.'

'Against their husbands? Is that likely when all six have already been named as witnesses for the defence?'

'It is worth a try. One or two might feel aggrieved enough or ashamed of their spouses' treachery to feel the urge to vent. If nothing else, it will give me an idea how best to question them in court. Perhaps find clues to their Achilles heels. How goes your side of the investigations?'

Fortunately, never one to miss an opportunity to talk about business, Lord Fennimore gave him an extensive rundown of everything the King's Elite agents had been working on all week. He barely paused for breath, which meant that Hadleigh could pretend he didn't sense Penny as she came back into the room, nor did he have time to allow his gaze to linger as she filled his own cup with coffee and he managed to mumble his thanks. In fact, by the time old Fennimore was done, the servants had cleared the plates, the ladies had all left and only the pair of them and Flint remained.

Penny walked past the dining room for the third time and for the third time that hour had to resign herself to not speaking to him any time soon. He was thoroughly engrossed in his work and attempting to interrupt him to have a word seemed trivial, when she still had no earthly idea what words to use.

What exactly did one say to the master of the house after shamelessly plastering herself against him and kissing him with such enthusiasm her lips were still swollen from her fervour?

Excuse me, my lord, but did you mind me kissing you?

Mortifying. Because of course he had. He had put a stop to it.

Shall we draw a veil over last night? We were both tired...

Her toes were cringing inside her slippers at the lie, because she had never been particularly good at lying. She *had* been tired. Then she had been wide awake and willing. Shockingly willing.

She had lain awake for hours, her body all aquiver and positively throbbing with need, trying to think of a believable reason to knock on his door on the off chance he might want to continue what she had patently started. Or had he? The start of the kiss was a bit of a blur, it was all so overwhelming. The middle was a fuzzy haze of scandalous sensations which had fizzed around her body like freshly released champagne bubbles. The end had been awkward. He had said goodnight and she had been left yearning for more. Which probably meant she had instigated the kiss because he had had to extricate himself from it.

Gracious! She had been all at sea. Still was, truth be told. So much so, she barely recognised herself this morning at all. Her breasts still resolutely refused to feel anything like her own. She kept glancing down at them, convinced they had grown twice their size overnight they felt so heavy.

Perhaps the best course of action was to wait for him to speak first? Simply carry on, pretending nothing whatsoever had happened at all. Just as she had when he had walked into breakfast and she had spontaneously combusted while simultaneously scolding one of the guests under her charge. Yes! A positively spectacular piece of acting on her part that had been! She should have hung a sign around her neck—*I kissed Lord Hadleigh like a wanton*—not that it would hang particularly straight now that her breasts had ripened.

Just as she had ripened.

Obviously, the world had gone quite mad—she was now actively considering inviting another man to her bed, when she had been thoroughly determined to empty it of the first. But she couldn't deny a newly awakened part of her was considering it. If Lord Hadleigh's kiss was anything to go on, it had been nothing like the aggressive, intrusive and sloppy kisses her husband had foisted upon her when drunk. Nor had her body felt violated at his touch. Most striking of all the comparisons was that she had been actively part of the proceedings last night and not pretending she was elsewhere during the intimacies. A first for her as the only way to tolerate Penhurst's intrusions—because she couldn't think of any other word to accurately describe the distasteful, brisk coupling she had suffered with him—had been to be elsewhere in her mind while it was occurring to such an extent, she rendered herself numb from the neck down.

There had been no need to do that with Lord Hadleigh. Her body had screamed for his touch. Welcomed it. Craved it still. What was she going to do about that?

Absently, she wandered back down the hallway, completely forgetting she was actively avoiding the ladies after her ridiculous display of gaucheness over breakfast.

'There you are!' The Dowager beckoned to her through the open door of the drawing room. 'We have been looking for you!'

Penny attempted to paste on her diligent housekeeper's mask. 'Would you like some tea?'

'We have tea,' said Harriet, patting the seat next to her on the sofa ominously, 'What we need is some juicy gossip to go along with it. We are all dying to know what all that was about this morning.'

'I am not sure I know what you mean.' Penny didn't sit. Didn't dare.

'Oh, come on, Penny! You are among friends here. What the blazes was all that?' The Dowager waved her arms about frantically. 'All that stuff between you and the handsome lawyer? You were both blushing...neither of you could hold the other's eye...'

'There was a distinct *frisson* in the air, I thought.' Harriet smiled knowingly. 'The sort of *delicious* frisson which only occurs when a man and a woman have something to feel guilty about.'

'Honestly, he startled me. I am not used to him being there over breakfast.' She felt guilty blotches bloom on her neck at the flagrant untruth.

'Ah...*bon*...of course.' Even Jessamine was clearly unconvinced, although for some reason, with her French accent her agreement sounded like an accusation. 'He never stays the night, so *of course* you were startled to see him. That vivid blush had absolutely nothing to do with the cosy chat the pair of you had in the middle of the night. The one which you wore your nightgown for and Lord Hadleigh attended in a state of scandalous *dishabille*...'

'How did you know about that?' The guilty blush exploded in all its shameful glory, making her uncomfortably warm in her new wool dress.

'In this house of spies, nothing happens without somebody knowing about it.' Harriet patted the spot on the sofa again and, mortified, Penny perched upon it. 'An agent told Flint and Flint told Jessamine.'

'And *obviously* Jessamine told us.' The Dowager giggled. 'Although we all thought it was only a matter of time. The pair of you have been doing a great deal of looking these past few weeks. And looking invariably leads to touching, in my experience, and then nature takes its course.'

'He stumbled across me trying to get Freddie back to sleep and assisted. We drank some hot milk and then went to bed.'

'Together?' Harriet had leaned forward expectantly.

'Certainly not!' This was getting out of hand. 'You are all making gross assumptions about a perfectly innocent conversation.'

'So there was not even a kiss?' The angry red blush turned instantly purple and her mouth hung slack for several seconds before she attempted, too late, to deny it. 'I knew it!' The Dowager slapped both hands on her knees. 'She has the look of a woman who has been recently kissed. That dress, the flirtatious hairstyle...'

'It was an accident.'

'Tripping over a rug is an accident—unless you tripped over the rug and inadvertently found your lips flying towards his as a result.' Harriet patted her hand as if she were a child. 'Why don't you start the story again properly? He stole a kiss...'

'Actually, I think I might have been the one to steal it.' Penny buried her burning face in her hands. 'He ended it. And now I have made everything so awkward I have no earthly idea how to fix it.'

'Oh…' Jessamine sounded sympathetic. 'By ended it, he rebuffed your advances…or did he join in and *then* end it?'

'What difference does it make?'

'Oh, my dear—a great deal!' Harriet wrapped a reassuring arm around her shoulders and hugged her close. 'Men are simple creatures when it comes to women. They can take what they want without caring. Take what they want because they cannot help themselves or deny what they want out of some misplaced belief they shouldn't be taking it in the first place. Does that make sense?' None whatsoever. 'Therefore, the most pertinent detail we need to consider before we acknowledge he ended the kiss, is if he kissed you back first.'

'Well, I suppose he might have.'

'If you have to suppose,' said the Dowager sagely, 'it couldn't have been much of a kiss.'

'It was a lovely kiss.'

'Passionate?'

At Jessamine's question Penny hid her face back in her hands. 'Yes. A little too passionate.'

'There is no such thing as too passionate, darling.' Harriet again. 'A kiss is designed to give your body ideas and by the sounds of things, it gave your body quite a few of them. Should we ask if the ideas were…reciprocated?'

Penny nodded miserably. She had felt his desire and practically glued herself to it. 'Splendid! Then it sounds as if both of you are in the same hideous place. Both mad with lust and longing and not quite sure what to do about it. We have a strong foundation to build upon.'

'There is nothing to build upon.' Despite their delight at her situation, this needed to be nipped in the bud. 'It was a mistake for so many reasons.' Three faces stared back at her blankly, clearly not understanding her dilemma at all. With a resigned sigh, Penny started to list them. 'For a start, I am a housekeeper and he is a viscount.'

'Weren't you once a viscountess?'

'Which leads me to my second point, that being the sordid fact that I am a traitor's widow. Lord Hadleigh was the man who tried my husband! It's all very messy.'

'But you hated your husband. You testified against him.' The Dowager pushed a cup of tea into Penny's hand. 'Why, only the other day you admitted to Jessamine and me that you never shed a single tear when you heard he had been murdered. Good riddance to the brute, you are well shot of him.'

'Which is exactly why I cannot plunge headlong into a relationship with another man! I've been a chattel and I have no desire to be again.'

'To be his chattel, you would have to marry him and he would have to be the sort of man who makes his wife a chattel, which I am entirely convinced he is not.' The Dowager gestured to the other ladies. 'We all know Hadleigh well and can categorically vouch for him being a thoroughly decent man. But you are missing the point, my dear. This has nothing to do with marriage yet and nor does it need to be. One of the biggest benefits of being a widow is the *freedom* it gives you.'

Penny blinked incredulously, not at all understanding the bizarre turn this unwelcome conversation was taking. It was Harriet who said the unthinkable and rendered her totally speechless. 'What she means, darling, is it is perfectly acceptable for a widow to take a lover. Nobody would blink an eyelid. It's positively expected. I certainly enjoyed a few of them after my first husband died—and before I met Cedric, of course.'

The Dowager nodded, raising her eyebrows suggestively. 'What better way to forget the chore of your marriage bed than finding passion with another who is willing. I'll bet Hadleigh will not be an atrocious lover. That man is far too *diligent*. And your position here is only temporary, after all, Penny. Soon you will move on and so will he. And thanks to Cedric and the government's generous fifty guineas it's not as if he even pays your wages. So you see, there is nothing *messy* about your situation at all.'

Chapter Fourteen

By late afternoon that day, when he had failed completely to track her down, Hadleigh had left Chafford Grange in a state of total wretchedness. It was obvious she was avoiding him and had clearly chosen to traipse to the village to run an errand rather than see him and listen to his apology. Therefore, all the awkwardness between them would still be hanging in the air upon his return today. An awkwardness that his three-day absence would only serve to feed.

Not that he had intended to stay away so long. He had meant to return the next day and make things right, but he had approached the first of the traitor's wives, the Countess of Winterton, and, just as Penny had said, the woman had wanted to talk. Her extensive and damning testimony had led to more unforeseen work as Hadleigh had followed up each of the new leads. At least he could tell Penny that and thank her for opening his eyes.

One other wife had also co-operated, perhaps less enthusiastically than the Countess, but now he knew that there were undeniable links between the leader of the smuggling ring and the peers she had lured to be part of it, because both wives had known that their husband and the traitorous Viscountess Gislingham had been lovers at some point. The Countess of Winterton had even given him love letters sent to him by the other woman, although love didn't really feature in the graphic list of sexual acts the Viscountess had promised to bestow upon the man. Just like Penny's husband, he had been seduced to stray.

Although that put the blame wholly at the door of the seductress when as much lay at the door of those unfaithful husbands who were agreeable to straying in the first place.

Hadleigh didn't understand that at all. If Penny were his, he doubted he'd notice another woman if she were sprawled naked on his bed and it went without saying he would honour his marriage vows. His father had taught him that by default, too. Why marry at all if you wanted to live like a bachelor all your days? Besides, if he failed to honour his, he could hardly expect his wife to honour hers and the thought of Penny kissing anyone else made his blood boil!

Had he just thought the words Penny and wife in the same sentence? Yes, he had. Twice, apparently. And, more importantly, why did the prospect not terrify him as it should?

Good grief, this was all spiralling out of his control. When his mind should be occupied with suspected treason and the trial, his was filled with her. Not more than a few minutes went by before she encroached on a thought. Last night, despite being bone weary and despite the lateness of the hour, he had forgone his unappetising cold supper, put away the pile of work on his desk begging for his attention and taken himself to an inn to eat instead. Simply because she had wanted him to look after himself and rest.

He turned his horse on to the drive and was halfway down it before he realised he didn't feel queasy at the prospect of going home. He supposed he had her to thank for that, too. While he wasn't looking forward to stepping inside the house, that was more to do with the humiliating apology he had to make to Penny rather than the usual dread he suffered at the mere sight of those forbidding four walls.

Things were changing. At speed. But, bizarrely, he was keeping up. Last week, he would have rather died than sleep a night under that roof. Yet folded neatly in his satchel were two clean shirts, cravats, drawers and stockings in case he happened to find himself sleeping here again. Or was that wishful thinking? Brought about by one too many fevered and erotic dreams over the last three nights involving a certain brunette who had all too briefly fitted so perfectly in his arms.

So much for his new resolve to redouble his efforts to concentrate solely on the case now the Crown had insisted it be brought forward. Another reason why his return here had been delayed. Against his sound and reasoned arguments to the contrary, the Attorney General had scheduled the Gislingham trial to the second week of December instead of January. Which meant he had two weeks to put it all together now. Two weeks to dot every *i* and cross every *t* and try his hardest not to think about that kiss and that woman at all.

An agent stepped out of the stables to take his horse. 'Where is Mrs Henley?' Because the King's Elite would know her exact movements. Something he perhaps should have thought of before he'd taken advantage of her so thoroughly in her room.

'She took her son for some air in the gardens not half an hour hence, my lord. They were headed towards the lake.'

The fact she was outside came as a relief and Hadleigh set off at pace to find her. It would be easier to apologise to her without the usual audience and he didn't want to worry her by summoning her to his makeshift study where they would be alone, or, heaven forbid, turn up unannounced and uninvited at her rooms again.

He spied her as promised at the closest edge of the lake, holding Freddie's hand as he toddled along beside her. She must have sensed him, as she turned and momentarily stopped as if surprised. Hadleigh raised his hand in greeting and sprinted the last few yards towards her in case she got any ideas to flee before he had said his piece. He had rehearsed his apology throughout the hour's ride to get here and needed to get it out to be able to move on.

'You are back, my lord.'

'Yes, a little later than I would like.' Because she was still walking he fell into step beside her, wishing he didn't feel so relieved to be with her again. It really didn't help his cause. 'But you will be pleased to know I followed your advance and questioned the wives.' He was stalling. Pathetic, really, but he reasoned he was easing himself in gently.

'You did?' Her blue eyes locked with his, curious. 'Was it fruitful?'

'What you mean to say is, were you right?' She merely smiled slightly in confirmation, staring off to the lake. 'And, yes, you were. The Countess of Winterton was very eager to talk. The Marchioness of Nethway less so, but thanks to you I now know both of their husbands enjoyed a particular sort of friendship with the Lady Gislingham. As a consequence of those conversations, I have left both men in no doubt I have enough evidence to link them to her treachery, so I am hopeful they might come to their senses soon and confess to their crimes. I doubt either of them relish the thought of having the ugly truth spilled by their own spouses in court. As we know, juries have a great deal of sympathy for wronged wives.'

She frowned at that statement, her eyes finally locking with his in disappointment. She had to be thinking about the kiss. There was clearly no putting it off any longer. This woman was peeved. 'I came here to apologise for what happened the other night.' The words came tumbling out. 'It was a mistake... I was tired, you were vulnerable...'

'Vulnerable? An interesting choice of word.' Hadleigh cringed at her annoyed tone.

'What I mean to say is, it was wrong of me to take advantage of you as I did. I am heartily disgusted at myself, if it is any consolation. It won't happen again.'

She exhaled slowly and he assumed she was considering his apology. 'Is that how you see me still—the wronged wife?'

What was he supposed to say to that when it had nothing whatsoever to do with their kiss? 'You were wronged...'

'Of course I was. The world knows that...only that is not the way I see myself. It is such a small part of who I am, yet it appears to be the version of myself others are most content with accepting as if it is a fait accompli. Chiselled somewhere into stone in perpetuity. Maybe I should have it written on my forehead to make it easier for people to decide how to view me? Poor, downtrodden Penny! Rather that, than as that brave women who spoke out in the dock. Or the woman who *is* a good mother or *was* a good daughter. Or the diligent housekeeper here at Chafford Grange who has things running like a well-oiled wheel? I was a wife for just three out of my near twenty-five years. For twenty-two of those nobody would have dared call me *poor* Penny at all.' She was staring straight ahead, her expression slightly wistful for a moment, making him wonder if the flash of temper he had just witnessed was gone and she was merely reminiscing. 'I was an heiress. A catch, if I say so myself. When Clarissa and I first met and became friends, I was vivacious and witty, a little daring, quite outspoken. Certainly not your average debutante by any stretch thanks to my upbringing. Some gentlemen even considered me rather pretty and told me so at every opportunity. They sent me flowers and poems and asked me to dance.

'Before that I was considered resourceful and level-headed by all those who knew me. My father thought me an asset to his business. Until he sold it, of course. In fact, as my mother's health began to decline, I ran Ridley's for a time. Did you know that? I was barely nineteen, but I could negotiate with hardened merchants, balance the books, organise the staff and sell practically anything to anyone. I had her eye, too—I knew which pieces to select, exactly how to price them and they flew off the shelves. Papa said I had the knack for making money. A talent for charming people. An apple which didn't fall far from both the trees which made it.'

She paused again while Freddie kicked some leaves about and Hadleigh tried and failed to come up with a suitable response, completely confused by the strange way the conversation had turned. He had barely uttered a tenth of his apology and, while she had every right to be angry at him for taking advantage, he got the distinct impression it wasn't the kiss that pinched her lovely features with blatant irritation or made her voice positively sharp.

'I am not entirely sure what you want me to say.' Because he had worked out she did expect him to say something. Or at least he thought she did, although lord only knew what about.

'I suppose what I am trying to say is this: simply because the cap fits, a person shouldn't be expected to always wear it when the world is joyously filled with different hats and we, as individuals, have the right to choose, try them on for size and discard them as the mood takes us.' She began walking again, taking the path towards the house which went through his mother's beloved rose garden. He would have attempted to lead her on a different route and subtly avoid it, except he could see she was in no mood to be led. Now he was trapped. Cornered. Petrified. *He wasn't ready.*

'Let us take you, for example. Who are you, Lord Hadleigh? Are you the dedicated and dogged lawyer your reputation claims? Or are you the wealthy Viscount who owns this grand house? The good friend to the Flints and the Leathams and the Fennimores of the world? Or the charming, thoughtful fellow who sweeps up flour and rocks little boys to sleep? Or perhaps you are that remorseful man I met fleetingly in the kitchen the other evening, who wished he had done more to help his mother? The one who fears the memories inside that house more than he cares to admit and feels responsible for all abused women everywhere.'

Her astuteness brought him up short and he realised she had brought him down this path on purpose. His mother's beloved roses now flanked where they stood. The prickly bushes dormant, only a few inches of their barren stems protruding from the ground. 'Which one of those many hats fits you best?'

'All of them, I suppose…alongside a few more.' He took her arm, tried to turn her, but she refused to budge. Although now that she was stubbornly stationary, at least they weren't moving forward.

'Of course! Because people are more than one thing. We are all multi-faceted and complex in our own way. Brave and afraid. Clever and daft. Downtrodden and proud. Stubborn and charming and annoyingly overbearing.'

'This is a very *philosophical* conversation so early in the morning.' Confusing, more like. She was running rings around him but, for the life of him, he couldn't fathom her intention or dismiss the growing unease.

'I am in a very philosophical mood.' She gripped his arm and purposefully dragged him round the bend and there it was.

His mother's grave.

He had placed her here on purpose, he suddenly recalled, so she would be among the flowers she had always tended with such care. Upon it were three hothouse roses, left by the old gardener perhaps, their pretty blooms withered by the biting winter frost. Much like his rehearsed apology and his hope to smooth things over.

'Why is she here when the family plot is on the other side of the lake?'

'She loved this rose garden.' The past was suffocating him. He could barely breathe.

'And your father is safely and symbolically buried on the other side of the lake under a thick block of granite. *She* is out of harm's way.' He didn't deny it. Instead he schooled his features to become unreadable to hide the guilt and pain which simultaneously hit him square in the gut like punches.

'I remind you of her, don't I? That is why you paid my rent and that is why you now heavily subsidise my wages. Do not bother denying it because I have checked.'

'I failed to help her and have regretted it ever since.' His fixed his gaze on the gravestone. The cold, hard rock seemed a safer option than looking back into Penny's perceptive blue stare and admitting she was right. But he felt her stare regardless and wondered if he'd made a total hash of things yet again. Because she had reminded him of his mother once upon a time...

'Tell me, out of interest, when you look at her headstone what do you see? An abused wife... or more than that?' A little of his rigid composure cracked. Hadleigh felt his eyebrows furrow as she forced him to see more of the past than he was prepared to. 'Because you do her memory a gross disservice if that is all she has become to you, for the woman who put together this magnificent home, filled this garden with summer roses and raised you to be the crusading, vexing man that you are wore many different hats and I'll wager she preferred all of them over the one you have consigned her to eternity wearing.'

Penny had allowed him to stalk off, not caring that he had been obviously angry by what she had said because she was livid at him. And livid at herself for believing him when she should have trusted her nagging doubts about his miraculously convenient and fortuitous offer of employment. What had her father always said? If something appears to be too good to be true, then it usually was. Ugh! She knew that!

Yet instead of squirrelling away the six guineas she had in her hand, she had frivolously spent them, confident she would soon have more than enough to do exactly what she wanted. Freddie had indulgent new toys and she had treated herself to five new dresses. Dresses she adored which were nothing like the shapeless, dull garments Penhurst had forced her to wear because he knew she loathed them. Now she was stuck here, unwittingly beholden and feeling very silly to have been so easily convinced.

Lord Hadleigh had got one thing right, though—he had taken advantage! Although not in the way he thought. He had taken advantage of her desperation for employment and presented her with an offer he had known full well she would have been mad to refuse.

Logically, she knew it was hardly a betrayal in the true sense of the word. She liked it here and there truly was a job for her which the government were still paying her handsomely for. Fifty guineas for less than three months' labour was astonishingly generous for a housekeeper by any standards—and her role was so much more than housekeeper. She was a confidante, an advisor, the essential component to the smooth running of a house filled with government spies and secrets. It was a unique role and not one just any old housekeeper could adequately fill. It needed Penny's unique experience and insight—he hadn't lied about any of that. Nor had he expressly ever told her the government were specifically paying *all* her wages. She had to give him that, too. In part—

But he had certainly omitted telling her the truth he so rigidly claimed he stood for with every fibre of his being. After she had realised he was doubling the ridiculously generous salary out of his own pocket, she had gone through the wording of her contract and not once had it stipulated where the money came from either, nor mentioned the exact sum she would receive. But it had certainly been worded to make her think the government were paying '*the sum agreed*'.

Just as his convincing words the night of the flour had heavily hinted at their involvement.

'*We suggest an amount of ten guineas per month... We will recruit the staff... We cannot risk anything leaking to the defence, or, heaven forbid, the press before the trial.*'

A great many 'we's had been flung about to embellish things with the right amount of gravitas to get her to believe him. And procuring the refund from Mr Cohen had been a masterstroke on his part. It had made it appear he had listened to her assertions about standing on her own two feet and respected them. Except, he hadn't believed her truly capable of managing her own life in the long run, what with her being nothing beyond the tragic abused wife who needed rescuing and thus had felt the need to become her anonymous benefactor once again.

Quite frankly, if she hadn't grown to like the man so much, or grown to understand what a complex, wounded and thoughtful character he was beneath the inscrutable lawyer's mask, she would cheerfully roll up that duplicitous piece of legal parchment and bash him over his irritatingly noble head with it!

But she did like him and she did understand his motives, even if she fundamentally found them exasperating at the same time. Somewhere in his irritating and noble head he had decided to appoint himself the rescuer of abused women everywhere, because obviously they all needed rescuing, the poor things. When, in actuality, in doing it the way he had, by assuming control, he'd labelled her as hopeless and stuffed her unwillingly back in the same box she had been desperate to get out of. Couldn't he see that she loathed *Poor* Penny and everything she had stood for? Wasn't it obvious she wanted to take the whitewash to those awful three years and paint them out of her memories, pretending they'd never happened? That was not who she was! She was more like the old Penny again now. Perhaps had always been the old Penny, because despite the enforced subjugation, inside she had always railed against it. Her thoughts and her actions were different, that was all. And only out of dire necessity.

'Penny…can I come in?.' She had been expecting him. So much so, she had even gone to the trouble to indulge in a little of Clarissa's staging in preparation.

'Yes.'

The door to her private sitting room opened and, because she purposely had her back to it and was facing the fire, she made no attempt to turn when she heard him softly click it shut again. He came to stand awkwardly in front of her as she embroidered. He had no choice but to do otherwise as she had dragged the big chair far away from the others, giving him nowhere to sit. She wanted him to stand and squirm.

'We need to talk, I think.'

She dropped her embroidery into her lap, face down in case he saw it, and stared up at him. 'There is no *we* in this situation, Lord Hadleigh. If there is talking to be done in my chambers, then I will do it.'

'Fair enough.' He looked ridiculously handsome and uncomfortable, and she hardened her heart against the way it fluttered at the sight.

'You lied to me. Perhaps not to my face, but certainly by omission. I am not entirely sure where such a deed stands in legal terms—but know that you would call foul if faced with similar deceptions in court. Worse, you wilfully went behind my back again when I expressly asked you not to.'

'I was only trying to help.'

'Perhaps—but dishonestly. Although I am sure you convinced yourself it was for my own good.'

'All I wanted to do was give you and Freddie a decent start after the government saw fit to—'

Penny held up her hand. 'Fifty guineas *is* a decent start and it is all I will take with me once this job is done.'

'Oh, for goodness sake!' He had the gall to look exasperated. 'It was not meant like that and you know it. You are choosing to be offended, Penny, by something that was only well meant.'

'Be careful, my lord, as it sounds as though you are on the cusp of justifying your actions by telling me it was all for my own good, when we both know this is more for *your* own good, ultimately, than anyone else's.'

'That accusation is unfair. I stood to gain nothing from it, nor did I expect anything in return.'

'Really? Nothing?'

'If you are alluding to that kiss and suggesting my motives were—'

'This has nothing to do with that kiss and

everything to do with whatever nonsense you choose to believe in your head!' Penny stood then, clenching her fists at her sides rather than grabbing him by his shoulders and shaking him. 'How dare you underestimate me! How dare you trivialise all that I have achieved in the last six months to assuage your own guilty conscience!' His face had paled, hardened. 'You once took great offence at my calling your *benevolence* blood money—yet you are a hypocrite, Lord Hadleigh, for that is exactly what it is! I know next to nothing about your mother and her suffering or your part in that—but I do know that you cannot use mine to try to make amends for your guilt regarding her! Because it will not work. You can give me your entire fortune, spread it liberally among every abused wife and Christendom if you think it will help, but those demons will still be there waiting for the day you finally choose to stop being a coward and face them.'

His body jerked backwards as if she had slapped him. Then he stalked out of the room, slamming her door hard behind him.

Chapter Fifteen

Hadleigh buried himself in his work for two days and avoided the wench. For the first day, he had been outraged. Royally so. That she could take something noble, something well meant and selfless and throw it back in his face with such venom beggared belief. He had ridden home on the cold, dark road to London imbued with the justified anger of the self-righteous and then lain awake all night castigating himself for poking his nose in when, patently, he should have left well alone for all the thanks he received. There was proud and there was stupid.

Why should he care what became of her? She wasn't his responsibility. She was nothing to him... Nothing!

Except he couldn't quite bring himself to believe *that* lie—because she was something to him. He wasn't entirely sure what, or entirely certain what he felt about it, but he did know he hated to think of her co-existing beneath the same sky as him and hating him.

That uncomfortable truth proved to be a gateway for many others and forced him to do a great deal of introspection over the subsequent day while he licked his wounds in town. Hiding again, but this time from a woman who barely reached his shoulder rather than a house he would rather forget he owned, and one who had the power to prick his conscience, prod at his heart and who called to his soul without uttering a word.

Thanks to her, it had been the single most unproductive day of his professional life. He couldn't focus on his pressing case preparations at all, so in desperation had headed to Newgate to see if he could break the last remaining three traitors who were determined to take their chances with the jury. A huge error of judgement, because he lost his temper, when he prided himself on never losing his temper. Yet for some reason, the cool, calm, reasonable lawyer he was had packed his bags and disappeared somewhere on the long road from Chafford Grange alongside the emotional numbness he felt so comfortable with.

He blamed Penny entirely for that. Thanks to her and her blasted hat analogy, he couldn't stop remembering his mother. His mother had loved a hat. Ridiculous confections with wide brims and tall feathers that always matched her vivid gowns. For a woman with sedate tastes in decor and furniture, her vibrant choice of gowns might have surprised some, but they matched her character to perfection. She had been vibrant. Fun, whimsical. He could once again hear her laughter, which he had adored, and her horrendous singing, which had grated on each one of his nerves. Yet despite her lack of talent, she had loved to sing and dance. She had taught him to waltz one weekend when the snow had been so deep outside they couldn't risk going out. He had been reluctant. She had been relentless.

A force of nature.

Much like Penny in many ways. Neither woman had allowed the pockets of bad in their lives to suffocate their spirit. Neither liked to wear the hat of victim. Both were proud and stubborn and not afraid to put him in his place. His mother would have approved of Penny.

Good grief, he missed her. Missed the sight of her in the mornings before he started his working day, missed the quiet way she made him take regular breaks or ensured everyone's comfort. The lilting sound of her voice in the hallway. The glimpses he stole of her with Freddie in the garden every afternoon, where she swung him around and laughed with such joyful abandon he was always tempted to join them, but never did because he didn't want to encroach. The proud set of her shoulders when she refused to budge. The way he could always see the truth swirling in her lovely blue eyes. The way his body reacted to her presence every single time she was near. The way she had kissed him. Made his house feel a lot like home again.

His rooms in the Albany felt so impersonal and empty now. Soulless. He longed for home. He longed for her.

Then Hadleigh had sat bolt upright in bed. Wondering why the blazes he was trying to sleep when he needed to make it right? Hastily, he had pulled on fresh clothes and stuffed more in a bag. Necessity meant he had to head back there in the morning anyway, he reasoned. There was so much work to do, travelling back and forth would only waste time. It was his house, for pity's sake—his *home*—so he was perfectly entitled to stay in it and if he was there, constantly under her nose, they would have to muddle through all the awkwardness anyway and reach an accord. Besides, he had things to tell her. So many things he had no idea where to start or how to explain it. But she was right, damn her. He had to face his demons, because since she had forced him to see how they controlled him still, he now realised how much they defined him…when he was so much more than that.

Like a madman possessed, he'd piled papers and documents and legal reference books on to his desk, then scratched out a note to his valet ordering to have the lot delivered to Chafford

Grange as soon as he woke up, alongside more clothes and his shaving gear. Only then had he retrieved his bewildered horse from the stables and ridden it through the small hours to be where she was.

Now that he was here, he realised it was still more night than morning. The house was plunged into darkness. And while there were soft lamps burning for the men on the watch, there were still a few hours before the first servants would rise and a few more before he would see her at breakfast.

He considered heading directly to the music room and working, but knew he would be incapable of concentrating until he had spoken to her, so instead took the servants' stairs, creeping quietly to his memory-free guest room to wait out the rest of the night and try to get all the words he wanted to say in an order in which they would be coherent.

'Lord Hadleigh?' Her dark head appeared out of a crack in her door and he winced. 'Are you aware that it is only three o'clock?'

'I'm sorry… I didn't mean to wake you.'

'You didn't. Freddie did. Again. Over an hour ago and now I am wide awake.' Her eyes drifted to the fat satchel in his hand and then back up to his with alarm. 'Please tell me you didn't just ride all the way here…all alone? In the dead of night when anything could have happened to you!'

That sounded encouragingly like she still cared, and he found himself smiling. 'I couldn't sleep...and I have all these *things* whirring in my head.' It was late. He was irrational. But so relieved to see her. 'I don't suppose you could spare me an hour tomorrow to tell you a long, rambling and doubtless disjointed story which will probably make no sense? Only I seem to have lost the ability to be thorough and meticulous because I need to get it out.'

Her door opened fully and she stood in the space with her arms folded, her bare toes just poking beneath the lacy hem of her nightrail. 'I could spare you an hour now, if you'd like.' She gestured behind him with a nod of her head. 'Why don't you drop of your bag while I fetch you something to drink? You look frozen to the bone.'

It had been icy, he supposed, because he recalled how his breath had made clouds swirl around his face, but he had been so consumed with the need to get to her he had ignored it— but it explained why his hands, feet and nose felt numb. Yet, for once, the rest of him didn't. There were feelings, hundreds of them, all so confusing and jumbled, vying for attention and a good airing, he didn't know where to start to attempt to unpick them.

But he did as she asked, dropping the heavy satchel on his mattress and wandering back to her room. Discarded next to her chair was her embroidery hoop. Without thinking he picked it up and chuckled. The design was crude, the colours garish, the stitching uneven. How marvellous. She was no embroiderer, but persisted regardless. How perfectly… Penny.

'It's a shocking mess, isn't it?' She was carrying a decanter and two glasses. 'But I cannot bring myself to give it up. Despite my lack of talent, I've always found it relaxing.'

'My mother used to embroider.'

'Was she any good at it?'

'She was. Excellent, in fact. But she often used her skills for evil. She sent me off to university completely unaware that she had stitched flowers on my drawers for her own amusement. Roses, periwinkles, daisies…a different, huge and flamboyant display on every single pair.'

'Poor you.' But she was smiling as she poured them both a brandy and handed one to him before sitting opposite him. 'That was evil.'

'There was, apparently, a practical reason, too.' Inadvertently, the memory had offered him a way in. 'She wanted those flowers to make me think twice before I—' how to put it delicately? '—sowed too many wild oats.'

'Did she succeed?'

'Not entirely… I sowed my fair share…but I had more pertinent reasons to be discerning than the bright pink peonies festooned over my unmentionables.' Hadleigh took a deep breath.

Sat forward in his chair. It was long past time to tackle those demons head on. 'My father had syphilis. Was riddled with it, actually. It is what killed him. Frankly, hardly a surprise because he was an indiscriminate and *undiscerning* philanderer. The disease ate at his brain and rendered him mad by the end. He was only fifty-five.'

'Is that what made him violent?' Clearly she understood he needed to purge himself.

'No. That was there all along, he always had a violent temper, but it exacerbated it. He was a cold man. Uninterested most of the time in anything not about himself. The awful temper only showed itself occasionally. Of course, I might be wrong for we rarely saw him. After I was born my parents lived largely separate lives. He stayed in London, in close range of the hells or brothels he enjoyed, or with his latest mistress. He always had at least one on the go. Usually more. He never hid that and if my mother disapproved of his lifestyle she hid it well. Even as a child I understood she disliked the man she had married. It was a loveless union and she did once confess not of her choosing. But she loved his estate. Loved living in this house.'

'The pride she took in it is evident everywhere. This is a beautiful house.'

'She would be pleased to hear that...' It would be easy to change tack now and avoid the demons, but it would give him little temporary relief rather than exorcise them as he knew he should. Purging himself here with Penny was a necessary first step. 'As the disease progressed, that part of his character became more prominent until eventually there was nothing else left.' Hadleigh took a sip of his brandy. Dutch courage. The amber liquid felt smooth and warm on his tongue, but did nothing to ease the pain. 'I suppose I first learned of the violence the summer I turned fifteen. He had been ill and had come home to convalesce. I have no idea if that was anything to do with the syphilis or even if he had the pox at that stage. My parents kept it from me, but I do know that the oasis I had grown up in changed that year. The smallest thing would ignite his temper and the way it exploded and stole away all reason was terrifying. They would argue behind closed doors—usually in either his bedchamber or hers—although now that I think about it, those arguments were one-sided. I heard his ranting, never hers. That's when the *clumsiness* started with a vengeance and she would tell lies about how she acquired the bruises.'

'She wanted to protect you.'

'And I wanted to protect her, but she wouldn't let me. It was my mother who locked the doors to prevent me barging in. I assume now that was to ensure he never took his temper out on me, but I would rather he had. I felt so powerless. And I hated him! So much it began to gnaw away at me. I planned to kill him. A foolish, childish plan which I had all meticulously worked out. I was going to shoot him late one night on the toll road and blame it on footpads. I had stolen my grandfather's old pistol from the gun cabinet, lead and shot and I spent that entire summer learning to shoot the damn thing. I took out so much anger on those targets...'

His voice petered out and he sighed. 'But when push came to shove, I couldn't do it. I had him in my sights. Drunk on the road, exactly as I had envisaged it, yet I couldn't pull the blasted trigger.'

'Of course you couldn't.' He felt her hand brush his arm and brought his other up to capture it, needing the contact. 'You are a man of high principles. Never regret refusing to compromise them that night. It would have been a dreadful burden to bear.'

'Better than knowing my father killed my mother when I was too busy studying for my own selfish reasons far away? I don't think so.'

'He killed her.' She intertwined her fingers with his, her expression distraught on his behalf, and he gripped them for all he was worth. 'Here at Chafford Grange?' He watched fat tears gather on those ridiculously long lashes, swell, then trickle slowly down her cheeks. Tears for his mother. Tears for him. Tears that humbled him. His own eyes prickled with a decade's worth of unshed tears. He bit his back and tried to be matter of fact to get the rest of the gruelling story out.

'Yes. Here. I am not altogether sure how it happened, but it was late. Past bedtime. The servants heard him shouting and her trying to placate him, but by the time they had run to her aid it was too late. They found her at the bottom of the stairs.' Hadleigh felt his voice choke. 'She was already dead.'

'You blame yourself.'

'I should have been there.' He practically gulped down the rest of his brandy as he allowed the anger to burn. Feeling more comfortable with that than the grief which sliced like a sabre and demanded release. 'I begged her to leave not a week before, asked her to come back with me to London, but she refused to leave her home or him in his hour of need. She felt sorry for him, can you believe that? Didn't want him to have to face dying all alone when even his wits had deserted him.'

'That she could was testament to the sort of woman she was.'

'She was stubborn.'

'A trait you both share. What happened to your father?'

'He died a few months later. Unlike her, I happily allowed him to do so all alone and good riddance to him. That was nearly ten years ago. I keep thinking what a significant milestone that is. *Ten* whole years when I remember it all as if it were yesterday.'

'Of course you do. From my own experiences of losing a parent, the pain never goes. You just find a way to cope with it. For me, I always try to focus on the good memories for they are the most fitting tribute to the two wonderful people who raised me.'

'My memories are too bad. Too painful. Wrapped in guilt and layered with regrets.'

'Is that why you never came here?'

He nodded, swallowing past the tight knot of emotion which was making it so very hard to breathe. 'I'd managed to avoid it and block it out of my mind till you came along and I reopened Pandora's box.' He sighed, accepting defeat, and shook his head. 'That's not entirely true...' They both deserved the truth, although whatever that truth was he was yet to rationalise it. 'This year I killed a man, Penny... Saint-Aubin.'

'The monster who imprisoned Jessamine?'

Hadleigh nodded. 'And the strangest thing is I am not the least bit sorry for it. In *that* moment, when faced with the stark choice of either killing him or allowing him to kill my friend, I aimed and fired without a second thought—but that has stirred things up in here.' He tapped his head. 'Reminding me that I had the chance to do it before and failed to step up to the mark.'

He must have allowed the full extent of that burden to show on his face, all the guilt and shame at his inadequacy, because she cupped his cheek tenderly, smoothing the lines of pain which etched themselves deep in his face, and sighed. 'You are wrong to punish yourself.'

'Am I?'

'You are hardly comparing like with like. The decisions we have to make in the heat of the moment are different from those which are premeditated. I am hardly surprised you found it easy to do one and struggled with the latter. For a man who lives determined to right wrongs, I know you would not have been able to live with yourself if you had murdered a defenceless man on the road. That would have been wholly and morally wrong—and you are too noble. Nor would your mother had wanted you to carry such a burden. She would have been devastated to have caused it. We mothers are conditioned to only want happiness for our children at whatever cost it happens to come to for ourselves. And as much as you claim you are not the least bit sorry for killing Saint Aubin, killing another human—no matter how monstrous they happen to be—would weigh heavily on the mind. Especially when one is so dedicated to upholding right over wrong as you are. The trauma of that decision, the knowledge you had ended another's life, would always have deep emotional consequences. Therefore, it is hardly surprising it dredged up the last time you aimed a gun at a man as a frightened boy and the tragic, senseless death of your mother years later. But you are wrong to question yourself. In both situations, you acted justly.'

'Maybe, but it's forced open Pandora's box and now I cannot, for the life of me, shut it again...' Unpleasant noise and destructive chaos. He fought the overwhelming urge to weep, not because he thought she might judge him because her tears were still openly flowing, but because he knew that if he allowed just one tear to escape, then the dam would burst and he wasn't entirely prepared for those most powerful of emotions yet. 'So to finally answer your question from the rose garden, yes, you do remind me of her a little bit. Or at least your situations do. Penhurst and my father were cut from the same cloth. You and my mother both suffered at their hands. Those similarities, alongside the niggling echoes created by passing the milestone of a decade, churned it all up and I've been mired in the past ever since. It is as if my past has decided enough is enough. It's there. Hovering. I can't hide from it and I can't ignore it.'

He risked looking at her then and something peculiar happened to his heart. Beneath his ribs it felt as if it was opening like one of his mother's summer roses, reawakening after a long hibernation. More feelings swamped him and this time he let them. This was necessary. Cathartic. He was tired of running from it or burying it. Tired of keeping it all locked within because it was eating him from the inside. The protective numbness was lifting and leaving him vulnerable. Burying himself in his work no longer worked. For some reason, his mind had taken itself back ten years and was demanding the right to process thoroughly all that had transpired.

'I realise I need to face it, because you are annoyingly correct. I cannot make amends for my guilt regarding my mother by bestowing it on you. Helping you is something I find myself naturally wanting to do.' He allowed his thumb to trace circles on her skin. Accepted the strong emotions he felt towards her. Not pity or guilt at all, but affection. Tenderness. Absolute trust. Probably more. 'And being able to be there for you makes me feel…content, but Pandora's blasted box is still there lurking in the background. Waiting for me to properly look inside and face it.'

'And do you now know what is in it?'

'My mother.' Easy to answer. 'Guilt—misplaced or otherwise. Regret. Sadness. Pain. I've spent the past two days thinking about her. It probably sounds daft to you, but I haven't allowed myself to think about her since it happened. She died and

I felt numb. I still felt numb when I put her safely in the ground and then I carried on with my life.'

'It sounds to me as if you didn't allow yourself to grieve.'

'Again, my clever Penny, you are annoyingly correct. I am not comfortable with emotions. It was easier to bury myself in work and hide behind the numbness than face it all. My mother would be livid. She was always so adamant she wanted extensive weeping and wailing. She enjoyed a bit of drama.' He smiled at the memory, felt a single tear form and allowed it to fall, closing his eyes as her thumb gently brushed it away, feeling entirely overwhelmed and totally lost. Clearly, the dam which had held firm for a decade was about to collapse and it was unlikely to be pretty. 'I should go…' Although he didn't want to. He was so tired of being all alone.

'Please stay.' Before he could stand, she did. 'Extensive weeping and wailing should never be a solitary pursuit. Besides, just like you, I am exceedingly good in a crisis. It is one of my strengths. Let me be here for you.' She wrapped her arms around him and enveloped him in what felt a lot like love, that one elusive and powerful emotion which had been missing for far too long. For the first time in years, and despite all the overwhelming grief threatening to engulf him, Hadleigh no longer felt all alone. When he heard her quiet sobs on his behalf, they proved to be his undoing and he stopped fighting. Burying his face against her middle, he finally let the dam burst.

Chapter Sixteen

He had no clue how long he wept for, but he was grateful she was there. Was grateful for the reassurance of her unwavering embrace, her strength, her mumbled soothing words of comfort, her tears, the feel of her fingers in his hair and the steady beat of her heart against his ear. All reminded him that there was life beyond the pain—but that this pain was necessary to move forward. When the worst was over, she seemed to sense he now needed space to recover from it all, insisting on fetching him hot tea from the kitchen because everything was better after a cup of tea. It gave him time to compose himself, rinse his face with water and ponder the unstoppable explosion of uncomfortable emotion properly.

Bizarrely, although undoubtedly hugely embarrassing, noisy and chaotic, it had been cathartic. And completely draining. He felt as if he could sleep for a week, which would indeed be a blessing if he could manage it. It had been too long since he had slept soundly.

She appeared at the doorway with a tray and smiled. 'I've brought some biscuits up, too. I seem to recall I ate a phenomenal amount of them after my mother died.'

He felt awkward and stupid and vulnerable, but ridiculously happy she had returned. 'Did they help?'

'With hindsight, probably not, but they gave me something pleasant to do between the constant bouts of crying. I had Freddie by the time my father passed away, so he kept me occupied.' She deposited the tray on the table and passed him the entire plate. 'How are you feeling?'

'Odd. Not quite myself. Embarrassed that you had to witness it.'

'Would it make you feel less foolish if I told you that I am vastly relieved that you finally found the courage to grieve? When I first met you, I found your ability to conceal your emotions unnerving. In truth, it was a little off-putting. I like that you feel things deeply, that you are human and care. My father was a very sentimental man. I grew up in a house where his stiff upper lip would constantly quiver—usually with happiness or pride or nostalgia. After living with a man who was incapable of feeling natural human emotion, let alone display it, it restores my faith in men to know that it was my husband who was abnormal. Besides, I am contractually obliged to keep secrets, remember, so it's not as if I would dare to tell another soul even if I had a mind to. Which of course I don't. You needed to face your fears and you did. If anything, I am inordinately proud of you and I dare say your mother would be thrilled she finally received some decent weeping and wailing.'

'She would and she was due it. So was I. Because I now see that beyond the pain and guilt there are a million other memories—all surprisingly happy. In ruthlessly blocking out all the bad to keep the pain at bay, I lost sight of all the good. Not at all a fitting memorial to the woman who made me what I am.'

'There is still time to make proper amends and honour her memory as it should be. We all grieve differently and time and tears eventually heal all wounds. That I know, too.'

'You are a very wise woman, Penny.' He smiled and realised he wasn't sad or confused or angry any longer. He simply felt better. Purged. Not completely, but the process had started. 'For the record, I blame your hat analogy entirely. It forced me into uncomfortable soul-searching.'

She smiled. 'Analogies will do that. My current one involves coins, ironically, but has done much the same thing. Clearly the last few days have been a time for soul-searching for both of us.'

'Was yours as fruitful?'

'Very.'

'I'd love to hear it if you'd like to share your findings.' Because he wasn't ready to leave her yet. The cosy atmosphere and intimacy in this room felt special and necessary. Like a balm to his soul. A soul that was, perhaps, a little less troubled now that he had bared it and said it all out loud. Over the coming days he would face it all. Confront every fear, remember everything which deserved remembering, empty out every nightmare inside the locked box in his mind, probably allow himself to cry a good deal more and try to find enough peace with it all to let it go.

'Well… I've been thinking about me and the hats I want to wear.'

'I thought this analogy involved coins?'

The giggle was accompanied by a playful nudge. Hadleigh enjoyed both immensely. 'Did I interrupt you during your crisis?'

'A fair point. Do continue.'

'Since the trial, I've been so busy trying to invent the new Penny, I had forgotten the old. When, in truth, they are both two sides of the same coin… What was there beforehand combined with what has been tarnished by life's experiences. And I have come to the conclusion, there is no new Penny—nor can there ever be. Does that make sense?'

'Not really. Other than the coin you are referring to is you. I think this new analogy of yours needs work.'

She laughed again and he decided it was the very best sound in the world. 'Then I'll go back to the hats, seeing that your poor, addled brain understands that.'

'A splendid idea. Thanks to Pandora, my brain has turned to mush. Which hat are we currently talking about?'

'The new one I've been trying for size. It doesn't feel right. I need to stop being the version of me I think I should be or the version other people think I should be. My "Poor Penelope the Viscountess Penhurst" bonnet and the fictitious Penny Henley's ill-fitting mob cap have been resigned to the rubbish pile where they belong. Neither suit me.' She shrugged and smiled wistfully. 'I'm going back to being Penny Ridley. Back to being what I am. I have decided I am going to take my fifty guineas and rent out premises in Cheapside and dust off my shopkeeper's hat. I'm going to reopen Ridley's.'

He couldn't hide his concern. 'Is that wise... it is still so soon? Once the newspapers get hold of it, then they will drag everything up again.'

'What better time than now? It's all bound to get dragged up again anyway with this new trial. Penhurst may be dead, but he was still part of all that. Yet life moves on and scandals pass. Ultimately, I never did anything wrong and so have nothing to be ashamed of. I need to stop behaving as though I have. I am done with hiding. Done with trying to flee the past or pretend it didn't happen. I don't want it to sneak up on me unexpectedly in the future and bring shame or scorn on Freddie. As you now know, it's better to face your demons because you cannot outrun them indefinitely. I intend to carry on regardless and refuse to let them define me. People might turn up their noses at the beginning, but I have my mother's eye for what will sell and my father's talent for selling it, so they will come around in the end.'

He felt immensely proud of her, too. 'Then allow me to correct my previous statement. You are a very brave *and* wise woman, Penny.'

'And you are a very tired and very brave man, Lord Hadleigh. You look exhausted and, I fear, urgently need your bed.'

She stood and dragged him up with both hands. Hands some devil inside of him refused to let go of. 'It is long past time you dropped the lord bit.'

'Because Hadleigh is so much more personable? I have never understood that about titled men. The title is always there regardless. An abrupt punctuation to prove to each other how important you all are. Hadleigh, Flint… Penhurst.' She rolled her eyes at the last and made a face. 'Yet another hat—but an ostentatious one.

Do you know I was never given leave to call him anything else? How ridiculous is that?'

'Then clearly it is also time to resurrect my Christian name, although it might take me a while to answer to it again. I haven't heard it for ten years...it's Tristan.'

'Like the medieval knight?'

'My mother was a hopeless romantic as well as an evil embroiderer and thwarter of inadvisable romantic conquests.'

'It suits you... I suppose a barrister is the modern equivalent of one of the knights of old. Defenders of justice and damsels in distress.'

A crusading righter of wrongs. Him in a nutshell. 'Even if they are no longer in distress.'

'I've long thrown away my distressed bonnet. I loathed that thing.' She tugged him to the door. 'Goodnight, Tristan...what's left of it. Sleep tight.'

As he was about to leave he remembered the items in his pocket. 'Here...seeing as tonight was a night for honesty, I wanted to give you these.' He pulled out the old jewellery and place the lot in the centre of her palm. 'I bought them back from the pawnbroker. Please don't shout at me.'

She stared at the precious pile of trinkets for the longest time before her eyes lifted again to his. They were swimming with tears again. Sentimental tears of happiness. 'Oh, Tristan...what am I going to do about you?' Then she kissed him.

* * *

She considered telling herself she had intended it to be an innocent kiss, merely a brief, chaste expression of gratitude for returning the last earthly remnants of her mother, but realised that had not at all been her intention the second her lips had touched his. But the truth was Penny had wanted to kiss him because he had thoroughly overwhelmed her with his thoughtfulness, with his openness and by simply being him. She felt affection for him, that was undeniable, but it was more than the sort of affection bestowed upon a friend or a family member. This was different because attraction and, miraculously, lust was involved. Something she never thought she would experience after Penhurst. Somehow, the man in front of her had sneaked past the walls of her hardened heart to the romantic core which clearly still beat at its centre.

Worrying.

Perplexing.

Thrilling.

Just as it had the first time, soft and tender quickly turned to more and she welcomed it, wanting to touch him and feel him touch her, happily surrendering to the power of the sensual spell the kiss created. Those sensations were all so new and gloriously addictive. But it was Penny who reluctantly ended it this time. She stepped away, smiling when he tried to tug her back. 'We are both tired…you are vulnerable…and I don't want either of us to continue this with anything clouding our judgement. Go to bed, Tristan, and sleep. Tomorrow, apparently, we have a house full. Eleven people and one mad dog? Followed by the Attorney General himself later in the week. Significant details you neglected to mention.'

He looked delightfully sheepish. 'Ah…yes. I meant to send you a message about that, but…'

'You were in high dudgeon.' She couldn't resist the eye roll. 'But fortunately, Lord Fennimore had the good sense to tell Harriet, who in turn passed word on to me. So I must spend tomorrow readying the place for them and you have hours of important trial work to do… Fortunately Harriet also mentioned the trial had been brought forward so I am expecting it will be all hands on deck.'

'Yes, it will. We are almost there. I want to present it in a completed state to the Attorney General when he arrives later this week. I've been cross-referencing all the evidence we have with witness statements, organising the order to present my investigation and call the witnesses. All in all, I am confident. I firmly believe we have enough to convince the Lords of the guilt of all seven of the treason as well as the smuggling.'

'The Lords rather than a jury?'

'Unlike your husband's trial where the Crown decided to make a point, the six peers charged alongside Viscountess Gislingham were not impeached before the trial. Therefore, they can elect to be tried in the House rather than the court, which they have. The defence clearly believes they might receive greater leniency by their peers rather than a jury of potentially lesser men.'

'Does that bother you?'

'It is standard practice for peers, regardless of the severity of the charges, to seek justice in Parliament. The structure of the court is the same. All the Lords can witness the trial, but the proceedings will be overseen by the Lord High Steward assisted by a smaller group of legally minded lords who will act as the jury. As in any trial, there will be witnesses called and the accused will be defended and prosecuted by trained lawyers—the only difference is those barristers must be allowed to speak in the House.'

'By that you mean they need to be peers—like you?'

'Exactly. Occasionally, being my father's son has its rewards—few though they may be.'

'Will they be more lenient, do you suppose?'

'With treason as part of the charges, and in view of the seriousness of this case and the way it has been widely reported, I sincerely doubt it. To be frank, the fact it is in the Lords might well work in our favour. Had I been defending those men, I would have cautioned against holding the trial in the House. If the evidence is strong and the arguments conclusive, it would take a brave peer to query it. This smuggling ring had infiltrated the highest echelons of the British aristocracy and threatened both the economy and the safety of these shores. Most will be keen to make an example of them.'

'To prove their own loyalty, I dare say.'

'There are other benefits. The proceedings will be closed to the press. They can hound the witnesses outside, but not within, as they did you.'

'There was one reporter who used to sit in front of me and draw me every day.'

Hadleigh sighed. 'I know. I used to watch him and regularly had to fight the urge to rip his sketchbook to shreds or bash him over the head with it. But you dealt with it with more grace than they showed. I was proud of you.'

'What doesn't kill us makes us stronger.'

'An adage I need to adopt. Right now, with all the past clouding my head alongside all the speeches and arguments I still need to construct for the case, I am in danger of becoming buried beneath it all.' He seemed suddenly deflated. 'If feels like a mountain to climb in only ten days.'

'One which you will climb triumphantly once you are rested, of that I am in no doubt. You are the most meticulous lawyer, after all. Everybody says so—not that I would need their word on the matter, having witnessed it myself.' And there it was again. The trial. Her awful marriage. Demons she had faced and come to terms with, yet still pieces of her past which she couldn't seem to whitewash over no matter how hard she tried. Maybe they would fade once this last trial was over?

'And what about us and that kiss? Both kisses, in fact? We are yet to discuss either and what they mean.' Her stomach clenched and she fought the urge to swallow nervously. Perhaps she hadn't faced all her demons, although to be fair, after Penhurst she had been certain she would never feel the inclination to need to face this one. Another man had never been on the horizon—even temporarily—so why bother?

But now she wanted to bother. Which meant she had to lift the lid on her own box, dredge up horrid memories and do some heart-searching of her own. 'Yet more confusion to cloud your judgement—do you really need that now?'

'I fear I will be mired in cloudiness unless I know. Please don't make me wait weeks for your answer?'

'Very well. Once the day is done tomorrow and we have pondered it all with clear heads, we should talk. Properly. And decide whether to blame it all on the fraught circumstances in which we find ourselves or whether it is something we…explore again when there are no excuses to stand in our way.'

'I know already which I want.' She watched

the golden flecks in his dark amber eyes turn molten and that sight alone made her wonder why she was stalling. 'But tonight *has* been fraught and, as much as it galls me to agree with you, I do feel, if not vulnerable, then certainly off-kilter. We are also both tired, so perhaps we do need time to digest it all with a level head. For me, that means considering more than kissing you. I doubt I'll ever stop wanting to do that.' He took both her hands in his, his gaze locked thrillingly on hers, and brought them to his lips. 'Until tomorrow, then…and cloudless heads. And no more excuses.'

Chapter Seventeen

Penny had been doing a great deal of further soul-searching all day, listening to the different voices in her mind and their conflicting advice until there was so much of it, none of it made sense. Two hours ago, once dinner was cleared and the house full of noisy guests were all happily ensconced in the drawing room with Tristan, she had returned to the privacy of her own sitting room, determined to come to a conclusion. She had played with Freddie, bathed him and stroked his silky curls till he fell asleep, then she had sat at her table with paper and a pen. Seeing that all else had prevented her from seeing the wood for the trees, perhaps one of Tristan's lists would do the trick? She would compare the pros and the cons and hope the truth would show itself.

Do you want to kiss Tristan again?

After writing those words, she underlined them to mark their importance, because this was not a decision she was prepared to take lightly.

Reasons not to: it muddies the water.

There was no denying that, whether it be employer versus servant or Crown Prosecutor versus Defence Witness, theirs was an unconventional relationship.

I don't know what I want from it?

His words last night had stayed with her and bothered her. *For me, that means considering more than kissing you.*

Did that mean he wanted an affair or was there a chance he was suggesting a future? She didn't know and needed to before any decision could be made. Penny had not considered another future with a man once since the day Penhurst had died. Not once. In all the scenarios she envisaged for her new life, the only male in them had been Freddie. She had assumed her horrid husband had succeeded in putting her off men for life. Apparently not…but did that follow that she wanted another man for life? In the short term, she was more than tempted. Anything more made her feel uneasy, so…

Is he worth sacrificing my new-found independence for?

She sat for several minutes mulling that one over and then shook her head at her own indecision. Why was she even thinking about such a thing after everything she had gone through? She liked standing on her own two feet and that was that. She scratched out the question and replaced it with a statement.

I will not give another person control over me ever again.

Much more decisive!

Am I ready for intimacy?

A tricky one, and doubtless jumping the gun, but one she had to face if she did kiss him again. Because kissing was not ultimately what she would be signing up for and, while his were quite lovely, the expectation would be that kissing turned into more and Penny had uncomfortable memories of *more*.

While she had indulged in a few kisses with other suitors before her hasty marriage and enjoyed them, and she had definitely enjoyed a certain handsome barrister's since, she had never been intimate with any man other than Penhurst. And while Tristan was nothing like him in character, looks or physique, the process would be the same. His body would join with hers in exactly the same way. It didn't matter that Harriet and the Dowager had come right out and said they had thoroughly enjoyed the physical aspect of their relationships and had reassured her it would feel entirely different with the right man. Their bodies weren't *her* body. Hers had never worked that way.

What if hers failed to feel any passion as things progressed to the act itself? With Penhurst it had been an intrusion, one she had endured with gritted teeth at first until she had discovered that she could block out his relentless pummelling simply by transporting her mind elsewhere. Would she have to resort to that with Tristan—and if she did, would he be able to tell she abhorred it? Penhurst had never given a moment's thought to her, so it had never mattered, but Tristan was too thoughtful and her lack of passion would wound him. He'd take it personally and then what? Or did she want to endure something which gave her no pleasure? Of course not. That would be merely jumping out of the frying pan and into the fire.

Will Tristan also find me unattractive?

This was a niggling, deep-rooted fear which had been newly reawakened since their first kiss. Because, as much as it galled her to give Penhurst any power over her now, even if she took a leap of faith and assumed her body could respond with passion, what if his constant complaints about her lack of allurements were correct? Their couplings had taken place in the dark, she had always been wearing her nightgown because he delighted in telling her that her naked body was not the slightest bit seductive. She had hardened herself to those criticisms, eventually coming to realise they were all designed to control and manipulate her, or to simply make her feel wretched like the unflattering dour dresses or the rationed time with Freddie—because Penhurst had bizarrely found excitement in her pain. But what if her breasts weren't big enough? Or her curves tempting enough? She had carried a child since the last time and that had left its marks upon her skin. What if Tristan's passions faltered at the sight of her? Could she bear that? Was she brave enough to face that with a man she was coming to care about a great deal?

She didn't know.

Reasons to kiss him: his kisses feel divine.

It was perfectly acceptable for widows to indulge in brief affairs.

Curiosity.

There was no denying that. It was driving her mad, wondering if things might be different with another man, especially as her body was responding to him differently already and they had only kissed twice. She recalled the Dowager's wise words and decided to jot them down as a point all by themselves.

What better way to forget the awful chore of the marriage bed, than finding passion with another who is willing?

I like him.

She stared at those insipid three words and shook her head. Good grief! If she couldn't be honest on her own private piece of paper, then she really was a coward. Decisively she drew a line through them and replaced them with the truth.

I have a deep affection for him.

He was kind and noble. The way he treated Freddie melted her heart. He was maddening and stubborn—but also not too pompous or proud to admit when he had done things wrong. And of course...

I find him very attractive.

She underlined this three times. Shallow, perhaps, but there it was. He was broad and golden and filled his breeches exceptionally well. And his eyes... Heavens, they were something to behold, especially when they burned with passion for her. Just thinking about it made her feel all warm and ripe and—

The light tap on her door had her jumping guiltily out of her skin. That was quickly followed by shame at what she was doing.

'Penny?' His voice was low and silky, filled with forbidden promise, and her insides melted like butter.

'One moment!' Guiltily she snatched up her list and looked frantically for a place to hide it quickly. Why were there no drawers in this silly room? In desperation she stuffed it under the nest of threads in her sewing basket and then scurried to the door, patting her hair and smoothing down her dress. Realising, too late, that this dress was a statement in itself. What had possessed her to change into it? Red was the colour of passion and seduction and the neckline! It was too daring for a sensible discussion about kisses. He would think she had worn it in invitation!

Which, of course, she had. Because...

She wanted to.

The list she had just made proved that. Four reasons against and five for. The truth in glaring black and white.

Her hand shook slightly as she opened the door and her knees felt weak to see him stood behind it. He was so handsome—and she was going to kiss him again.

Gracious!

'Come in.' Nerves had her pulse beating like an out-of-time drum in her head. She had no idea what to do with her hands, then felt a fool for clasping them behind her back. 'You should probably sit down.' And she should probably calm down or she was in grave danger of babbling and hopping from foot to foot on the spot like a ninny.

He sat on the sofa and she dithered, having no idea if she should immediately sit next to him or perch on the chair opposite. She stared at it, hoping it might give her the answer.

'Should I take your desire to sit there as a bad sign?'

'No! Er...no. I am just a bit nervous.'

'Then that makes two of us.' He smiled and she felt marginally less silly. 'Just sit, Penny.'

She did. On the chair. Then her mind went a total blank. 'I have no idea what to say.'

'Well, if we avoid what is bound to be an awkward preamble while we both dance painfully around the issue, I suppose it all boils down to one thing. Will there be a third kiss or not?' He looked her dead in the eye. 'And I am afraid that has to be entirely your decision. Because I shall go out on a limb and state I am all for it. I find myself quite besotted with you, Penny. So much so, I can barely think straight.'

Out of nowhere, massive butterflies began flapping in her stomach at his pretty and heartfelt confession and unwittingly her hand went to her abdomen to calm them. His eyes dropped to it, then rose to meet hers, staring intently while he waited for her verdict. For a second, she seriously considered running away, because this was a big decision. A positively *huge* leap of faith. One that frankly terrified her now that the time for mulling and pondering was done. She wasn't certain she was ready for it—and all that went along with it—but then would she ever be? There was every chance the longer she debated the wisdom of it, the less chance there was of her doing what her body plainly wanted her to do. And then, out of sheer cowardice, she was giving Penhurst power over her from beyond the grave.

That settled it once and for all. Six to four on the should. 'I suppose we could give it a try.'

He exhaled loudly and she watched his mouth curve upwards in amusement. 'Not quite the giddy yes I was hoping for, but I shall take it.'

Now what? 'Shall I fetch some tea? Some brandy?' Should she offer him a snack perhaps, or should she attempt some small talk? What exactly was the correct etiquette in this sort of situation? She risked glancing at him for some sort of direction and the wretch was still smiling. 'Are you laughing at me?'

'I am trying not to, but you are making it very hard. I have never seen you so jittery.'

'Perhaps we should just get it over with?'

'Be still my beating heart…' But he had stood and easily closed the distance between them. He took her hand and tugged her to stand. Then tortured her frayed nerves by gently brushing his index finger down her cheek. 'Have I told you that you look particularly lovely this evening?' His lips brushed her forehead, trailed down to the exact bit of her skin still tingling from his touch seconds before while that seductive index finger which had caused the tingles had now found the tendril of hair she had left loose by her ear. Involuntarily, she shivered as his warm breath caressed the sensitive spot just beneath it, then held her breath when his lips found it, too. 'I've been dying to taste you here.' His teeth nibbled her earlobe, causing goosebumps to erupt all over her body. He trailed soft kisses all the way down to her collarbone, making her neck arch of its own accord. 'And here.' Who knew clavicles were sensitive? This was all boding very well.

At some point her eyelids must have fluttered closed, because she had not been expecting his mouth to brush against hers just then. She sighed into his, her body instinctively pressed against him, her fingers closing around his lapels, then pulling him closer.

She felt one arm snake its way around her waist as the other cupped her cheek, then gave herself over to the delicious feel of her body opening itself to true passion for the very first time.

He deepened the kiss, but was in no mood to hurry, using his tongue and teeth to seduce her more thoroughly than she had ever allowed herself to be before. An exciting heat pooled between her legs. Her breasts ached to be touched. By the time he wrapped both arms around her, she was already draped shamelessly against his body, her hands fisted in his hair and her wits abandoned completely to the thrilling sensations her senses were bombarded with.

She groaned at Freddie's angry wail, refusing to remove her lips from Tristan's. Only when it became quite apparent her son had no intention of allowing her to indulge in her pleasure any longer, did she reluctantly tear her mouth away. 'I'm sorry... I'll be quick.' Silently, she prayed that just this once her son would settle swiftly.

'Take as long as you need to. I am not going anywhere.'

However, Freddie was in no mood to be compliant and the few minutes she had hoped it would take rapidly turned into half an hour as he insisted on drinking every last drop of the milk she had left warming in a bowl of hot water on his nightstand. Then, as if sensing the odd new tension in his mother's body, he flatly refused to settle until she had to practically wrestle him back to sleep.

When she returned to her sitting room, feeling suddenly self-conscious, Tristan was stood as cool as a cucumber at the window, gazing out. He turned as she entered, his expression odd despite his smile and she hoped the enforced break in proceedings hadn't irrevocably destroyed the mood. He walked towards her and took both of her hands in his, staring down at them. 'I suppose it is time for bed.'

Unease immediately replaced anticipation. 'I suppose it is.' Perhaps this time it would be different, because he was different. Only one thing was absolutely certain: unless she tried it, she would never know and always wonder. Thanks to him. Penny smiled, in what she hoped looked like encouragement. His slipped off his face the second his hands dropped hers and he started towards the door to leave.

He hadn't been referring to intimacies at all.

'Would you like me to come and kiss you again tomorrow?'

She wanted him to continue kissing her some more tonight. 'If you want to.' Disappointment replaced the unease rather than relief that she had been spared. Surely that said something?

'Oh, I want to.' His amber eyes positively sizzled with the truth of it, which in turn made her wonder why he was leaving. 'Goodnight, Penny.' His gaze raked her body slowly...possessively. 'Sleep tight.'

Chapter Eighteen

⟨ornamental divider⟩

There were some things you couldn't pretend were unseen. For Hadleigh it was Penny's list. He hadn't been snooping or prying. He had stumbled upon it by accident the second she had left him all alone to see to her crying child. Quite literally. He had been so consumed with the power of what he had now labelled the Kiss to End all Kisses, he had backed towards the chair on slightly unsteady legs, needing to sit, and tripped over her sewing basket. As he knelt to stuff the haphazard mess back into it, he noticed the paper. Then he saw the columns and then, before he could stop himself, he had read the blasted lot.

He still wasn't entirely sure what he felt about it despite leaving it all to ruminate for the day. Even the brisk gallop he had taken across the estate to clear his head hadn't given him any true clarity. Some of it had been very encouraging. She found him handsome, thought his kisses were divine, had a deep affection for him... All music to his ears.

It wasn't the reasons to kiss Tristan which bothered him. It was the reasons not to. Good lord, she had knocked the wind from his sails! There he was, racing headlong into a full-blown romantic attachment and he had given scant consideration to how she was feeling.

He had stupidly assumed she felt the same— excited, happy, consumed with longing and lust and need, when in actual fact she was scared. He had seen that for himself when he had tested her, his words intentionally ambiguous to see how she would react. Her intense reaction to *'I suppose it is time for bed'* had brought him up short. Her fingers had gripped his hands, not with passion, but with alarm, while it was fear which skittered across her expression before she quashed it with a brave, stoic smile which broke his heart.

He couldn't ignore irrefutable evidence. Penny had suffered. Words like *'Am I ready for intimacy?'* and *'forget the awful chore of the marriage bed'* suggested she had low expectations at best and at worst, she was dreading the prospect. Not that he had gone to her last night intent on immediately seducing her, but it had been on the cards at some point in the not-so-distant future because the passion had positively sizzled between them. And as much as he didn't want to have to think about her in the arms of another man, he now *had* to think about her with Penhurst, because the monster had clearly put her off it—or worse.

Worse! He felt sick. And so furious, he wanted to smash the furniture.

What the blazes was number five all about?

Will Tristan also find me unattractive?

What had Penhurst done to make her think such twaddle? Belittled her, no doubt, issuing criticism where there should have been compliments? Or worse?

Worse!

It was a good job The Boss had had him murdered because Hadleigh would have jumped on his horse last night and choked the life out of the bastard with his bare hands otherwise!

None of which would help Penny now—but he could. Hadleigh was going to have to broach the subject with her when the time was right, help her face her demons as she had helped him, then prove to her he would rather never have her than allow her to think it a chore. This was a wrong he could right and gladly so if she would allow him. Of course, she had every right to refuse and he would honour that decision. But if she didn't... well, then he would gift her with something she couldn't return once bestowed. With patience and tenderness. Rather than plunging headlong into full passion, he was going to kiss away her fears and her awful memories of the sexual act with Penhurst. Banish all thoughts of the ridiculous and unfair *number five* from her mind. She was a beautiful woman. Totally perfect. He would prove that to her while waging a sensual assault and a painfully slow seduction to initiate her into the wonderful world of carnal pleasure. Until she begged him to bed her rather than that trembling, martyr-like *'I suppose so'* he had heard last night. She deserved nothing less.

And the wanting was going to kill him.

It couldn't be helped. Penny needed to understand what it meant to be loved by a man.

Loved? He hadn't been expecting that and certainly had not expected to feel perfectly at ease with the concept—if indeed it was a concept. He didn't have to be *in* love with a woman to make love to her, did he? It was merely a turn of phrase. Wasn't it? Although…

He shook his head and decided not to torture himself by analysing one random thought when he had enough on his plate already, if the biggest and most important trial of his career or thoroughly seducing Penny or facing the demons of his past didn't kill him first. As he handed the reins of his horse over to the waiting groom, he took a cleansing breath and stared at his house.

'Hello.' She suddenly appeared from the stables, holding Freddie's hand in hers, her expression pleased to see him tinged with a little shyness. His heart swelled at the sight of her. He had no idea if the pink flush staining her cheeks was because of their kiss last night or the biting cold of the day. 'We've been petting the horses. Have you been riding?'

'I thought I'd best get some fresh air… I have this harridan of a housekeeper who is forcing me to take better care of myself. Can I walk you both back to the house?'

'Of course.'

Hadleigh took Freddie's outstretched little hand, snugly encased in a knitted mitten, and walked slowly alongside. Wordlessly, they both began to swing him as they walked, enjoying his babyish giggles as his tiny booted feet flew up in the air.

They came to the part of the path where it split and she naturally turned towards the kitchens, assuming that would be the entrance he intended to take, because that had been the entrance he had chosen to take since that first visit weeks ago.

'I am going to take the front door, Penny…it's long past time. But I would appreciate your moral support if you don't mind offering it.'

She simply nodded and he was grateful. She didn't offer platitudes or advice. Didn't allow either pity or concern to cloud her expression, instead she continued forward alongside him, both still swinging Freddie in the air.

He paused briefly at the wide stone steps before the door and she waited with him, watched the footman open it and allowed him the brief time he needed to prepare himself for the onslaught. Then together, Freddie still sandwiched between them, they climbed them.

In front of him was the staircase. The unforgiving stone steps rising in a twin arc either side of the imposing atrium. The hard, cold marble floor. He forced himself to look at it all properly, accept the tragedy which had occurred here and then push his memories beyond that. There were so many, they brought a lump to his throat. Good and bad.

The exuberant welcomes when he came home from school. The echoing, hollow sounds of his parents fighting upstairs behind a door. Snippets of long-forgotten inane conversations. *'Don't forget your gloves...'* She was obsessed with him catching a chill while out riding… *'I would like to see the ridiculous bright purple bird that feather belonged to...'* His mother had adored a tall headdress… *'It's a statement, darling!'*

Then came childish giggles and he looked down at Freddie, assuming it was him. But they weren't. They were from another little boy from another time. A little older than the one holding his hand. Sliding joyously down the banisters encased in the cage of his mother's arms.

'You are smiling.'

He was. His eyes had filled with tears, but he *was* smiling. 'It is not all bad.'

'Of course it isn't. Good always triumphs over bad.' She picked up her son. 'There will be hot tea and cake in the music room once you are done reminiscing. According to my mother, a cup of tea made everything better.'

'I'll take it in the morning room.' The room which he associated the most with his mother.

'Then I'll reinforce the tray with biscuits, too.' With that she left him, clearly sensing, now that he had found the courage to face it, he needed time alone with his past. All of it. Still wearing his coat and clutching his hat, he walked towards the stairs, steeled his shoulders and climbed them.

Penny intended to give him space for an hour before she checked on him, but then the day got in the way. The house full of guests was certainly keeping her busy. Alongside the Flints and the Fennimores, the other King's Elite agent Gray had descended the previous evening with his new wife, Thea, this time, alongside an excitable black dog whose tail wagged so fast it blurred. Freddie had fallen for the hound instantly, the pair becoming fast friends. Thea's Uncle, Viscount Gislingham, the husband of the main traitor soon to be tried, had also come in the same full carriage with his friend, Bertie.

The last two houseguests, Seb and Clarissa,

had arrived shortly after she had ordered Tristan's tea tray for the morning room and then her best friend in the world had insisted they have a proper catch up in Penny's sitting room. It had been just the two of them and for the first time in two months they reconnected as friends.

'You look well, Penny! Lighter, somehow… more your old self.'

By old self, she assumed her friend was harking back to the old Penny, the one she had made mischief with in ballrooms and garden parties while flirting with the many gentlemen who had buzzed around them like bees, rather than the downtrodden and largely invisible woman she had been during her marriage. Or the lost and broken shell she had been over the course of the arrest and trial.

'I feel like my old self. I love it here. Having a purpose was exactly what I needed.' A tiny dig, perhaps, seeing that Clarissa had been so against her seeking employment.

'I can see that. You seem to have blossomed. Is that all because of your new purpose?' She made no attempt to hide her intimation or her curiosity. 'Or has something else put the spring back in your step?'

'For the time being, it is the new purpose.' Penny wasn't ready to discuss all her confused thoughts regarding Tristan just yet—not even with her dearest friend. 'I'm going to reopen Ridley's. Nothing quite so grand to begin with, but from little acorns...' Excitedly, she confided in Clarissa all her plans and the reasons behind it, and even when she explained that she was intent on heading back to Cheapside, her friend didn't attempt to caution her against it. Instead, once she learned that the Dowager and Harriet were keen to invest in it, she offered her financial support, too.

'But what about you? If I have blossomed, then you are positively *blooming*. I hope you insisted on this private talk so you can finally confess to me you are expecting—although I've known for a while.'

'You have?' Clarissa appeared stunned at the news.

'The lack of appetite in the mornings...the need to constantly touch your stomach...those wondrous, secret looks you and Seb exchanged, constantly assuming I wasn't looking. Besides, you have always had an abdomen as flat as a washboard and suddenly you didn't. What are you—three months along now? Nearly four?'

'Nearly four.' Clarissa looked guilty. 'I should have told you sooner.'

'Yes, you jolly well should have! But you were so obsessed with wrapping me in cotton wool and protecting me from the world after the trial, I suspected you didn't think you should confess your own happiness in case it made me bolt sooner. I know you too well, Clarissa.'

'And I know you too well to have coddled you so. You always were made of stern stuff. I think we both lost sight of exactly who Penny Henley was. I just couldn't bear the thought of you all alone.'

'I know. It was well meant. For a little while I needed it, so I shall be for ever grateful. But it is time for us both to move on. The bright bold horizon awaits…'

'Seeing that we are talking of bright and bold horizons—how are things between you and my favourite barrister? Flint told Seb he suspects there might be a little romance brewing between the pair of you. Is that true?'

'Hardly a romance.' Because a romance sounded so much more permanent than she was prepared to consider at the moment. 'But we have shared the odd kiss.' Penny sipped her tea and tried to sound blasé about it all. 'After all, it is perfectly acceptable for widows to indulge in the odd affair.'

'Oh, it's *just* an affair then.' Clarissa frowned, disappointed. 'That is a shame.'

'To be frank, after Penhurst, that I would even consider an affair is a miracle. Not that it is an affair yet. Not in the strictest sense of the word.'

'So you haven't…'

'No! Not yet and nor may we…'

'Now that *would* be a shame. He is very hand-some and he has such fine and expressive eyes, don't you think? And I am guessing he would look very nice *out* of his clothes, staring at one hungrily with undisguised passion.' Two perfect blonde eyebrows lifted suggestively as she fanned herself with her other hand. 'I would, if I were you.'

'Clarissa! You are married!'

'Yes, I am. Deliriously so. But I'm not blind or dead and neither are you. Pour me a second cup of tea this instant and tell me all the gory details about those kisses, you saucy vixen! And I will warn you now I will be asking lots of questions and doing my best to convince you to sample him *sans* clothes. You are in dire need of some pas-sion. What is the point of an affair otherwise?'

Several hours later, after the rest of the gentle-men had long left Tristan's presence to change for dinner, Penny wandered to the music room in search of him, imbued with a new sense of dar-ing courtesy of Clarissa's enlightening conversa-tion. Not that she was truly ready to do the deed yet, but she was considerably more encouraged it might not be as awful as she continued to fear it might be.

Penny had no idea that it had been Clarissa who had first seduced Seb, nor had they ever discussed the physical aspect of a relationship between a man and a woman. But Clarissa had been very open about the passion she felt for her husband, blaming her scandalous lack of decorum before their marriage on the sinful way the man's kisses had made her feel from the outset.

According to Clarissa, they were so intoxicating she rapidly reached the point where if he didn't try to take more, she'd be forced to take matters into her own hands because the constant lust and yearning was sending her mad. Then she had confessed that six months of marriage had done nothing to dampen that lust either, which was how she happened to find herself thoroughly pregnant when they had both decided to give it at least a year to start a family. But then he'd kissed her one day in a carriage and that kiss had been so magnificent, the pair of them quite forgot to be careful in their haste to tear each other's clothes off in that bouncing conveyance to Norfolk and neither could bring themselves to regret the mistake.

That she might get to the same delirious state with Tristan on the back of his magnificent kisses was certainly food for thought. Food that was making her lips and other parts tingle with anticipation as she hurried along the hallway.

The sound of the pianoforte made her hesitate before approaching and she lingered outside the door listening. Mozart. She recognised the composer despite not knowing the exact sonata which was being played. Clearly one of the ladies had taken over his office in his absence. Whoever it was played beautifully.

Needing to know which of her guests was so accomplished, she silently cracked open the door and then stared agog, because it was Tristan. He sensed her and stopped, a wistful smile on his handsome face.

'I didn't know you played.'

'I haven't played in years and was intrigued to see if I still could.'

'I think Mozart would have approved of your efforts.'

'He was my mother's favourite and she adored the sound of the pianoforte, but alas, she had absolutely no musical talent herself so she insisted I take piano lessons. I think I was five or six when I started. She had delusions I would be a virtuoso and then we would travel around Europe together, playing for all the royal courts. It was our secret. My father never knew I could play. He wouldn't have approved of such pointless nonsense. He never considered I would ever do anything except run the ancestral estate.'

'He disapproved of your legal training, then?'

'He would have, had he not been stark staring mad already by the time I started.'

'And how did your mother cope with you dashing her dreams of consorting with European royalty?'

'Remarkably well, all things considered. She embroidered crochets and quavers over my favourite shirts and that revenge seemed to get all the crushing disappointment out of her system.'

'Dare I ask how your day went?' They both knew she was referring to his demons rather than the case.

'It was better than I expected and worse all at the same time. I find I now veer between happily nostalgic and horrendously sad. I am taking a leaf out of your book and embracing both stoically. What doesn't kill us makes us stronger, after all.'

'And you need to experience the bad to appreciate the good. There is a great deal of good, I suspect.'

'There is. I should never have let it go.' He smiled and watched his hand while he played another few bars aimlessly. 'I had forgotten how relaxing I find this. For some reason, sitting here helps my mind unclutter.' Then he stood and sauntered towards her. 'I intended to wait till later to kiss you, but I don't think I can. Do you mind?'

She had barely nodded when he dipped his head to hers and brushed a whisper-like kiss on her mouth. Then he looped his arms around her waist and smiled. 'I've been wanting to do that all day. Since breakfast, in fact. Or a little before if I'm honest. I think I deserve another kiss for being so patient, don't you?'

'Perhaps.'

But he didn't take it. His eyes dropped to her lips and then locked with hers, waiting. After what felt like for ever, she raised herself on tiptoes and closed the short distance between them herself. Only then did he kiss her the way her body wanted him to. Desire bloomed instantaneously and its presence gave her renewed confidence, or at least it did until she stopped thinking entirely. As he had last night, Tristan had the power to banish everything but the moment and she poured herself into it completely, not caring that her hands had gone exploring beneath his coat.

He was so solid, his body so unlike hers. When his palms began to do the same she welcomed it, moaning against his mouth in encouragement until one finally found her breast and she arched against it greedily. Because of the difference in their heights, he lifted her to sit on the piano and his big body nestled perfectly between her thighs as he kissed her breathless. Just when she thought she might die from the wanting, he stepped back, smiling, his index finger tangling in a wayward lock of hair which had somehow escaped its pins. 'You seem to have the ability to make me forget where I am.' As did he.

His eyes took in the shameless sight of her perched atop the pianoforte—hair mussed, rumpled skirts ruched up to display her legs below the knee, her mouth doubtless pink and swollen, her bosom rising and falling to the rhythm of her rapid breathing—then he grinned wolfishly before lifting her carefully back to her feet. 'Have dinner with us.'

'Out of the question!' But it was so lovely he had asked. 'It wouldn't be right.'

'It feels right to me and I doubt any of the others would care.'

'I would feel awkward...' Oh, for goodness sake, tell the man the truth! 'I don't want to have to explain myself to anyone just yet, or have anyone speculating about us. I never anticipated being tempted by a man again. All of this is so new and unexpected, exciting but a little unnerving. I would prefer to keep it between us rather than have the others poke their noses in and offer advice. They are curious enough already and I want to do this at my own pace. Besides, we have a house full—I still need to manage it for the next few weeks. That will be easier if we keep this separate.'

He sighed, but nodded. 'I understand.' He tucked the tendril back behind her ear. 'Can I visit you again later? Well away from the risk of prying eyes and gossip?'

The prospect thrilled her. 'Yes.'

'Will you stay a while now and keep me company?'

She glanced at the mantel clock. 'Dinner is in less than thirty minutes.'

'I dare say the world won't end if I'm still wearing this coat for it. Indulge me for a few more minutes. I want to talk to you.'

'What about?'

'You.' His finger trailed along her sleeve aimlessly. 'All the things I don't yet know about you, but desperately want to.'

'Such as?'

'What was it like being married to Penhurst, for instance?'

The question, so out of the blue, soured her pleasant mood. 'I don't want to talk about him. Besides, the world knows what he was.'

'I want to know more of you than the world sees, just as I want you to know more of me. Some things you already do. I've never spoken about my past with another living soul, but I trusted you with it. Trust me with yours, Penny. Allow me in here.' His index finger touched her forehead. 'I only know the bare bones rather than what happened behind closed doors. I know he was violent and malicious. Very controlling. I know you didn't mourn him. I also know you found the physical side of your marriage a chore...' Good heavens! She hadn't expected him to say that! Instantly, her face flushed with mortification. 'But I do not really know any more about those things and I suspect nobody does. I so want to understand what it was like for you, Penny. I think it is important...for both of us.'

His intuitive amber eyes were fixed on her intently and she found herself looking away in case he saw the truth. Or worse, expected her to discuss intimacies with him when she could barely bring herself to talk about them with Clarissa. Like a coward, she had allowed her friend to do all the talking when she had a hundred questions she had desperately wanted to ask. 'Heavens, I have no idea where I should begin with such a maudlin tale of woe.' Discomfort had her scrambling for a ready means of escape and avoidance. 'Besides, there is less than half an hour till dinner, so we hardly have the time today.'

'Why don't we start at the beginning, then?' He was being selectively deaf, drat him. 'Did you ever love him?' She made the mistake of flicking her gaze to his, briefly intending to brush it off and sidestep the question, but saw his concern and his pity. Saw the fact he truly cared loud and clear in his eyes. Realised she could trust him with at least part of the truth.

Honesty bubbled out before she could stop it. 'I thought I did—briefly. Ours was a brisk and speedy courtship. A bit of a sham really, in the end, because I believed he meant all the hogwash he wrote in his daily letters. I was ridiculously flattered that an eligible viscount wanted me—a shopkeeper's daughter—enough to pursue me with such ardour. That he would write to me almost immediately after we had collided at a ball or event, send me giant bouquets and hunt me down wherever I happened to be… Well, I am ashamed to say I saw all those inconsequential trimmings as evidence of his love and convinced myself my anticipation of all that was love, too. And my mother found it all romantic. She was desperately ill at the time and we all knew she didn't have that long left, and somehow that only served to spur me on. When he proposed weeks later, I happily said yes because I knew my mother would adore planning my wedding. My whole existence became that—the gown, the trousseau, the floral arrangements, the perfect menu for the wedding breakfast.'

'You and your mother had fun.' There was no judgement in his expression, only understanding. He took her hand in his and placed a soft kiss on the back of it which she felt everywhere.

'We did and those happy memories of that time with her are precious to me.'

'When did you realise he wasn't the man you had been duped into believing he was.'

'My wedding night.' Penny was not prepared to confess all the indignity of that night to Tristan. Some things were too private and some wounds too deep. She gently tugged her hand out of his in case she said too much. 'He was drunk and told me straight out he had only married me for my dowry. He felt he had married beneath him and I saw the truth of his feelings. He didn't love me. Didn't even like me. I was a means to an end. He needed my money and, seeing that he was stuck with me, he needed an heir. Unsurprisingly, things deteriorated quite rapidly from there.'

'Why didn't you leave him in those early days before Freddie?'

'Pride in part, I am ashamed to admit. Both Clarissa and my father had cautioned me against marrying him and I had ignored them.' Unconsciously, feeling exposed, she hugged herself, then quickly dropped her arms once she realised. 'But mostly I didn't want my mother to feel guilty for encouraging the match. She had been duped, too, you see, and I couldn't allow her to die knowing I was unhappy. So I lied. Then, by the time she passed it was too late. I was carrying Freddie. My father fell ill, following my mother to heaven soon after and I had nowhere to go. Penhurst had made it obvious he was happy for me to leave once his son was born—but despite the mysterious change in his fortunes, he made it perfectly clear he would neither support me nor allow me to take Freddie if I left. He had been quite specific, actually—if I left him, I relinquished my baby entirely.' She felt her shoulders rise defiantly. 'So I stayed. What other choice did I have? I had no family to run to.'

'I sympathise. We only children have no siblings to support us in our hours of need. And the law is an ass sometimes. Especially when it applies itself to women.' His hand again reached for hers and she found herself gripping it gratefully. 'I suppose he also kept your father's fortune?'

How like Tristan to ask such a pertinent legal question. 'Papa's illness came on so unexpectedly and suddenly that, although he had stated his intention to bequeath everything to his grandchild to keep it from Penhurst, he never got around to changing his will. But at least he lived to see his grandson born.' Tears suddenly filled her eyes, threatening to spill at the tragedy of it all. 'Penhurst couldn't take that from me.' Although he had tried. The punishment for her disobedience had been worth it. Without thinking, she touched the bridge of her nose and watched Tristan's eyes widen in understanding.

'Oh, Penny...' She found herself wrapped in his strong arms, enveloped in a hug which she hadn't known she desperately needed and one she returned gladly, clinging to him as she fought the pointless urge to cry. He held her for the longest time, not saying a single word, yet that simple, heartfelt act of affection soothed her far better than any words or physician ever could.

Chapter Nineteen

Penny kissed her sleeping son's forehead, then gently tucked him in. He'd had quite the week. They all had. It had whizzed past in a whirlwind of fevered activity, with Tristan ensconced in the music room from dawn till dinner methodically preparing each of the witnesses for their grilling in the dock. It wasn't only their testimony he was reinforcing, but the barrage of questions that the defence might ask them which might trip them up or catch them unawares. Penny sustained the proceedings with plenty of tea and coffee and made sure that everyone, including Tristan, ate properly.

It was fascinating watching him work. Even the little snippets she intruded on were eye opening. He had a knack for asking exactly the right thing at precisely the right time, his clever mind switching from one line of questioning to a completely different one in the blink of an eye as he deftly played the defence lawyers who would cross-examine them. The inscrutable lawyer's mask—for she understood it was exactly that now that she knew the real man beneath—served to befuddle and deflect as well as hide the powerful emotions he held so well in check. Even the experienced King's Elite agents Gray, Flint, Seb and Lord Fennimore, who frequently testified in trials as par for the course in their profession, left their sessions looking a little drained and battle weary after Tristan had put them through the mangle. Yet they all appreciated his efforts, leaving each ordeal better prepared for the real one to come than they would have been without his thorough tutorage.

But even in the thick of it, when Penny entered the room with tea, the mask he wore melted briefly as he smiled at her. Those amber eyes would heat, the message in them for her only, yet entirely clear.

This morning, the two traitors' wives had been brought to Chafford Grange for a few hours as he had readied them for the trial, too. Over all, there was a renewed atmosphere of confidence in the house with even the eternal pessimist Lord Fennimore conceding they were ready. Two years of dogged investigations, months of meticulous planning and a palpable air of anticipation as they all waited for that final sprint to the end. On the morrow, the Attorney General himself would arrive to hear the progress and the trial of the century was due to start two days after that on the Monday.

Tristan and the others were due to return to town on Sunday afternoon and then Penny's short but rewarding stint as his housekeeper would end. Or so she supposed. Neither of them had discussed the final days and while she pondered them, like him she had avoided bringing it up because she didn't want to spoil the time they had left together.

Because the past week had also been one of the most enjoyable and enlightening weeks of her life, too, especially when the nights drew in and Tristan came to visit. Those visits followed a reassuring pattern she looked forward to all day. He would come, often while Freddie was still awake so he could play with him and help put him to bed. Then they would kiss. Each time, since the first, things would go a little bit further than the last, but he halted things long before she was ready. Then they would sit and talk for at least an hour over a nightcap about everything and nothing. Their day, their good memories and their bad. Tristan opened up more about his parents' relationship and his difficult, impotent role within it and Penny found herself telling him about the nightmare which had been her marriage. Then they would kiss some more, she would feel his blatant desire against her body and revel in it, wishing each time he would take things further, then lying awake for a good hour after he had left her, castigating herself for her own cowardice at allowing him to leave her without asking him to stay.

Yesterday evening, for the very first time, he had loosened the laces of her dress and kissed her bared breasts. Torturing the sensitive tips of them with his tongue and his teeth until she had positively writhed beneath him on the sofa. Then the wretch bade her a goodnight. She had been left in such a state of frustrated arousal it had taken hours to drift off to sleep, only to suffer from the single most erotic dream she had ever had, awakening well before dawn broke feeling as needy and physically unfulfilled as she had been the night before when he had torn his mouth away and gazed down at her shamelessly bared upper body with undisguised carnal longing.

He had liked what he had seen, or at least she thought he might have. Had wanted to ask, but couldn't find the right words or the courage to do so. Yet she wanted to know desperately, almost as desperately as she wanted his mouth on her nipples again. The shameless things had craved his attention all day, alongside other parts of her anatomy which she had never been so thoroughly aware of.

She wanted things to go further. The wanting was sending her mad. Was that what Tristan intended? Or was he unaware of just how needy he made her body? Or—and this made her frown in irritation—was he being a gentleman on purpose because he thought that was what she wanted? Although, in fairness, she had never told him explicitly she always wanted more. Instead, she meekly accepted his termination and wished him goodnight right back. Did he need her permission to take scandalous liberties?

Drat the man for being so wonderful, because clearly he did. What had happened to her recently rediscovered backbone? For months she had promised herself to be a new, braver version of herself and, despite her ardent curiosity and permanently needy nipples, she wasn't being particularly brave with him at all.

Suddenly feeling very bold, Penny dashed into her bedchamber and stripped off her gown. Perhaps if she couldn't find the words to tell him she was ripe for the picking, greeting him in her nightgown would? She rummaged into the bottom of her trunk for the filmy concoction her mother had bought her for her trousseau. The only thing she had left from it and one she had never worn. It had felt too daring for her wedding night, and after that dreadful debacle she had certainly never been inclined to put it on afterwards. She hadn't wanted to give the man any ideas and had only kept it because it was the last thing her mother had bought her. But she wanted to give Tristan ideas and she wanted him to have them tonight before their time came abruptly to an end on Sunday.

One by one, she pulled the sensible pins from her hair, then ruthlessly ran a brush through her locks until they shimmered. Tonight, come hell or high water, she was going to whitewash the memory of Penhurst's vile intrusions and replace them with something else.

Something she had no tangible concept of other than the secure knowledge it couldn't possibly be a worse experience, not with the kind, noble, utterly beautiful man who made her nerve endings fizz just by looking at her!

Despite all her bravado, his knock on her door had her practically jumping out of her skin and dropping the brush like it was a slippery bar of soap. Penny had to suck in several calming breaths before she dared leave the sanctuary of her bedchamber and another two more before she composed herself enough to brazenly open the door as the new and daring woman she was thoroughly determined to be.

It had been a hell of a day. Relentless even. But for the first time since he had been appointed the Crown Prosecutor on this case, Hadleigh felt ready. Every *i* was dotted; every *t* crossed. His head was aching, his poor body was aching, even the tiny space between his eyebrows hurt like the devil because of all the blasted frowning he'd been doing as he pondered. Tonight, as much as he wanted to see Penny, he knew he was on his last legs and needed to collapse on his bed and simply sleep—he would definitely need to be on his game for the Attorney General in the morning. Something he planned to tell her from the outset, knowing she would understand, give her a quick, searing kiss to remind her he still adored her before excusing himself to rest.

Then she had opened the door and he forgot his own name, let alone all his lofty plans to impress his superior.

She was wearing just a nightgown.

One quite unlike the sensible sort he had seen her in before. This one had no high neck to disguise the creamy, perfect skin which graced her chest. Instead, he was greeted by the whole expanse of her décolleté above the deep V which ended mid-bosom, the delicate lace trim moulding itself to the upper swells of her breasts. The rest of the garment followed suit. He couldn't see through the fine silk with his eyes, but thanks to the way it whispered and brushed against her curves, he could imagine it. The tips of her breasts pebbled in the chill from the hallway, drawing his eyes and reminding his brain exactly how they had tasted the night before. How sensitive they were. How she had moaned and writhed in pleasure as he had worshipped them with his mouth.

And her hair…

He had never seen it completely unbound before, that thick plait she usually wore for bed had not prepared him for the sight of the dark, tousled silky curtain which now hung all the way to her waist. She had arranged it over just one shoulder, one finger twirling the ends of it like Eve tempting Adam.

He tried to swallow, but his throat was too dry.

Tried to speak, but his mouth wouldn't work.

Couldn't blink. Couldn't breathe. Couldn't move if his life depended on it. Instead, he stood rooted to the spot and stared. Every single drop of blood in his body suddenly rushing to pool in his groin. The damned woman was going to kill him.

'You're late. I was beginning to despair of you ever coming.'

'Work.' For a man considered a great orator by his peers, it was a miracle he could croak out that single syllable. But she had stepped to one side so he could enter and in doing so had stepped into the light of the flickering lamp behind her. It made several strands of her dark hair shimmer copper and gold. Turned her lovely blue eyes into deep lagoons he was helplessly drowning in. Turned a great deal of that seductive silk translucent.

As she moved to close the door, he saw her unbound breasts move and almost groaned aloud. How exactly was he supposed to maintain the rigidly slow and incremental seduction he had diligently planned when she came to the door looking like temptation incarnate? His eyes hungrily swept the length of her before he managed to choke out a sentence.

'Perhaps I should go… Allow you to sleep seeing that you are ready for bed.' Because neither of them would sleep if he stayed. 'I am *very* late.'

The seductress who had opened the door to him disappeared instantly and she suddenly seemed self-conscious. 'Oh… I thought you had come to kiss me?' Her soulful eyes were distinctly wounded. 'But of course it can wait if you don't want to tonight.'

He watched her hands clasp in front of her awkwardly a second before they burrowed out of sight in the billowing silk. Then he realised he had unintentionally hurt her feelings because she was dubious of her own attractiveness. Damn Penhurst to hell, the blasted fool!

'Hell's bells, woman! Of course I want to kiss you.' He gestured helplessly at the flimsy garment she was wearing and felt the pain between his eyebrows double. 'I am trying to be a gentleman, damn it…trying to give you time to get used to the idea of being with another man after the fool you married knocked all the confidence out of you…something I will fail miserably at

while you are looking like that.' His greedy eyes raked her body once again and he did groan. 'Have some mercy, Penny. I'm only human. Unless you want to be thoroughly ravished by a man rendered devoid of all sense at the sight of you, please, I beg of you, go put on something more substantial.'

Her eyes finally raised to meet his shyly. 'And what if I do want to be thoroughly ravished?'

'Then heaven help us both.' Hadleigh closed the distance between them in two quick strides and hauled her into his arms. 'Because right now I want you more than I've ever wanted a woman before and if I don't have you, it will probably kill me.'

He didn't hide the truth of those words in a gentle restrained kiss. Instead, hc poured every bit of his desire and unquenched frustration into it, plundering her mouth and running his hands possessively over her body. To his delight, her ardour matched his and she stripped off his coat as her mouth slanted passionately over his. As soon as it dropped to the floor, her fingers went clumsily to the buttons of his waist coat as she backed him against the wall. As soon as she wrestled it open it joined the other garment on the floor.

'I can't stop thinking about last night.' Her breath warmed his neck as her teeth nuzzled it. 'And the feel of your hands on me. I should have asked you to stay.' Her hands tunnelled beneath his shirt and splayed across his chest. 'I wanted you to stay.' Then they dropped to the waistband of his breeches and began to feel for the buttons of his falls.

It was all happening so fast. Too fast. She deserved the thorough and meticulous seduction he had promised himself he would give her for their first time, one that told her she was completely adored, not a fast and fevered coupling. Instinct told him she had suffered enough of those and he wanted this to be different. Damn it all to hell, it *had* to be different!

Hadleigh dragged his lips from hers and hoisted her into his arms, then carried her to the fireplace where he deposited her with precious little finesse. A mallet to crack a nut. Good grief, he needed to calm down. 'Wait right here.'

Breathing hard, he let himself into her bedchamber and stripped the eiderdown and pillows from her bed. He wanted nothing of this experience to remind her of the last. While she stood watching, bemused, he made them a little nest on the floor of her cosy sitting room. This had been the room in which they had shared most of themselves, after all, sat here, by the glowing fire, so the location seemed fitting. Finally, he reached out his hands and took hers, bringing both to his lips and doing his level best to ignore the insistent bulge in his breeches.

'I won't rush this, Penny. You are too important to me and this night is too important to us. I am quite determined to make *thorough* and *meticulous* love to you. And I'm afraid I am far too stubborn to be swayed from that quest.'

Chapter Twenty

Tristan kissed her again, tenderly this time, yet Penny could feel how valiantly he fought for control. Against her chest, she could feel his heart hammering against his ribcage, felt his body tremble as she touched him, felt the long, hot, hard length of him against her stomach. Solid proof he liked what he saw.

He deepened the kiss and smoothed his palms down her arms and then back slowly to her shoulders. She felt his fingers go to the lace which edged the scandalous neckline, felt him push it slowly over her shoulders and then stilled when she realised that that single, thin layer of silk was the only thing separating her naked body from his eyes. She extricated herself from his arms, hoping she still appeared confident and alluring and went to blow out the lamp nearest.

'Leave it.' He caught her gently by the wrist and tugged her back. 'I want to see you.' One finger traced her jaw, slowly caressed down the sensitive side of her neck before lodging itself once again beneath the lace. 'Let me look at you, Penny—all of you.'

She held her breath and nodded, dreading it, looking down rather than watch his eyes as he slowly smoothed the garment from her shoulders. As it was designed to, it slithered down with ease, puddling at her feet, and she heard Tristan's breath hitch. Was that a good sign? Proudly, she set her shoulders before daring to look up, then found her own breath hitching at the sight of the obvious emotions swirling in his eyes. Admiration. Desire. Lust so strong and palpable she could feel it.

The backs of his fingers grazed her cheek before tangling in her hair. 'Beautiful.' The word was like a sigh, a benediction. 'I knew you would be.' He kissed her mouth. Her neck. Ran his palms gently over her skin as if she were precious. 'Come…lie with me.'

Feeling exposed, yet oddly choked with emotion at his reaction, Penny allowed him to lead her to the eiderdown. She sat, wondering how to arrange her limbs to appear the most attractive and then gave up to hug her knees instead while he tugged off his shirt, seeing for the first time what she had only touched. Broad shoulders. The flat plain of his abdomen. The light dusting of hair, the same colour as the darkest shades of blond on his head, which covered his chest and arrowed down through his navel.

His fingers fumbled with the remaining buttons of his falls and she realised he was nervous, too, and that knowledge empowered her. 'Allow me.' She twisted around to come up on her knees, grateful her hair had arranged itself to cover a great deal of her modesty, and undid them for him, drinking in the sight as she pushed the fabric from his hips.

To her complete delight, naked, he looked nothing like Penhurst. Tristan's skin glowed in the firelight, encasing taut muscle beneath. The male part of him stood stiff and proud, much bigger and thicker than the other she had seen, but where that had made her want to avert her eyes, this made her want to stare. Want to touch.

Should she?

As if reading her mind, he settled his big body beside her on top of the covers, laying propped on one elbow as she stretched out next to him. He took her hand and placed a kiss inside her palm, following it with a trail of soft, open-mouthed kisses along her arm and shoulder that felt sublime. When he reached her mouth, he tilted his body to rest against hers and she marvelled at the sheer beauty of his skin touching hers.

What came next was equally as unexpected as his hands and then his mouth explored everywhere. None of it felt intrusive, nor could she even begin to detach herself from what he was so skilfully doing, as sensation after sinful sensation shimmered through her. He had promised to make thorough and meticulous love to her and he was true to his word. Not an inch of her body was missed. Fingers. Toes. Breasts. Belly. His tongue brushed her navel. His teeth grazed her hips. While his fingers wandered a lazy path from her knee to her thigh, then gently dipped between them to the place her body shockingly screamed the most for his touch.

She felt him smile against her breast as her body shuddered at the intensely intimate contact. 'Is that nice?' The tip of his finger had found the unexpected place where every nerve-ending apparently merged into one.

'Yes.'

'How about this?' It was such a small but deadly caress and her body involuntarily arched with the pleasure.

'Yes...' Then, as an afterthought, 'Please don't stop.' Because it felt so good. Overwhelming. Necessary.

Penny thought nothing could feel as wonderful, until he sucked her straining nipple into his mouth and teased it simultaneously. She moaned, surprised that such a wanton, abandoned sound had come from her lips and felt her legs fall open shamelessly, not caring that he could see her most secret place as well as touch it.

She was too lost by then, desperately trying to reach a place she couldn't see and did not recognise, to think of anything that extended beyond that tiny bud of nerve-endings and the splendid things he was to doing them.

When he shifted his position to lay above her and that part of him pressed insistently against her body, she welcomed it, her eyes fluttering closed as he slowly edged inside and moaned again when he completely filled her. By then, none of her past so much as occurred to her because he was moving so perfectly inside her, loving her completely with his body, so wonderfully thoroughly and meticulously, that nothing else existed beyond him and her. With each deep caress, she fell further and further. Further and further. Until the hot, molten, amber stars in his eyes seemed to explode and fill her heart with such incomprehensible but all-encompassing beauty, all she could do was cling to him helplessly as they fell together.

Hadleigh woke in pitch black darkness curled around her and decided there and then that was precisely how he always wanted to wake up. In his thirty years on the planet, he had never felt this sort of connection with another person. Or allowed himself to feel this depth of emotion voluntarily. The most splendid and surprising thing about it was he didn't feel like running or blocking it all out. Penny owned his heart. Odd really, that such a momentous thing should be so easy, yet it was. He didn't need to weigh up the pros or cons, test the evidence or debate the reasons. Some things just were and this was one of them.

He was in love.

The realisation had hit fully some time between her opening the door in that outrageous nightgown and as he had peeled it off with reverence, although alongside that realisation came another. He'd been in love with her for a while. Probably since the night of the flour, if he were honest with himself, or perhaps that first time they had kissed. Hadleigh wasn't entirely certain he could pinpoint the precise moment and decided it didn't matter. All that really mattered was that he loved her. And probably should tell her. Should have told her before she fell asleep in his arms, only then he'd had no words. He'd been so moved and choked by the honesty and perfection of their love making, all he could do was feel.

He was coming to believe intense emotions weren't all that dangerous after all. The grief he had allowed himself to experience was raw and painful—yet somehow in accepting that, the experience was cathartic. He had realised through it that this house wasn't just a house or Pandora's box filled with everything that was bad and painful, it was also the guardian of his most treasured memories. His mother was here. That invisible yet solid link to her was comforting and...pleasant. He was glad he had found her again. Glad he had found home.

Was the regret still there and the tragedy? Of course it was. But Penny was right. You had to experience the bad to appreciate the good. And now Penny would be intertwined with his memories of this place for ever. They had found each other here, bared their souls, shared their bodies. The most wonderful thing about all of that was this was merely the start for them. Life shouldn't be all about work. It deserved to be enriched with love.

He happily closed his eyes again and snuggled, only to hear the whimper coming from next door.

Freddie.

With a sigh of resignation, he carefully disentangled his arm from her waist and slipped out from the tangled eiderdown. Another new aspect of his life he was only too happy to embrace. He was going to be a father and already knew he had solid foundations to build that on. After all, thanks to his own father, he already knew all the things *not* to do. Poor Leatham was stumbling into the experience blind. Of course, Freddie was older and his friends would soon be confronted with a newborn, but Hadleigh would try to take that in his stride as he and Penny expanded their family—and she knew what she was doing there. Together they would work it all out.

As the fire had clearly long died, he groped around in the dark for his breeches and shirt, slipped them on and padded barefoot into the boy's room. The child was sat up, his small fists rubbing his eyes, and his expression suggested he was about to wail the place down at any moment.

'Come on, little man.' He hoisted him into his arms and kissed him. Warm milk was obviously required. 'Let's leave your poor mother to sleep, shall we?'

On stealthy yet quick feet, he swiftly manoeuvred the pair of them out into the hallway and headed to the kitchen, realising too late that he had left Freddie's bottle on the nightstand. After a fruitless search for a spare with the child balanced on one hip and the boy already fighting him, he decided the milk was more important than the vessel which housed it and set some to warm in the pan. He would spoon it into him if he had to. How hard could it be?

While they waited, he grabbed a couple of biscuits from the pantry and handed one to Freddie and munched on the other himself. This appeared to work wonders, as the boy seemed perfectly content to grasp the thing with both hands and suck it to death.

Milk warmed, Hadleigh sloshed some in a cup which he deposited on the table, then, predicting a royal mess otherwise, he snatched a towel and, with Freddie on his knee and ignoring the soggy remnants of biscuit his grabbing small hands smeared on his face, tied it around his neck. 'Right, young man. It's time to practise some cup skills. Proper young gentlemen do not drink out of bottles.'

He let the boy grip the handle while he supported the bowl, and helped him guide it to his mouth, smiling as the child pursed his lips and made a complete hash of drinking from it. Milk spilled everywhere and he congratulated himself on have the good foresight to grab that towel. 'That's it, Freddie, you can do this.'

It was an uphill battle, but one Hadleigh appeared to be winning. Each time Freddie lost patience, they would wrestle for control of the cup. To distract him, he blew raspberries on his pudgy cheek and was rewarded with delighted childish giggles complete with an endearing milk moustache. 'I suspect I might have a knack for this parenting lark.' Which boded very well for the additional children he fully intended to plant in Penny's belly as soon as humanly possible. He had been careful last night, out of respect for her and because they hadn't yet discussed the future, but once they had and if she was agreeable, he saw no reason not to start straight away. 'Can't leave you a lonely, only child, can we, Freddie?' Because both he and Penny had been and then, when their parents passed, they'd had no one until they had found each other. Siblings would have helped.

'There you both are.' A very rumpled, very ravished-looking Penny appeared at the door, her lips still beautifully pink and swollen from his kisses, her hair a thoroughly shocking tangle he could proudly claim full responsibility for. No doubt for proprieties' sake she had forgone the seductive nightgown in favour of a very sensible thick one done up to the neck and an equally bulky shawl. They made no difference. His mind could see through both of them and thoroughly enjoyed what it saw.

'We didn't want to wake you up.' And because he couldn't help himself. 'Did you miss me?'

She smiled shyly and nodded. 'I thought you had gone back to your own room.'

'Why on earth would I want to do that?'

'The floor was hard?' Then she blushed prettily, no doubt remembering just as he was exactly what they had done on that floor. 'Here, let me take him. You have an important day tomorrow.'

She reached out her arms and he caught one of her hands, brought it to his lips. 'I thoroughly enjoyed tonight.'

'So did I.' She looked down at their locked hands rather than directly at him. There were unshed tears swimming in her eyes. 'Thank you... I had no idea it could be like that.'

'It's not always like that.' He needed to let

her know how it had affected him. 'That was particularly wonderful. If you want the honest truth, I had no idea it could be like that either.' She gifted him with the most beautiful smile, his heart skipped a beat and the words he had been thinking happily tumbled out. 'Marry me, Penny.'

He had expected another smile at his proposal at the very least, not her stunned and pained expression. 'Don't ask me that.' She tugged her hand away, took Freddie and put some distance between them.

'Why not?' The look of distaste on her face wounded him. Her sudden need for detachment made him panic.

'Because I can't.'

'Can't or won't?'

Reasons not to kiss Tristan number three: *I will not give another person control over me ever again.*

'This is all too sudden.'

'Not for me it isn't. I love you. I want to spend the rest of my life with you.'

One of those unshed tears spilled over her ridiculously long lashes. 'Don't say that.'

'Don't say that?' What did that mean? Were his feelings one sided? But he'd seen them written with his own eyes.

I have a deep affection for him.

Was deep affection not quite love?

'I am not ready to hear it…or even think about it… I've been married and hated it.'

'That was him!' The unfairness and the pain made him snap at her. 'Not me!' He saw Freddie's little eyes widen and fought for calm. His next words came out more measured and reasoned. Imploring her to understand. 'I am not like that and you know it. I don't want a chattel or a subordinate, Penny. I am neither cruel nor callous. I don't want to control you or stop you doing what you want. Rebuild Ridley's. With my blessing and without any interference. I won't stand in your way. I simply want to be with you.'

She began bouncing Freddie on her hip with more concentration than the task warranted and shot him a pleading look, tempering her voice maddeningly. 'We don't have to change things, Tristan. We can still be together.'

'What? In secret? An illicit affair when we have no reason to hide it?' Reasons to kiss Tristan number blasted two! 'How will that work, Penny, when the trial is done?' He was hurt by her distinct lack of faith in him and couldn't hide it, but he kept his voice low for Freddie. 'Or is this only a temporary liaison borne solely out of *curiosity*? Will I be receiving my marching orders at some point once the trial is done?'

'We can make it work. I am moving back to London…your work keeps you in London…' Her tone was reasonable, but it did nothing to placate him. He thought making love had immeasurably changed things between them. Ratified and clarified their relationship as something unique and special. It certainly had for him.

'Oh, how splendid. I get to sneak into your lodgings at night time and creep out before dawn in case anybody sees me? I don't want that. There is no future in that. I don't want a mistress or an affair, Penny. I am not like my father. And I am nothing like Penhurst!' Temper leaked out and he couldn't stop it. How dared she? *How... dared...she?*

'I don't want an occasional lover. I want a wife. A home. A family.' His eyes drifted to Freddie and he tore them away. He'd had plans for the pair of them, dreams of a gaggle of siblings and a house filled with laughter. Teaching them how to slide down the banisters, play piano, ride...

'But I don't want to be a wife again. Surely you can appreciate the reasons why?'

'Oh, I appreciate them, Penny!' For the first time since he had met her, Hadleigh was totally disappointed in her. She didn't believe in them. Wasn't brave enough to fight for them. A different sort of grief ripped through him and his voice shook as he fought against it. 'You are the hypocrite, not I. You were disgusted at me when you thought I was comparing you to my mother and trivialising all that you were. You told me, quite rightly, that I couldn't change the past or rid myself of guilt for it by bestowing it on you. Yet you are allowed to compare me to Penhurst—to damned Penhurst, of all people!—and I am supposed to blithely accept that and not mention the dreadful unfairness?' He threw up his hands in the air. 'Well, I won't. I've seen your list, Penny!' He looked momentarily forlorn despite the level and measured tone of his voice. 'Reasons to kiss Tristan, reasons not to, and I've done my best to prove all of your doubts wrong. But if I have failed to do that in my actions and my deeds, I flatly refuse to be the discreet affair that makes you forget the chore of the marriage bed and I'm damned if I'll allow you to use me out of curiosity! I'd rather have none of you, Penny, and suffer the heartbreak than only ever have the leftover scraps from your table!' He stalked to the door. 'And I won't be compared to a monster from your past to allow you to justify not facing your demons there. I am nothing like blasted Penhurst and you wound me by thinking it.'

Chapter Twenty-One

Hadleigh stared back at the house and set his jaw. He was back to loathing the damned place again. It was funny how a few hours and a few words could shift everything. 'It definitely looks like snow.' He stared at the angry beige sky to prove his point as he loaded another box of papers on the carriage. 'I won't risk months of hard work on the weather. Better to leave today than chance leaving it till Sunday. Especially now the Attorney General is no longer gracing us with his illustrious presence.' Although it wouldn't take a house full of spies long to realise it had been he who had dispatched the express before dawn changing the day's plan and informing his superior he would meet him instead this afternoon at his chambers.'

'I think you should at least say goodbye to the ladies. They'll be expecting you at breakfast.'

And see her? Not a cat's chance in hell. Thanks

to her, all he had left was the tattered remnants of his pride and a thoroughly broken heart. 'For pity's sake, Seb! They are your wives, not mine. I doubt any of them will care that I'm gone.' She thought he wasn't good enough. That was the long and the short of it. She'd happily share his bed and his body, but she did trust him enough to give up her *freedom*. As if he would ever try to curb it.

'I told you they had had a row.' Gray saw his angry expression, nudged Flint and winked. 'The agent on the watch last night said he was positively fuming when he stalked back upstairs in his shirt tails.'

'In his shirt tails, you say?'

'Well, he had been to her bedroom again—like he has been every night this week—except this time apparently, he didn't return to his own room at a reasonable hour. He *stayed*...' Hadleigh tried his best to ignore Gray's raised eyebrows. 'But what I want to know is what happened after the lady arrived looking all tousled and scandalous in the kitchen? Because the agent said she practically *floated* down the stairs.'

'Do we suspect *tomfoolery*?'

Any second now and he was going to punch Flint. His friend had been shooting him knowing looks all morning. Except they didn't know the half of it. Hadleigh had thrown himself headlong into love. She had guarded herself against it. He wanted marriage. She wanted a *discreet affair*. Pathetically, he felt used and undervalued. More than a little betrayed.

'Undoubtedly. I suspect he showed her his *credentials*.' Gray tapped his nose and winked again. 'Perhaps they were unimpressive...'

Huh! Lewd analogy aside, clearly she did find his credentials unimpressive if she refused to see he was nothing like her hideous husband. Hadleigh was a man of integrity. One who cared. One who would never lift a finger to hurt another. A righter of wrongs and a defender of justice. If he likened Penny's actions to the trial procedure, she had found him guilty first and used hearsay, speculation and false witness testimony to condemn him. A true miscarriage of justice if ever there was one. And it hurt. On top of everything he hadn't thought he was capable of more sadness—until this. So of course he had stormed off. It had either been that or beg as he had been sorely tempted to. Or weep again at the tragedy of it all.

'And he's such a tall man, too...it's a great pity he failed to measure up.'

Hadleigh growled at Flint, 'Enough! Have your fun elsewhere! I've got a trial to prepare for.' As Seb was aiding much too slowly, he hauled the last box of documents into the back of the coach himself, prompting his friend to shake his head in exasperation.

'Go talk to her. Find a compromise. There's always a compromise. It's obvious she's as miserable and upset about the argument as you are. She's been moping around all morning. Or apologise for whatever you did wrong. Women like a man who knows when to apologise.'

At that, he snapped. He had nothing to apologise for. Nothing! Aside from loving her significantly more than she cared for him. *Great affection* wasn't love. It clearly fell a good way short. He jabbed his finger at Seb.

'As if I would take advice from you! Everything you know about women could be written on the back of a calling card and even then there'd be space for the Lord's Prayer! And as for you two…' his finger waved menacingly at the grinning Flint and Gray '…make one more innuendo about Penny and me and I swear I'll wring both your blasted necks!'

With that he stalked off to the sounds of their irritating laughter, keen to put as many miles between this house, his foolish heart and the woman who had pitilessly stamped upon it, vowing never to come back.

Penny learned he had left from Seb, who patted her arm sympathetically, gave her a little speech about compromising and apologies, despite clearly knowing nothing whatsoever about what she and Tristan had fought about, how

Hadleigh had a tendency to crack a nut with a mallet…whatever that analogy meant…? and reassured her he was sure it would all come out in the wash. She wasn't reassured.

She still had no idea what to say or what to do to make things better. Her inner thoughts were at war with themselves. Why couldn't he see her side of things? What was the rush? What should she do? Was he right? Was she? Surely it had all come about far too soon? And if so, why was she painfully mourning the loss of him and dangerously close to tears?

He was clearly in high dudgeon and had typically gone off to lick his wounds as was his wont. Except this time, she doubted she'd see hide or hair of him until the trial was over and who knew how long that would take? The trial—yet another thing which worried her. Because surely he should be approaching the biggest trial of his career with a clear head and now he wasn't thanks to her hurting his feelings and the guilt of that was overwhelming. If she could turn back time…

Why had he proposed to her last night when she was barely awake, let alone able to comprehend such a momentous thing? Everything about her relationship with Tristan was so unexpected, she would never have predicted things would gallop along at such a rapid pace. He had caught her completely unawares and then she'd mishandled it. She hadn't even told him she loved him in return, which might well have softened the blow of her reluctance to consider his proposal had she been thinking straight. But she hadn't been thinking straight and that was his fault.

He'd made tender love to her. Twice. Leaving her thoroughly and delightedly exhausted from the experience, then threw her completely with a proposal on the back of it when she was barely compos mentis and still completely befuddled by all the new emotions their intimacies had stirred up. Emotions she was still to properly examine and digest. She wouldn't be herded into a future when she still didn't know if it was what she wanted, too. Despite his excellent closing speech, which she kept listening to over and over again in her mind.

Feeling despondent and wretched, she had gone about her day, furious at the man for leaving her to deal with it all alone when it had been he who had kicked the hornets' nest. He who had opened Pandora's box. What to do? What to do? Was she in the wrong? And if she thought of one more annoying analogy she was going to scream!

Stop it!

'Stop what?' Good grief, she had said it aloud. Loud enough that Jessamine had put down her book and was staring at her as Penny cleared away the afternoon tea things in the drawing room.

'Nothing. I'm preoccupied. So much so, I'm

clearly talking to myself. There is a lot to do before you all leave tomorrow. I don't want any of you to forget anything.' Like leaving without saying goodbye or giving her a chance to think things through.

'If we forget something, we shall muddle through. Besides, it will give me a good excuse to come back here. This is such a lovely house, isn't it? I will be sad to leave it. And you.' At her feeble attempt at a smile, Jessamine frowned. 'Penny—what is it? You've been in an odd mood all day? Is this to do with Hadleigh?'

'No.' Penny grabbed the last cup and snatched up the tray. Then dropped it noisily back down on the sideboard. 'Maybe it is. I'm all at sixes and sevens with the dratted man.'

'Sixes and sevens! *Mon Dieu*...that sounds serious. It sounds exactly the sort of thing a lady needs to discuss with a friend. And I am your friend, *non*?' She patted the seat next to her on the sofa. 'Would it help to know that anything involving sixes and sevens and dratted men would never be shared with another living soul?'

'Yes... No.' Penny covered her face with her hands. 'This is mortifying.'

'Ah! If your face is red and your whole body is cringing as it is now, we are talking passion. Have you and Hadleigh finally done the *deed*?'

'You know about our little affair then?'

'The whole house knows. It is the only exciting

gossip any of us can talk about.' Jessamine smiled to soften that news. 'Being stuck inside waiting for the trial, things have been a little dull and repetitive. Watching the pair of you and speculating what you've been getting up to every night when he tiptoes to your room, then tiptoes out all dishevelled and grinning, has been the only thing making life tolerable. And is it really just a *little* affair? The ladies will be disappointed. We all believe it is quite serious. From the heated looks the pair of you have been exchanging these past weeks, I confess we all assumed it was more than a dalliance.'

'I had originally intended it as a dalliance. A discreet affair to help me move past the memories of my husband but… Tristan proposed last night and I don't know what to do about it.'

'But you are considering it?'

'I turned him down. He didn't take it well.' An understatement. By the devastated expression on his face and the way he had slammed the door in his haste to stalk out of the kitchen and then this house, she had hurt him badly and desperately wished she had handled things differently.

'You turned Hadleigh down?' Clarissa, Harriet, Lord Gray's redheaded wife Thea and the Dowager practically fell through the closed door, making no apology for the fact they had all clearly been listening at the keyhole. 'Whatever for?'

'How long have you all been there?'

'Long enough to know you've done the deed, thought it was nought but a little affair and he's taken your rejection very badly.' Harriet waved it all away as she sat down in the chair directly opposite. 'What possessed you to turn him down? He is a such a fine specimen of manhood.'

'I can't marry him.' Penny wanted to weep. In case she did, she covered her face with her hands. 'Despite his obvious physical appeal.'

The Dowager bustled over and enveloped her in a perfumed hug. 'Did he turn out to be an atrocious lover?'

'No!' She didn't lift her face from the Dowager's shoulder. They might find it perfectly natural to talk about intimacies—but she was new to that world. In both the talking about them and indulging in them. 'He was a lovely lover.' Passionate. Attentive. Could do positively sinful things with his mouth. And his hands. And his other parts. Made her heart burst with the joy of it all. 'Excellent, in fact.'

'Well surely that's a point in his favour?'

'This has nothing to do with intimacies and everything to do with me. I don't think I want to marry again. I don't understand why we can't continue exactly as we are.' But Tristan didn't want the scraps from her table.

'Because—and I've said this before, darling—men are surprisingly simple creatures.' Harriet gestured for Thea to ring the bell. 'Order us some tea. And cake. Such a deep and meaningful conversation requires some sustenance, or we'll all get indigestion.' Then she turned back to Penny sympathetically. 'And your Hadleigh is one of the simplest of them all. Undeniably brilliant as he may be, that man is entirely black and white.' She slashed the air decisively with her hand. 'I mean, seriously—things are either right or wrong with him. Yes or no. Truth or fact.'

Marry me or have none of me.

'That's true.' Clarissa perched on the arm of Harriet's chair. 'Seb says he makes pages and pages of lists. Always with two columns—never three. For a man like that, he is either madly in love or he isn't. There is no in between.'

'He said he loved me, too.' And that he was heartbroken. That thought only made the knot in her own chest tighten further. 'But this has nothing to do with love.'

'Forgive me if I am wrong, *ma chérie*, but surely if a marriage is about anything it should be about love?'

Penny couldn't stop a tear escaping as she replied to Jessamine, 'I've been married. I hated every second of it.'

'Then this is not so much about Hadleigh as Penhurst?' Which is exactly what Tristan had accused her of. Five heads nodded in understanding. 'You worry a marriage to Hadleigh will turn out the same?'

'I don't know. I made one horrendous mistake because I married in haste—I won't risk another.'

'Then let's discuss your suspicions and get to the bottom of them. Between us, I'm sure we can dig to the root of the problem. We are all married ladies, after all—and all of us are your friends, Penny dear.' The Dowager appointed herself the prosecutor. 'Do you suspect he might harbour a violent temper?'

'Of course not! Tristan storms off when he's angry or hurt.' Because by his own admission, powerful emotions made him uncomfortable. And then he sulked. That was his second worst trait, the first being his overbearing stubbornness in what he believed was best.

'You found the marriage bed a chore with Penhurst—does that put you off?'

Penny shook her head miserably. Her body had wanted Tristan last night and still wanted him now. It was like an itch tucked inside a tight boot, that nothing so far had managed to scratch. Yet another fitting analogy and not one that made her feel better.

'Is this about Freddie, then? Do you worry that he won't take to the child of another man?'

'No... Freddie adores him.' And Tristan was a natural father. He'd even managed to get her son to drink out of a cup for the first time last night, which was more than she had managed. And he blew raspberries on her son's cheek which made him giggle. Oh, how the sight of that had disarmed her last night.

'Has he objected to you reopening Ridley's?'

Penny shook her head. 'He said he wouldn't interfere.' And she believed him.

'Do you love him?'

'Yes.' Completely. Which was what made this all so hard.

'Then perhaps that is enough.' Thea spoke for the first time. 'We can't know everything about a man. Sometimes, you have to take a leap of faith.'

'This has nothing to do with any of those things. This is all about control.' Clarissa sighed and offered her a sympathetic smile.

'Tristan can be stubborn sometimes and you've seen the lengths he will go to get his own way when he thinks he knows what's best for me when he doesn't always,' Penny said.

'I see your dilemma.' Jessamine reached out and squeezed her hand. 'It is hard to trust again after you have been treated so dreadfully by another. Penhurst beat you and made you a prisoner in your own home and Hadleigh tried to anonymously give you and your child money when you had none… If you don't mind me saying, you are comparing poison mushrooms to strawberries. His actions might have been clumsy, but they were never meant with any malice. A good man will always move heaven and hearth to protect you.'

Not even Jessamine, a woman who had suffered at the hands of a vile man herself, understood the crux of the matter. 'I spent three years wishing I was free—praying for it—I'm not ready to give that up yet.'

'Then let us hope you don't spend the next three years regretting that decision,' said Harriet matter of factly as the tea tray came in. 'Because then you'll not only have let a good man go, you'll have let Penhurst win when the monster deserves to rot in hell.'

'This is all so sudden.'

'So slow things down.' The Dowager sighed. 'Take advantage of the fact the dratted man has high-tailed it back to London and embrace the conundrum. And have a proper think about what truly matters here. Make one of Hadleigh's lists… maybe that would help.'

'I did that before and it's what got me into this mess.'

'It's not a mess, darling,' said Harriet. 'It's an adventure. Possibly life's greatest. The past is the past, but the future is unwritten. None of us can truly ever know what that path holds. The best we can do is hope we've made the correct decision as to who we walk down it with. Such a decision allows for some dithering at the crossroads. Cake?'

Chapter Twenty-Two

While one of the defence lawyers paused the proceedings to talk to his client, Hadleigh slipped the piece of foolscap from under his neat pile of notes and stared at his list.

Should I have proposed to Penny?

He was fairly pleased with the reasons for.

I love her.

Despite currently wanting to strangle her he couldn't deny that. It was responsible for making him beyond miserable.

When you love someone, you marry them.

Something which was so obvious it required no further clarification. At least to him. She, of course, didn't view things with the same lens.

Which brought him neatly on to the next obvious point. The one he had underlined three times.

I am nothing like Penhurst.

He was still smarting at the comparison. How dared she? How *dared* she?

Hadleigh found himself frowning, so skipped down to the next point.

We fit together well.

He meant that in the literal sense rather than the physical, although there was no denying the latter. But they understood one another, complemented one another, usually got along very well. When she wasn't being grossly unfair and stubborn.

The house feels like home when she's in it.

And he missed them both. So much so, that unless he wasn't in the thick of work, images of her in it skittered across his mind as he tried to picture exactly where she was at that precise moment of the day. Like now, for instance, at around two o'clock every afternoon or thereabouts, she would be in the garden playing with Freddie. It hadn't snowed yet, which was just as well, as he wanted to see that little boy's face when it did. Watch him toddling about in it, trailing his tiny footprints all over the blanket of snow on the lawn. Teach him how to roll a snowball, make a snowman, control his frequent temper tantrums…good grief, he yearned for that sort of noise and chaos.

At that point, he picked up his quill and briskly added another item to the column.

They are my family.

That made six damn fine reasons for. Now for the tricky part—seeing it through her eyes. Something he was usually very good at in his professional life, it was what made him such a force to be reckoned with in court. He anticipated the opposite arguments, mitigated against them and then obliterated them under cross-examination. Although he was prepared to concede he might not do it quite so well in matters concerning Penny.

Reasons why I shouldn't have proposed: it was a little hasty.

Yes, it had only been a few weeks, but surely that didn't matter? What one person might call hasty, another would call romantic. And if it felt right it felt right.

She was half-asleep.

With hindsight, perhaps he should have waited till Penny was wide awake and in charge of all her faculties...and he had tired the poor thing out. He'd made love to her for hours. It had been a wonder she could stand, let alone think.

She was previously married to Penhurst.

Hadleigh frowned at that one, then allowed the inevitable fury to smoulder. As much as he wanted to put that marriage behind them, he hadn't been the one to experience it. Listening to her talk about the way she was belittled, bullied, controlled and beaten by the brute was hard enough. To imagine what it must have been like for her, day in, day out, was impossible. Because...

Penhurst made her life a living hell.

Ergo, it was perfectly reasonable that she would be wary of another marriage.
Perfectly reasonable.
Damn.

She fears being controlled again more than anything.

Again, perfectly understandable given her past and she only had his word that he wouldn't attempt to do the same. Which put his foot-stamping temper tantrum before he'd stormed back to town into an entirely different perspective. When she had shown reluctance, he should have smiled and told her he would prove her wrong, not waved his arms in the air and chastised her for not being as enthusiastic about skipping down the aisle as he was.

Food for thought. Especially in view of what he knew about her. With a heavy, guilty heart he jotted down the next two points in quick succession. Both made him ashamed of his heavy-handed behaviour.

It usually takes patience and diligence to break down her defences.

I only thought about what I wanted when I asked her.

Seven. And all without giving it much thought. There were probably more he could add, too. Like the fact she had a child to consider, or that she had married in haste once before and lived to rue the day. Or that she hadn't been free for a year yet and that year had hardly been easy for her. Her home had been taken away, her life, her status, even her purpose had been ripped from her and she had been entirely powerless to stop it. He knew all that.

Knew it!

He practically groaned aloud. He'd made a hash of it again. A mallet to crack a walnut, forcing her to put on a hat she wasn't ready for and all the other blasted analogies which doubtless summed up what an idiot he had been that night.

This wasn't about him, it was about *them*. And the fact there would be no them if he continued to force his agenda to the detriment of hers. She wanted to rebuild her life. Reopen Ridley's. Stand on her own two feet. For a man who prided himself at presenting irrefutable evidence to get the correct verdict, he had been going about this entirely wrong. And it would be at least another week before he could go home and tell her.

Out of the corner of his eye he saw Lord Fennimore approaching and slipped the damning list back under his papers. 'Do we know what the delay is?'

'The Earl of Winterton is apparently having a change of heart. There are whispers he is about to change his plea to guilty!' The older man chuckled. 'Nothing like the cold light of day and the harsh realities of irrefutable evidence, eh?'

'No. Nothing like it.' Damn it. Idiot! *Idiot!* Perhaps he should write her a letter...

'You did an excellent job this morning, Hadleigh! Three down and four to go, although I'll wager Burmarsh will be next. Look at the blighter sweating over there.'

Lord Burmarsh looked decidedly green and totally petrified. Hardly a surprise. Westminster Hall was packed to the rafters with the great and the good. Everyone in possession of a peerage seemed to have turned out today, crammed in even the highest rows of the gallery benches squeezed between the ancient buttresses of the imposing hammer-beam ceiling, none wanting to miss a moment of the trial of the century. Outside the huge arched door, another circus was in full swing: reporters, agitators, curious onlookers from all walks of life held back by the reinforced lines of soldiers drafted in to keep them in check and out of the building.

'This just arrived for you.' Flint strode in and handed him a note. 'I'm to await your reply.'

Hadleigh aimlessly cracked the seal and scanned its brief contents.

Should I accept Tristan's proposal?
Reasons for: I love him
Reasons against: I'm scared

His heart leapt. 'She's here?'

'Outside, in fact. Talking to the press.'

Hadleigh dashed outside and there she was. Staring intently at an arc of reporters as she spoke to them and they hurriedly scratched down her words. Wearing another bold new dress and matching wool spencer in peacock-blue—the exact shade of her eyes. She filled both beautifully.

She sensed him and turned. Smiled. Went to move away.

'Lady Penhurst! Lady Penhurst!' She looked back at the reporters with an exaggerated frown.

'I am not Lady Penhurst any longer, thank goodness. I am Penelope Ridley again. Of Ridley's Emporium.'

'The one that used to be on Bond Street?'

'The one that will be *back* on Bond Street in the not-so-distant future. This city has been deprived of true quality furniture for far too long. Don't you agree?'

Hadleigh held back, folded his arms and simply watched her answer a barrage of questions which she handled perfectly. She wanted to stand on her own two feet. She didn't need to be carried. He simply had to prove he deserved to be the one to stand beside her. Not that she needed him at this precise moment, when she had the press eating out of her hand.

After several minutes, she extracted herself, promising them she would be back shortly to talk to them again and walked towards him. 'You got my note.'

'I did. We need to talk, I think.'

'We do. We could have talked sooner if you had not stormed off in a huff.'

'A fair point.' The press had started to gather around them, so he led her past the guards and back into the hall, saying nothing until they were all alone inside the small anteroom he had been assigned as his office for the duration.

'Have you read it?'

'I have.' To vex her, and as revenge for her pointed *huff* comment, he made sure he was wearing his lawyer's mask.

'Then you see my dilemma...'

'I do. I retract my proposal.'

She hadn't been expecting that and blinked. He couldn't help finding some pleasure in her obvious disappointment. 'You retract it?'

'Yes, I do. Because I realised...' He sighed and snatched off his wig and shook it at her. 'You and your blasted hat analogy. I have a whole speech worked out which I simply cannot say while wearing my lawyer's hat.' He tossed it on the table and stripped off his gown. 'Let me start it again in my Tristan hat—the hat I only wear in front of you, I might add. But back to that proposal.'

'The one you just retracted.'

'Yes. Because I have an entirely different proposal for you.' He took her hand. Dropped down on one knee. 'Penny Ridley, I adore you. So much so, I cannot bear the thought of you marrying me with an ounce of doubt in your mind. You married in haste last time and, because I want this to be nothing like the last time, I am proposing we wait. In actual fact, I am proposing a trial marriage. I have this charming estate just outside London. Close enough that we can both easily travel there from our respective careers, but blessedly far enough away that nobody will disturb us. Where we can live together as man and wife without all the complicated legalities which permanently bind and to give me all the time I need to banish away all your fears.' He placed a kiss inside her palm and closed her fingers around it. 'And then, once you are entirely convinced of my worthiness, *you* can propose to me.' He was giving her all the control. 'I doubt it will take you long.'

'Oh, really?' She was smiling. Beaming, in fact. 'If you don't mind me saying, that is very cocksure. And why, pray tell, are you so confident?'

He kissed her then, long and slow and utterly perfect. 'Because, my darling Penny, I am *meticulous* and *thorough*, famously so. And I intend to bathe you in my meticulous thoroughness until you'll be begging me to marry you.'

'Meticulous *and* thorough.' He felt her heartbeat quicken against his. Watched her lick her lips. Stare at his.

'Indeed. Doggedly and determinedly so. Week in, week out. Day *and* night. So, do you accept my proposal?'

'Well… I suppose you'll need someone looking out for you to check that you eat.' She kissed him this time, quite vigorously until the clerk knocked on the door and summoned him back to court. Then she helped him on with his gown, repositioned his wig and straightened his lapels. 'Go. Be brilliant. And I shall see you later, my trial husband.'

'That's a yes, then.'

She kissed him and smiled against his mouth. 'It's a definite maybe… I'm certainly looking forward to your opening arguments.'

Epilogue

Chafford Grange—November 1830

'To the next ten years!' Seb raised his glass and the four friends clinked theirs against it, not caring that it was barely midday.

'Ten years?' Gray shook his head, disbelieving. 'Where did they go?'

They were gathered in Hadleigh's drawing room as they did every November each year. The reunion had become a ritual now that their lives had scattered over time, one Penny had started to celebrate both their enduring friendships and the annual anniversary of all their marriages. Not that she and Hadleigh had married that year like the others. She had made him wait till the following February for the legalities. Neither of them had needed them, though. They had been married in their hearts from the first moment he had triumphantly carried her over the threshold after winning the biggest trial of his career at that point and they had never looked back since—other than nostalgically.

Ten years?

What a significant and wholly wonderful milestone. Ten years of love and family. Ten years of friendship and happiness. Ten years of noise and chaos. Especially during November when they all gathered *en masse*, dragging nannies and nursemaids, dogs, toys, wives and children. For a man who had once thought he preferred a solitary lifestyle, it still surprised him how much he adored his house full. If he was lucky, he managed a few solitary hours a day now if he was working and found it was he who would push his notes aside at some point and seek the company of his family.

'For my part, the last ten years have been blurred with more than my fair share of female histrionics.' Flint stared pointedly at his four blonde daughters alongside Gray's titian-haired youngest. They were practising their lines with their grandmother for the show they would put on for the adults tonight, another annual tradition, failing completely to disguise the obvious love in his eyes. Only those who knew him well would see beyond the icily calm spymaster who now worked secretly within the Foreign Office, co-ordinating all British espionage. Like his father and grandfathers before him, being a dedicated agent of the Crown was in his blood.

'I must have been cursed in a past life. Gird your loins, gentlemen. Despite last year's *King Lear* debacle, rumour has it we are being subjected to selected readings from *Hamlet* tonight.' He shuddered and adopted an entirely put-upon expression. 'I loathe Shakespeare in general and especially the tragedies. Doubtless we shall have to sit through the dreaded soliloquy. My girls, I am convinced, love them solely to vex me.'

'I rather like having only daughters.' Gray grinned and slapped Flint heartily on the back. 'But then I have only two and mine aren't hoydens. They are merely spirited, thanks entirely to my excellent training.' Something Gray had abandoned the unpredictable life of a spy for five years ago for his first love: horses. He and Thea now raised thoroughbreds in their Suffolk home and were making quite a name for themselves in equine circles.

Seb gaped and chuckled. 'Like you trained your dog?' All eyes flicked to the untrainable Trefor spread-eagled belly-up on the sofa, jewels shamelessly facing skyward, his glossy black coat now flecked with white around his face. 'I thought old Fennimore was going to kill him this morning when he stole that sausage off his plate.' Seb had only recently left the King's Elite for pastures new. He had been expressly recruited by Sir Robert Peel to help build and establish a dedicated police force in London to combat crime.

A very positive step forward as far as Hadleigh was concerned. As in everything, with the march of time the law was changing. The archaic and grossly unjust Bloody Code was all but gone, replaced by a more robust and humane system where prisons had been reformed and the death penalty was reserved only for the most heinous of crimes. They still had a way to go, of course, but change was in the air. Gathering momentum as it should. The public demanded it and for-ward-thinking politicians and judges, like him-self, were forcing it through.

'Old Fennimore loves that mutt. Just look at the pair of them.' Like the dog, the newly re-tired former commander of the King's Elite was sleeping soundly on the same sofa, Trefor's head nestled comfortably in his lap. 'Why else would he and Harriet have adopted not one, but four of Trefor's pups?'

'Hardly conclusive proof when we've all had Trefor's pups foisted upon us over the years.' Seb had three himself. One for each of his sons. Hadleigh had drawn the line at two, because like their snoring sire they had proved themselves to be thoroughly untrainable and brought more than their fair share of noise and chaos into his already noisy and chaotic house. Both his dogs were cur-rently intently watching all the boys rehearsing a magic show over by the fireplace. Something they had been doing constantly since yesterday, when the travelling troupe of entertainers Penny had hired to divert the children had left them mesmerised by the unexplainable cosmic powers of the Great Rodolpho.

The conjurer had produced coins out of ears, handkerchiefs out of noses and, much to Penny's horror, had whipped the tablecloth from beneath her finest Meissen tea set without rattling a single cup.

As the oldest, Freddie had appointed himself chief sorcerer and was currently swathed in an ancient red silk-lined evening cape they had found in the attic. Lord only knew which of his ancestors the garment had belonged to, but like all the old clothes the servants of yore had lovingly stored, they were now in the dressing-up trunk. Gray's other redheaded daughter was being pinned by Harriet—who for some reason was wearing a tricorn hat—into a boldly patterned polonaise that once belonged to Hadleigh's mother. The sight of the dress brought nostalgia, but in a pleasant way. Hadleigh had long accepted the truth that he couldn't run or hide from the past. None of them could. It was always there regardless. It shaped who a person was, affected the present and influenced the future. Therefore, it was best to embrace it.

He did not need to have seen her in it to easily picture that bright and confident polonaise on his mother in her younger days. How splendid and daring she must have felt in it. Seeing it on Gray's confident and tenacious daughter, watching her joy as she wore it was fitting.

Old memories making new memories.

He liked that. Perhaps even more than having the house full.

'I hope the ladies aren't going to be long. I am starving.' Not for the first time, a slightly belligerent Seb turned wistfully towards the open door and the smells of cooking coming from the kitchen. 'What possessed them to go out walking now—so close to luncheon?'

'It's our penance for playing cards and drinking till all hours last night and leaving them with the children.'

'We were catching up! And looking after the children for an hour is hardly penance.' Hadleigh swept his arm to encompass the entire room, quietly pleased with himself and life in general. 'Look at them all playing so contently. I've always had a knack for this parenting lark. It's simply a matter of keeping them occupied, your eyes peeled and trusting your instincts...' He frowned, noticing one pertinent and worrying missing detail. Another sweep of the room confirmed it. 'Freddie, Charlie—where is your sister?'

'She stormed off when Freddie said *she* couldn't be the Great Rodolpho.'

'Yes,' said Freddie with the arrogant authority which came from being the oldest child in the room at the ripe old age of eleven and a half. 'Girls cannot be magicians. Everybody knows that.'

Oh, dear.

His daughter was a fiercely independent, re-sourceful and stubborn creature who wouldn't take such a slight or set back lying down.

As one, he, Flint, Seb and Gray exchanged a worried look, then spread out searching for her. They reconvened in the hallway a few minutes later, shaking their heads just as the ladies came back in. 'Is everything all right, Tristan darling?'

'Yes…of course. Perfectly fine.' So much for being meticulous and thorough when he had mis-placed his own daughter. The daughter his wife had specifically tasked him to watch intently. The daughter responsible for more than her fair share of the chaos in his life. 'There's tea wait-ing for you all in the drawing room.' Surely the miniature termagant hadn't gone far? He would hunt her down, drag her back and Penny would be none the wiser of his gross incompetence. He had just ushered Thea and Jessamine in when there was an almighty crash that stopped them in their tracks.

'Mon Dieu!'

Trefor barked. Lord Fennimore sat bolt up-right. All the ladies' eyes widened.

Hadleigh simply ran as fast as his legs could carry him towards the dining room, his long-suffering wife and the three other sets of parents dashing after him. He flung open the door and took in the scene.

Carnage.

Utter devastation.

Every glass, plate and bowl laid out waiting for them on the dining table lay shattered on the floor among the cutlery. The giant tablecloth was rumpled in a heap, half-hanging off one end. Some sort of sauce was soaking into the Persian. A lone ham sat spinning on the parquet. Next to him, Clarissa was staring open-mouthed. He could feel his wife glaring in accusation.

'I looked away for a second. Perhaps a whole minute...'

The tablecloth quivered and he stalked towards it, ripping it back and there she was. Hiding beneath the wide brim of his mother's favourite purple hat. He grabbed the now bent and ridiculously tall feathers sprouting out of the top of it and hoisted it from her mischievous dark head. Blinking amber eyes gazed back at him guiltily.

It took all of his twenty years of legal training and courtroom experience not to shout in accusation because he prided himself in always seeking the truth. The evidence. Irrefutable facts. He believed entirely in the concept of *habeas corpus*—despite the fact that this was *his* daughter. The most stubborn, most tenacious, most lovable, most incorrigible seven-year-old hoyden to ever set foot on the earth. The daughter he should have named Trouble with a capital 'T' the second he had first clapped his emotional, tear-filled eyes on her.

'Would you like to explain what happened?' Why was his comfortable lawyer's mask always so ill fitting in dealings with his own family? His children regularly took him to the very end of his tether daily.

'Oh, Papa! It was awful! Would you believe a pigeon swooped down the chimney and…?'

He folded his arms and took a deep breath. 'The truth, if you please.'

'All right, it wasn't a pigeon. I lied about that to protect him. For it was Trefor. He saw the ham and…'

Hadleigh stared heavenwards and prayed for strength, sure he could hear his mother laughing out loud in the distance. This was exactly the sort of nonsense she would have thoroughly approved of.

'When I asked for the truth, be in no doubt, Daughter, I meant *the* truth, the whole truth and nothing *but* the truth. So shall we try that again please. The truth… *Pandora*.'

* * * * *

COMING SOON!

We really hope you enjoyed reading this book. If you're looking for more romance, be sure to head to the shops when new books are available on

Thursday 25th July

To see which titles are coming soon, please visit

millsandboon.co.uk/nextmonth

MILLS & BOON

Coming next month

MRS SOMMERSBY'S SECOND CHANCE
Laurie Benson

'How can I help?' he asked, tilting his head a bit as he looked at her with a furrowed brow.

'I'm stuck.'

'Pardon?'

'On the hedge.' She motioned to her back with her gloved hand. 'The lace on my dress is caught on a branch and I can't move. Would you be so kind as to release me?'

He glanced around the small wooded area she was in and even appeared to peer over a few of the lower hedges as he made his way closer to her. When he stood a few feet away, the faintest scent of his cologne drifted across her nose as it travelled on the soft breeze.

Clara was petite in stature and had to look up at him as he stood less than two feet from her. Facing him, without the busyness of the Pump Room, she was able to get a better look at him. His firm and sensual lips rose a fraction in the right corner, softening the angles of his square jaw. Although he was clean shaven, there was a hint of stubble on that jaw and on his cheeks. She appreciated impeccably groomed men so it was surprising that she had the urge to brush her fingers against his skin to see what that stubble felt like.

He leaned over her and her breath caught as his lips

drew closer to her eyelids. His finely made arms, defined through the linen of his blue coat, came around hers. He could have easily stood to the side of her to free the bit of fabric, but being surrounded by all his quiet masculine presence, she was glad he had decided not to.

'You truly have got yourself caught.'

He looked down at her and flecks of gold were visible in his blue eyes. 'I know I haven't spent much time in your presence, however, this is the quietest I think I have seen you,' he said with a slight smile.

'I don't want to distract you.'

'You already have.'

She lifted her chin and now their mouths were a few inches apart. The warm air of his breath brushed across her lips. The last time she had kissed a man was ten years ago. And even then, she couldn't ever recall her pulse beating like this at the thought of kissing her husband.

Continue reading
MRS SOMMERSBY'S SECOND CHANCE
Laurie Benson

Available next month
www.millsandboon.co.uk

LET'S TALK
Romance

For exclusive extracts, competitions
and special offers, find us online:

 facebook.com/millsandboon

🐦 @MillsandBoon

📷 @MillsandBoonUK

Get in touch on 01413 063232

For all the latest titles coming soon, visit
millsandboon.co.uk/nextmonth

MILLS & BOON

HISTORICAL

Awaken the romance of the past

Escape with historical heroes from time gone by. Whether your passion is for wicked Regency Rakes, muscled Viking warriors or rugged Highlanders, indulge your fantasies and awaken the romance of the past.